I0535355

The Good Samaritan

by

Jolie Mae Miller

The Good Samaritan

ISBN-13: 978-0692335444
ISBN-10: 0692335447

Copyright © 2014 by Jolie Mae Miller
Publisher: Jolie Mae Miller - LLC
Editing: Tiffany Tillman,
www.RedheadBookServices.com
Formatting: Deena Schoenfeldt, www.ebookbuilders.com
 Heading image of Richmond Skyline shutterstock_94785175 manipulated by E-BookBuilders
Cover Designer: Laura Hidalgo, www.BookfabulousDesigns.com

All rights reserved. In accordance with the U.S. Copyright Act of 1976, the scanning, uploading, and electronic sharing, or any other means, of any part of this book without the permission of the publisher constitutes unlawful piracy and theft of the author's intellectual property. These acts are illegal and punishable by law and will be actively pursued if committed. If you would like to use material from the book (other than for review purposes), prior written permission must be obtained by contacting the publisher at info@joliemaemiller.com. Thank you for your support of the author's rights.

Without limiting the rights under copyright reserved above, no part of this publication may be reproduced, resold (as a "used" e-book), stored or introduced into a retrieval system, or transmitted, in any form or by any means (electronic, mechanical, photocopying, recording or otherwise), without prior written permission of both the copyright owner and the publisher of this book.

This book is a work of fiction. Names, characters, places, and incidents are the product of the author's imagination or are used factiously. Any resemblance to actual events, locales, or persons, living or dead, or historical events, is coincidental.

Contents

A Note from the Author

As an independent (aka "indie" author), I can tell you it's not easy! We are 100% responsible for all facets of our books. In other words, we don't have big publishing houses helping us. The previous page discussed the legal terminology of copyright protection. In layman's terms, books are pirated through "sharing" sites, therefore, stolen, every day. If you obtained this book through channels other than reputable retailers, PLEASE delete it now and purchase through legitimate sources. Authors spend <u>countless</u> hours working to provide you with entertainment and we put everything into our books. In the scheme of things, the cost is minimal. Probably much less than that coffee you just bought and provides far more hours of interest. *PLEASE* adhere to the law.

On a more fun note, indie authors NEED your assistance by supplying feedback/reviews wherever possible. If you enjoyed it, TALK ABOUT IT! Share the link on Facebook, Twitter, Goodreads, and anywhere you're asked about a good romance or book boyfriend. Word of mouth is a powerful tool and is the only way we indie authors can survive!

Thank you! End of rant... now on to the sexy part.

Dedication

My beautiful parents have taught me that no matter how old you are, no matter what has occurred in your life, it's never too late to wish, hope or dream for what you deserve or truly want to achieve.

In that spirit, to my beautiful children:

Never stop reaching or be afraid of change. My unending love always!

Synopsis

Can money really buy you happiness?

What would you do to support your family?

The *Macintyre* family faces struggles of alcoholism and severe financial hardship after having it all and losing everything. Jeremy is forced into the ranks of the long-term unemployed, destroying his family with his alcohol addiction, and leaving Lizzie Macintyre to provide for the family in a most unconventional way. Just how far is Lizzie willing to go to save her family?

Jack Loving Jr., of the *Loving* family, is sole heir to Richmond's most philanthropic family's Trust. He and wife, Victoria, work hard to honor his family's long-standing tradition of serving the less fortunate, forcing Jack to sacrifice his lifelong dreams. Jack faces serious challenges when someone close betrays him, turning his world upside down. Can Jack create happiness for himself?

When Jack has a chance encounter with Lizzie, never could they imagine their families would eventually need one another.

"I just pray that our children ultimately learn the real joy and satisfaction you receive from having money can be very comforting, and comes when you can spend it not on yourself, but by making a real difference in someone else's life."

    By...*Jack Loving, Jr.*

Prologue:

Jack Loving, Jr.

(age 16)

"Shh! It's almost time, settle down."

"I know, Mom, but I'm so excited I can't sit still."

"Well, you need to behave. It's not every day one receives Richmond City's Award for Citizenship and Heroism."

"Yes, ma'am. I promise to make you proud-Dad, too."

"We're already immensely proud of you, son, but saving someone's life is a very big deal, you know."

"I don't feel I deserve an award for doing something anyone would have done."

"Apparently, they disagree. Look, you saved a man's life because you had the presence of mind to keep him talking until help arrived. Suicide is a very final act and you were a hero that day."

"I've been thinking about something, Mom. I know Dad dreams of me joining the family law firm, but I'm possibly interested in becoming a police officer."

The shocked look on her face as she turns pale white and the drastic, lengthy pause tell me very clearly she isn't at all happy. Finally, she swallows hard and says, "Jack that is a very dangerous profession, as admirable as it may be. You have a different path in life you must follow. Our family has many blessings, financially speaking, but to whom much is given, much is required. Before long, you will inherit a vast fortune in your Trust. But the terms are very clear: as my only living heir, you must provide to those less fortunate than us. Your path was predestined for you, as mine was, but I encourage you to be creative. Find an outlet that allows you to help others—safely from your desk as opposed to running from bullets on the streets. I love you with all my heart, dear, but as much as I have tried to provide a normal childhood over these last sixteen years, sometimes there are mitigating factors. You can work with law enforcement as an attorney. You'll end up better than your father. I just know it."

I sit and absorb her words carefully. I adore my Mother, but sometimes I wish my family didn't have lots of money. It's terrible of me to say, but I have cursed fate many times for taking my twin brother away. I miss my best friend so much and I selfishly wish he hadn't gotten sick and died, leaving me with this impossible future to face on my own. Nonetheless, I know deep in my soul what I really want to do with my life. The real challenge is being respected as an average guy doing the job I want to do, when I'm a multi-millionaire whose destiny is to be a Good Samaritan to others.

Prologue:

Victoria Winfield

(age 9)

I stand at the front window, impatiently waiting for Daddy's car to appear in the driveway. I have worked all day trying to complete my latest painting and I'm so excited to give it to him for his office. I love my Daddy so much. I love Mommy, too, but Daddy is really special.

Finally! He's home. "Mommy, he's home! Daddy is home from the store! Yeah!"

Opening the door, I can hardly stand still and can't refrain from jumping up and down and pushing my work of art into his hands. "Well, hello, sunshine. Did you make something display-worthy today?"

"Oh yes, Daddy! I worked really hard today to make you proud." He looks at my masterpiece and I can't help but see the frown lines. My heart drops because I know he is displeased.

"Oh, Victoria. You need to keep working at it. It will improve if you keep trying. Maybe less pink next time in favor of blue." He sets my painting on the table and walks away in search of my mother.

"I'm home. Where's my scotch?"

(age 17)

"You're heading off to college. Stay focused. Don't forget your goals: study hard, act like a lady, and find a husband. We're counting on you. Our entire family is counting on you to save the business. You must not settle for an average Joe. You're going to The University of Richmond, for goodness sake. It's full of rich brats. We're blessed to get that scholarship, but don't tell a soul because they'll think you're trash." My mother's words rip off her tongue like the many times before. "You've been blessed with gorgeous assets. Use them, but use them smartly. You can only give your virginity once. Only once. Land a husband and your father will be so proud of you. He needs this desperately, Victoria. The business is failing and you're our last hope. Our future is in your unfortunate hands, so you'd better not let us down."

Every time my mother grants me her special brand of love, I feel more desperate. I can't fail my entire family. We financially support my father's special needs siblings, twin sister, and brother, who are kept in a nice facility. They were almost drowned by their post-partum mother, leaving them permanently impaired. My dad saved them and now carries the financial burden to support them

"I know what I have to do, Mother. I won't let Daddy down."

"Well, see that you don't."

Prologue:

Jeremy & Lizzie Macintyre

(2008)

eering amongst the helium balloons that cover nearly every surface of our expansive backyard, I take a moment to absorb the scene before me. Our custom built home overlooking the James River is full of friends and family celebrating our son's second birthday. Everyone is happy and it shows—not with fake, plastered-on smiles, but genuine ones. I run my fingers over the impressions in the concrete wall we made just last year when we moved in. They are my daughter and son's handprints next to a set of our own. I'll never forget the look on Lizzie's beautiful face when I surprised her with plans to build on this site. She thought we were out for a picnic and had no idea we already owned the land we were sitting on.

I'm met with the most joyous sound of my wife's giggle and I can't help but admire her body from her long, wavy brown hair to her full breasts and nicely shaped ass. Even after two children, my dick stirs to life whenever my eyes roam her body. Suddenly, my legs begin moving, my hands desperate to touch her. Reaching from behind, I slowly and firmly grab her around the waist, moving toward her ear, and gently kiss and nip her earlobe. In this moment, it doesn't matter that I probably have fifty people surrounding us. All I see is my beautiful wife. My Lizzie. "If I haven't told you recently, you look exquisite and taste even better," I whisper to her.

She leans back into me, giving me her weight, and turning to find my eyes. Smiling up at me with heated eyes, she whispers back, "You *did* mention that at least twice this morning." She scans the area to be sure we're not heard, "And told me I tasted better after you filled me." She presses her ass into my groin, and suddenly I'm at the crossroads of a dangerous point of no return, at the most inappropriate of times.

"Lizzie," I warn. It takes all my willpower not to drag her into the pool house for a quick shag. Inhaling deeply, I will myself to calm down, but touching my wife is like sniffing out an impending orgasm, so walking away with blue balls is not fun to do. Holding her firmly with my hands, I whisper, "Tonight, baby, after all, these lovely people leave and the kids are asleep, I want your sweet ass spread out on the pool lounger. I intend to celebrate all the good things in my life—great job, beautiful home, amazing children—but at the top of that list is *you*. I love you, baby."

"I love you more, Jeremy."

Chapter One

Silver Lining: *BOB* Never Snores...

Lizzie

I spend the evening hiding away in my meditation room, as I refer to it. It's the only place of solitude and peace where Jeremy won't bother me. I've learned he has a strong dislike for scented candles, soothing music, and my antique furniture. My mistake was assuming he would once again sleep the night passed out on his comfy man cave couch. He catches up to me getting dressed for bed at the exact moment I am naked. His eyes widen and the sudden smirk on his face tells me he has plans for us.

Knowing the thoughts clearly written on his face, I try to dismiss him to no avail. "I said, come here Lizzie, now," he smarts off. My brain yells at my legs to move but they stand still. As the redness moves up the back of his neck and eventually covers his face, I know I will regret what is about to happen, yet again.

"Please Jeremy, I'm really tired and I was just getting ready for bed," I say as sweetly as I can muster.

"Oh, you're getting ready for bed all right. You're gonna suck me off real good. Now." With a serious determination, he moves onto the side of the bed and stares at my body with ferocious intent. "You know what I need, Lizzie, so come on over here and get to it."

Standing before him, I watch as his upper body sways back and forth. The strong smell of bourbon which permeates his pores seems to burn my nostrils. I remove his shirt, unable to ignore the stench. Gently, I push his torso onto the bed and begin unbuckling his belt. Jeremy just lays there, eyes closed, with a few mild escaping moans. After some struggle, I manage to remove his jeans. This is *not* how I envisioned crawling into my bed, getting some much-needed sleep. I move in between his legs and lower myself on my knees. As I stare at my husband before me, the last fifteen years seem to zip by on some fast-track timeline. Gone is my beautiful and supremely handsome, well-manicured guy who stayed physically fit. The guy who cared if his clothes were pressed and had impeccable southern manners. The avid sportsman who enjoyed the outdoors and everything that came with it from hunting to golfing, deep sea fishing to flag football. More importantly, my gentleman who knew the art of lovemaking and why foreplay and after play were the true prizes. This guy before me is a slob. No other way to say it. Gone is the southern gentleman. Disappeared is the athlete. Dust has now covered the golf clubs, football, fishing rods and the like. The intense lovemaking of our past has been reduced to the scene before me. This man who barely shaves would rather watch television all day as opposed to going to the gym. I'm saddened, but I'm embarrassed to say, I'm somewhat ashamed.

Jeremy raises his head up and motions his hands to get on with it. "Any day now would be nice, ya know," he says flippantly. I hold his cock in my hands stroking him up and down firmly. Not seeing much reaction, I lower my mouth to take him fully in my throat. Paying particular attention to the vein running down his penis, I suck and use my tongue to pleasure him the best way I know how. After about thirty minutes, I stop. It's hard not to consider this a personal failure but I know my oral skills have always been applauded.

"It's been a long day. I guess I'm just more tired than I thought", he explains.

I release him from my mouth, and with a large sigh, I gather my courage. "You have to stop drinking. The reason you cannot have, much less *maintain* an erection, is because of the alcohol, Jeremy. You've dulled your body to the point that not even your dick has feelings anymore. I love you very much, but I have needs, too. I want to feel you inside of me. I'm tired of relying on BOB for my orgasms!" I practically spill the words without much thought as if they were on my lips and had a brain of their own.

"What do you mean, Bob? Who is Bob and why is he giving you orgasms?"

"Oh, Jeremy, BOB is a what, not a who! B-O-B stands for battery operated boyfriend. It refers to my vibrator which sees far too much action these days."

"Well, if you didn't stay cooped up in that room of tranquility maybe you'd see some action every once in a while."

"I couldn't get action if I wanted it because you can't get hard long enough to give me an orgasm!"

"Really, Lizzie? I get plenty hard!"

"No, you don't, Jeremy. The truth is you use alcohol to numb your pain. The alcohol numbs your dick and you can't maintain an erection. Ever since you lost your job three years ago, you are not the same person. I know you are having a hard time. We both are having a hard time and it has affected our kids. You, on the other hand, have stopped living. You don't enjoy life anymore and you especially don't enjoy intimacy with me anymore. So what if we have zero in our savings account or had to give up the Country Club membership? At least we are blessed to have each other. I miss you, Jeremy! I miss feeling your touch and your breath on my neck. I need to feel like we aren't losing each other in all this turmoil."

He jumps off the bed and reaches inside his nightstand. A hidden bottle of bourbon in the back of the drawer is suddenly turned up to his lips. *Glup, glup, glup* and lips smacking dominates the silence of the room. Then, a loud crash, and all I see is the spray of glass in the corner of the room. "You don't think I can fuck you? You think my drinking gets in the way of our, what did you say, intimacy? Do you want to have sex, Lizzie? If you love me, you will have sex right now with me!"

"Of course I love you, but I just want it like we used to have it! I want to enjoy it," I state with as much sincerity as I can muster.

"Fine. You want foreplay and all that shit? I'll give you foreplay. Lie down in the middle of the bed." I gingerly move to the middle of the bed as requested. Jeremy crawls over top of my body and begins to lightly kiss my neck and shoulders. His feather soft wetness leaves a delicious chill in his path. My nipples begin to pebble as chill bumps slowly cover my body. He moves his hands to my breasts and gently pinches my nipples. As moans begin in the back of my throat, the undeniable tingles beginning to form in my most neglected area are suddenly craving his touch. My body, so eager from neglect, suddenly feels on fire. Then the worst thing happens, again. Suddenly, it feels like a bucket of cold water has been thrown on me. The sound I despise most in all the world is encasing me in a spectacle of vibrations. Snoring has to be the sickest joke of all and in this moment of finally getting much-needed physical affection, he passes out. He couldn't even grace my twat with a single lick before the alcohol took him under. I am so FUCKING PISSED!

There has to be something better out there. I ache so badly for tender touches and crazy sexy monkey love. My heart is broken from the inevitable split down the middle. I took a marital vow and that means something to me. So why do I feel this pull to find comfort at any cost? Even though the snoring ape is acting like a loser, I still feel like I should endure all the crudeness he delivers. The problem is my sanity or lack thereof. I didn't sign up to be the wife of a drunk who is used for ad hoc pleasure. I need a better life for me and my children.

Dammit. Why does this always happen? I push with all my might and it's useless. Maybe if I squeeze his nuts hard enough, he'll wake up and get the hell off me. I blow out in frustration, and with one strong push I'm free. I guess old habits die hard for my drunken husband. It seems every time we have sex, it always ends this way: me, brokenhearted, with tears streaming down my face.

Chapter Two

Moving Day...

Lizzie —6 months later

I'm physically exhausted. No other words can express how weak my legs and back are feeling at this point. I'm pretty sure I damaged a few vertebrae with all the heavy lifting I've done these past two weeks. Tomorrow, I will begin unpacking the sea of cardboard that exists in my new apartment. I truly won't allow another self-pity moment. That day came a few weeks ago when our local Richmond, Virginia sheriff deputy served us with legal papers ordering us to vacate the property.

We lost our home when it was taken away. We saved for years and built it with painstaking attention to detail. Jeremy hired Richmond's premier architectural firm to create my oasis, as he called it. He said he wanted me to have the most beautiful home in the river city. I'll never forget the day he surprised me with a surprise picnic overlooking the James River. He blindfolded me and hand fed me the most amazing food and desserts from Jean-Jacques Bakery. He capped off the afternoon with a set of blueprints which detailed our amazing new home. His loving words that day are permanently written on my soul, "In your hands are my plans for our future using lumber, concrete, and steel. These tangible things will undoubtedly fall without you, as you are the true foundation that allows my soul to breathe. Without you, I am just a shell of a man. A lifeless soul walking the earth without any direction or meaning. I love you more than life itself."

Today, Jeremy is far removed from the romantic guy overlooking the water that day. In fact, he has stayed in a drunken stupor since I confronted him with the eviction notice. His lies caught up with him when he realized I finally knew he was spending our mortgage money on god-knows-what. The web of deceit-unraveled. Our beautiful home representing glorious dreams for our future gone. He hasn't bothered to help pack anything, *nor* did he make phone calls to find us a place to live. That fun task was totally left to me. Hope and Ethan's hurt feelings or soothing their hearts for the friends they will undoubtedly lose due to the move—it was all irrelevant to him. I have tried so hard to shield our hardships from them and just allow them to exist as peacefully as possible. That façade disappeared when they happened to open the door to the sheriff holding the eviction notice. Confusion quickly turned to fear which evolved into anger directed straight at Jeremy. His cover-up was blown to hell in a single moment. Instead of consoling their broken hearts or answering their flood of questions, Jeremy simply grabbed his keys and walked out the door without a single word or backward glance. *Selfish bastard.* At the moment, he is passed out in the passenger seat of my car. It's been almost four hours since he's even moved; only his wretched snores assure me he is alive.

So I need to look to my future. I have to be the strong, independent woman my Mom preached about and put myself in a position where I don't need a man to survive. I flashback to our insightful conversations and recall them fondly. "Men are like a new dress…you feel good when you slip them on, but at the end of the night, you still look sexy in a pair of ripped up, ass fitting jeans. They are accessories that make life fun, but relationships do not 'complete you' as movie characters would have us think. You have to be a whole person inwardly, standing independently before you can truly offer anything to anyone." I think I finally understand why Mom was so emphatic that I be independently successful. My kids are relying on me and it looks like Jeremy is, too. Our basic needs and survival depend on me charting a new course and finding new income.

Chapter Three

Mother Knows Best...

Jack

"Mr. Loving, your mother is calling on line one," comes through my phone's intercom. I inwardly groan because I know why she is calling. She wants my answer requesting that I MC her fundraiser for the Children's Museum Christmas Gala she's co-chairing at the historic Jefferson Hotel this year. I think it's absurd that these things have to be decided nine months prior to the event but that's my mom—the epitome of organization, beauty, and class, not in any particular order, of course. Her well-refined social stature and grace comes from impeccable southern roots and breeding. She is, after all, the only daughter and living heir to the Bowes family Trust left by the tycoon, Rudy Bowes, who made his money in farming. Since I am her only living son, I too have a certain expectation to play the social circle games of the elite. Truth is, I adore my mother and can't really say no to anything she asks of me and she has a tendency to use that against me on occasion.

"Thanks, Patricia, I'll take it," I reluctantly reply.

"Oh, Jack, dear. How are you today? Father said you weren't at the club this morning and missed your tee time. Is everything okay, sweetheart?"

I see news travels fast amongst members of the Country Club of Virginia. Mother never seems to miss out on my comings and goings. "Yes, Mother. I had an emergency client meeting that I needed to attend. No need to worry."

She huffs and releases a slight giggle, "Well, I'm your mother. It's my job to worry. Why didn't Father know about this meeting? Aren't law firm partners generally aware of each other's cases?"

"It came up suddenly and I'm sure you're not really calling about my missed tee time or client meetings. So what can I help you with on this beautiful day?"

"I was genuinely concerned, but in any event, I was making my reminder call that I need a firm commitment from you to MC the Christmas Gala to benefit Children's Hospital of Richmond. It's an important fundraiser and they rely on our annual contribution to fund much-needed programs for the sick children in desperate need." She pauses, waiting for my answer, but I decide to tease her a little longer before answering her. "Jack, please stop torturing me. You know my fallback is Scott Harrison, and by extension, his wife. I detest the frump and frumpette. He was a real bore last year and the frumpette was blitzed before dinner was even served. I cannot go through that agony again this year. Everyone loved the job you did two years ago. You were so funny throughout the auction and you have such a way of making people spend their money. So please, just spare an old woman. Agree for my sake because you love me and you cannot bear denying sick children much less, bored auction attendees."

"Yes," I reply immediately. I knew she would eventually twist my arm with the ill children, but Scott Harrison was pretty dull last year. I just dislike the penguin suit and the schmoozing that invariably comes along with the pre-event details. I have accepted my family's philanthropic position within the community often requires my attendance and sometimes participation. So it comes with the territory—like it or not.

"Well, why didn't you say so? I figured you would," she teases. "So… I will see you, Victoria, and the children for brunch on Sunday at the Country Club, right?"

"Yes, ma'am. We will be there as usual."

"Lovely. Please be a dear and make sure the children are well mannered. I swear they are always so loud and Victoria never seems to —notice—"

"Mother! Please don't start in on Vickie's abilities. I assure you they will behave appropriately and look presentable for brunch. I really need to run, though, I have work awaiting me. I love you and we'll see you on Sunday—"

I barely have a chance to finish saying goodbye before she ends the call with, "Okay, dear. Thanks again for agreeing to MC the event, kisses!"

As I listen for the call to disconnect, my thoughts are consumed with Victoria. Mother is exactly right, although I don't want to always admit it to her. Victoria does seem preoccupied with her own social calendar these days. She doesn't work a traditional job but is quick to correct me that her charity work is a full-time job. When she married me, she essentially took on my crazy life as well. Marrying into a philanthropic family put social activities on her shoulders to manage and organize. She has become hugely essential to me, handling matters pertaining to my Trust, and I rely on her greatly. Since my full-time job is a criminal defense attorney, my time is limited.

When I married Victoria, I immediately set parameters in which she would be involved in every aspect of my Trust—financial meetings with investment bankers, strategy meetings to consider which worthy causes we would support, and all other matters pertaining to my accounts. It was very important to me, early in our marriage, that there would be no secrets—complete transparency between us. I didn't want her to feel any less important considering the disparity in our assets.

Over the last ten years, Victoria has been completely dedicated to our mission: supporting worthy, local charities. She's done a fabulous job and it's evidenced by the number of persons we've been able to affect with our work in local Richmond charities.

It would be naïve and remiss of me to say she isn't equally as invested in her own, self-absorbed, mission: enjoying the finer things money can buy. There are many days it irks me, far greater than it does my Mother, who has never needed a full schedule of weekly appointments to pamper herself. In the past, I never wished to deny Victoria anything she liked for herself because it is expected that someone of her social standing would keep her appearance looking particularly nice. She is in the public eye frequently and let's be honest, my dick stirs every time I see her smoking hot, tight little body. So, at the end of the day, I make a lot of money in a job I dislike. I can afford to give her the finer things that make her happy. Therefore, I do it.

However, when you examine the month-end expenses for twice-weekly skin and hair appointments, almost daily shopping excursions, body treatments, personal fitness training, and everything else she does to maintain her image, it is glaringly obvious she spends more time on herself rather than taking care of the children. She says we're paying good money for a nanny so she should give the woman a full day's work. Additionally, our housekeeper, Ingrid, whom has worked for my family for many years, runs a tight ship at home. So, other than the occasional exchanges I witness between her and the children, I'm not exactly overjoyed with the level of attention to their needs.

Victoria loves our twins, Bryce, and Grace, of this I am completely, unequivocally positive. They show her great affection as well. There are times, however, when I seem to notice disconnection between the children and their mother. I can't place my finger on exactly what it is, and sometimes I feel guilty for even thinking something like that could happen.

Grace craves her mother's attention. She longingly hangs on her mother's every word when speaking to her or giving her words of praise. You can just see the desperation sometimes in little Grace to have Victoria's approval. I prefer she know she is loved unconditionally and doesn't need to impress us to feel our love. Victoria, for whatever reason, doesn't go out of her way to spend one-on-one girl time with Grace and I think that's a mistake. She's at a very impressionable age and needs guidance and support from Victoria. I questioned it once and an argument ensued with her claiming I thought she was an unfit mother. Now, I walk on eggshells, quietly observing, always monitoring my sweet, baby girl.

Bryce, the outgoing chick-magnet, already loves sports and blows me away with his mature, old-soul point of view of life. He's a really cool kid and incredibly fun to be around. Making friends easily, he's the center of attention at school and at home.

Whereas Bryce is outgoing, Grace can be shy. He is incredibly protective of her; we've had a few calls from school already because boys disrespected his sister. I'm secretly elated he punched the brat for calling Grace a fat, snobby bitch. Victoria, at times, can be a little obvious with her comfortable relationship with Bryce, whereas it's noticeably absent with Grace. However, Bryce's affection is often cool toward his mother. The dynamic is an interesting one, to say the least. I just want my kids to feel the love and affection I did growing up. My parents were amazing, and if I can do half as well as them, Bryce and Grace will end up being great kids.

As for Victoria, I guess deep down my denial is thickly embedded. I always knew she was mainly focused on herself and the material possessions my money can buy. I was so entranced with her beauty and may pay a bigger price for that, in the long run. Who knows?

I just pray our children ultimately learn the real joy and satisfaction you receive from having money can be very comforting and comes when you can spend it not on yourself, but making a real difference in someone else's life.

Chapter Four

Shocking Revelations...

Jack —2002: University of Richmond

*L*ooking back, I met Victoria as a junior in college. She was a business major, and, of course, I was a law student at the University of Richmond. I was totally enchanted with her beauty. Her waist-length blonde hair and gorgeous blue eyes that reflected off the lake on campus seemed to glow. Her body was perfection—not a thin skeleton like so many girls at school. Victoria was genuine woman with impeccable curves in all the right places. Her tight ass and wavy hair swayed sexily as she walked. She was so striking that my jaw dropped, leaving me at a total loss for words when I was introduced to her, my usual swagger gone.

Normally, the ladies flock to me. In fact, I was involved with an older woman, Erin, whom I cared for very deeply. When she left Virginia to pursue a music career in California, I was crushed. The relationship was extremely sexual in nature, and considering the age difference, she was the teacher and I was her eager student.

When she left, I became obsessed with researching all matters pertaining to sex while I was in college. I sought out everything about sex from mastering positions and delving into the world of BDSM, to researching cultural differences and opinions. Additionally, I wanted to understand our sexual anatomy and the psychology of erotic lovemaking. Quite simply, I was determined to become the most educated, perfect lover. What began as a crush with Erin, turned into a research project.

I enjoyed spending time with various women and never had a problem with them being attracted to me until I met Victoria. Immediately, I thought she was incredibly special. In fact, I pursued her. Relentlessly. Victoria? She couldn't have cared about me in the least! She was a northerner from New York City, so my southern manners and Virginia-boy, gentile ways did nothing to entice her. My efforts to persuade her to date me proved unsuccessful because she constantly turned me down. I was determined if I could take her out, I would win her over for sure. It became a challenge for me *all junior year*.

By day, my damn nuts were seemingly shriveling away because I wanted her body so badly. My pathetic jealousy even extended to her silky hair, as it lay sexily against her cleavage, where I *wanted,* change that, *needed* to be. Obsessively, I daydreamed about running my tongue over those generous mounds. I wanted to hold them in my hands, squeeze and massage them. My imagination ran wild thinking about licking her body from her neck to each ear, whispering hot, sexy things to her. Most of all, I was desperate to taste and smell her. It was all planned out in my head—knowing exactly how I would consume her most intimate areas ever so slowly and greedily. I craved watching her orgasm, screaming with reckless abandon as her nipples would undoubtedly harden. So many days, I would become lost in my thoughts, imagining how they would feel pressed firmly between my lips as I ran the tip of my tongue over them, pebbling them. My hope:

she was incredibly responsive to touch and planned to make our first interlude a long, patient one.

I thought about the guys she had undoubtedly slept with and hoped they were sexual idiots. Since I was extremely fascinated with sex, some might say *obsessively* fascinated with learning about sexual technique, I spent much of my free time researching all things erotica. I wondered if she had ever experienced the elusive g-spot orgasm because I *really* preferred to be the first to blow her mind with that little trick.

My goal: be an incredible lover to this beautiful goddess, to catch her in my spell so she wouldn't even *want* to look at another man. She would want a life *with me*, building a future *with me*. In my mind, over the course of junior year, she was *my* woman. Maybe she didn't realize it just yet, but I was laying the groundwork. I was going to have her. Reality was a different story. She flirted with me unmercifully, but in a weird, from-a-distance kind of way and I never got past second base. She liked to flirt with all the guys. Thank goodness I didn't have to watch any first or second base action because I just may have laid them out cold.

We spent time together going to a few movies and on-campus events. She came to rely on me quite a bit, and sometimes I did resent the appearance of companionship and endless cold showers, but I knew I wanted her. I ached more and more for her every day. Toward the end of junior year, we had a Spring Fling dance. Of course, I wanted us to go together and she kept teasing me and was non-committal. My friends gave me shit all year, calling me a desperate bastard who couldn't close the deal. Still, I waited blue balls and all. I could have fucked other girls if I'd wanted to, but something about this girl kept me interested.

Everything changed, night to day, a week before Spring Fling. My parents, both alumni of the University of Richmond, were co-sponsoring the event. Victoria and I walked past the ticket table and she noticed their names on the banner. When she questioned if I was related to Jack Loving, Sr., I had no choice but to confirm it. I was pissed as hell because I didn't realize our names would be publicized so heavily. It was my understanding that our foundation name would be used, not *my* freaking name, or that of my father, I should say. She was noticeably taken aback and almost speechless.

I had been very careful to keep my family separate from my education for lots of reasons. Initially, it was because I didn't want others to think I had curried special favors to obtain entry into a prestigious law school. Secondly, I wanted to be accepted as a normal guy, not a rich Trust Fund kid with a rumored wealth of three hundred million dollars. Rumors always made me chuckle because that number was laughable considering I was the only child of two independently wealthy parents. People always forgot to add in my eventual inheritance from them as well. I have been used and abused by very close, trusted friends. I wanted to have a small amount of anonymity on campus for as long as possible.

In the blink of an eye, average Jack ceased to exist in Victoria's eyes. I could almost see her pupils change into the shapes of dollar signs right before me. Suddenly, she was very touchy-feely, kissing my cheeks and neck. Her hands constantly roamed my body, leaving electrified impulses in their path. The hunter became the prey in a snap. A stronger, smarter man would have seen the obvious insults. A sexually-starved man who was totally captivated by this beautiful woman, led around by his dick, put aside feelings of financial insults in favor of the ultimate prize: tasting her sweet, sweet honey. It was no surprise Victoria immediately purchased a new dress for herself and soon we made plans to attend the Spring Fling dance. The transformation was so obvious to my friends, and many of them looked at her in a negative light. One of the only fights I ever had with my best friend, Stephen, was about his growing distaste for Victoria. He didn't trust her and feared she was a gold-digger. I vehemently disagreed with him. No matter what, I knew Stephen always had my back. We were as close as non-blood could be and he did *not* like Victoria as my companion.

The night before the dance, Victoria insinuated she may have a surprise for me. I grew very excited as she ran her fingernails down my chest and kissed me ever so softly on my lips. My cock naturally began to swell and my hips slowly pushed into her pelvis. In past situations, she would shut my progress down cold. For the first time, she kissed me harder and didn't seem to mind my cock pressing against her soft body. Things began to progress very quickly. Whimpers left my throat, and I was unsure they even came from me in the first place. I was reduced to a hormonal teenage boy in a man's body, desperate to climb, scratch, or crawl my way out to experience the pleasures of Victoria's flesh.

Somehow, I grabbed hold of a much-needed lifeline when sanity reminded me I was desperately close to the most embarrassing moment of my adult life. I didn't want to ruin all of my plans that had consumed months of wet dreams by losing it in my boxers. Hell-to-the-fuck-NO! As I gently began to surface for much-needed air, I pushed slightly away. "Oh, baby, as much as I have waited and prayed for this exact moment, this is not how I see this happening for us." I began giving her light, delicate kisses mixed in with my staccato words. "I want to lay you down." *Kiss.* "Spread your legs wide." *Kiss.* "Part those sweet pussy lips and bury myself so deep inside you, your body will quake and burrrnnn... through its release from the inside out." *Kiss, kiss.* "I don't want a quickie with you, Victoria. I want to experience every square inch of your delicious body, my sweet, and I won't stop 'til I have you."

Appearing shocked by my filthy mouth and blunt words, she looked at me with her large eyes almost as if seeing me for the first time. "Oh, Jack, I want you so badly," she said breathlessly while grinding her body into mine. "When you touch me, it feels so good. It's like my skin is on fire."

As much as my dick was organizing a revolt in my pants amongst my sperm soldiers, I managed to find clarity. "I know, baby. I have waited for this moment all year, and I gotta have you, but I want you in my own way. I want to treat you like the lady you are, but I want to make you scream for me."

Something fleeting crossed through her eyes, but she recovered quickly. "I need to tell you something, Jack. I'm really scared, though."

"Victoria, if this is about whether I'm safe, I totally am. I had a full medical exam before school started, and I don't know whether you've noticed, but I've only had eyes for you."

"No, it's not about that. I trust you if you say you're clean. It's just…well, it's that I haven't—"

I could sense she was struggling and my heart ached for her. "What, you haven't been with anyone in a while? Victoria, honey, talk to me. I want this to be special for the both of us and I need to know what's on your mind."

"Well no, it's definitely not that. I don't know how else to say this other than to just blurt it out," Victoria firmly stated.

Trying to anticipate and calm her fears, I said, "You can tell me anything, baby. Just so you know, I plan to use protection. You never need to worry about that with me."

Looking relieved, she said, "That's good to know."

"So what do you need to say? I can handle it."

"I've never, I mean… I have never had sex, Jack," Victoria whispered so quietly I almost missed it.

"Wh-What?" I was shocked. *No, I must have misheard her completely.*

"I'm ya know, a vir- virgin," she said with a little more conviction, almost as if she was trying to figure it out as well.

"I don't understand. You've never had sex before? But we've made out hot and heavy. You flirt so damn well my balls have been in a constant state of arousal around you. I've seen you come on to other guys and I've wondered if you had sex with them. I was so fucking jealous thinking they got to see you naked and put their hands all over your body. It drove me fucking crazy, Victoria."

"Just because I may flirt a little doesn't mean I sleep with every guy I talk to. Jesus, Jack. I'm not a slut! I'm saving myself for someone special. I care so much about you, Jack. I want my first time to be with someone I may have a future with. You're a great guy. That's what I was talking about earlier. My surprise for you tomorrow after Spring Fling is me. What better gift can I give you than my virginity?"

I'm totally shocked and dumbfounded. Never in a million years did I suspect this new information. "I don't know what to say. I'm surprised but also strangely relieved. The idea of being the only man who has touched you felt you intimately all over your body, it's very intoxicating, Victoria. I have wanted to put my face between your breasts for so long and to know no other man has done that, well let's just say… I think I *need* some air because I'm on the verge of embarrassing myself." *I need some distance, like right fucking now.* Trying to quell the range of thoughts in my head, I made a decision. *My cock will definitely revolt.* "So, I think it's best if I go to my room. Alone." The look on her face makes me immediately question my decision.

She sighed, looking relieved, and whispered, "'Til tomorrow then." She kissed me lightly on the lips and I reluctantly walked away. Boner and all. I walked to my room with a level of suave confidence. *Damn, she's a fucking virgin! I never saw that shit coming. She's fucking hot and tomorrow night, I get to finally have my way with her.* I knew then I wouldn't sleep a wink, thinking that twenty-four hours from that moment I would be buried balls-deep in her warm folds. I had a huge responsibility, though. I owed it to her to make her first time special. I didn't want her to rename me "jack-ass" so I needed to adjust my well-thought-out plan of taking her hard and strong to soft and sweet.

In any event, all I knew was that it was a heady feeling to know she was untouched: she would be *mine*. All *mine*. Only *mine*. And forever *mine*, if I had anything to say about it.

Chapter Five

Bare, Triangles, Runway Strips Or Au Naturale?...

Victoria —2002: University of Richmond

I can't believe tonight is finally the night. I'm finally giving my v-card away to a worthy guy. I have waited *so* long for the *right* guy. It's been really hard to hold out, but Mom is right that I have a big gift to give, and I need to use it to attract the *right* prospect.

When I found out Jack's parents were school alumni, and co-sponsoring the dance, my wheels were turning at warp speed. *Could it be that the guy who has been hanging on me all year is rich and I didn't know it?* Damn, what a stroke of major luck. After I found out the connection, I did a bit of research and discovered a treasure-trove—literally.

Apparently, Jack's mom is some major heiress of a Southern plantation family. She's loaded! Jack's father and namesake is pretty wealthy, too. He came from a blue-blooded family, but he is wealthy in his own right as the most famous lawyer in Richmond. His law firm is huge and his downtown offices overlook the city. They are well-regarded philanthropists and seem to have their names as benefactors on all the major local charities. Bottom line, Jack is my path to a financially secure future. He can provide me with the lifestyle I need and deserve. My family is relying on me: I must strike it big! My dad is working so hard to save the family business and support his siblings. I have a chance to help my family and I need to do it.

I spent the day preparing for tonight. A morning shopping spree consisting of sexy lingerie, a quick drug store run for condoms since I don't want to take any chances getting pregnant (at least not yet, anyway), and a quick trip by the cologne counter to buy Jack a gift of cologne. I buff myself to a complete shine—a manicure, pedicure, and shaving all my girly-bits. Although, I'm really stressed about whether to do a close, bikini trim or be bold and go bare. I decide this is too important to make a mistake and disappoint Jack, so I elect the narrow, "runway landing strip." Taking my time, making myself look as attractive as possible, I apply perfect makeup and perfectly style my hair. I do everything a girl can do to make herself beautiful. There's so much riding on this night. I need to make myself completely irresistible to Jack for a long time to come.

It's not a hard task by any means to spend time with him. Besides, he's a gorgeous man both inside and out. Incredibly sexy, built like a brick shithouse, spending lots of time in the gym. I guess spending years as a high school athlete conditioned him to stay fit and healthy. I just hope my inexperience doesn't bore him after one encounter. He knows I'm a virgin, but I'm not completely innocent. In high school, I had a boyfriend and I only allowed him to go down on me. He just thought I was saving myself for marriage. Little did he know, my family's livelihood relied on my plan to stay a virgin, and attract a wealthy man. It may sound cold on my part but I'm a Daddy's girl and I hate to see my dad struggle day after day. We need an influx of cash and what better way than to marry into a family of millionaires.

At five p.m. sharp, my doorbell rings and I rush to the door to find a tuxedoed Jack carrying the largest bouquet of pink roses I have ever seen. I don't want to make it obvious by counting, but there have to be at least three dozen. They are gorgeous and smell so divine. I can barely conceal the massive and probably goofy smile on my face.

"Beautiful flowers to honor the most beautiful girl at Spring Fling." He then proceeds to take a bow before me. The man is totally charming, not to mention amazingly good looking. He oozes sex appeal with every step he takes.

As I motion him to come inside, I reach for the bouquet and my nostrils are filled with their sweetness. "Thank you so much. They're beautiful, but you really didn't need to get me so many. You must have bought out the whole flower shop."

Jack walks through the door and gently places his hands on my hips. "No, not really, but you deserved it." He takes a small step back to admire me more closely. "You look absolutely stunning." His eyes begin roaming my body slowly, up and down. His breath slightly hitches as he takes in my body with his eyes.

My royal blue, sequined dress with its off-the-shoulders and magnificent plunging neckline shows off my breasts, which he seems to admire quite frequently. The dress has a tightly fitted bodice and close fit, which hugs my ass so perfectly and includes a small train. I look sexy as sin if I do say so myself. He steps closer to me and gently lifts my chin with his index finger. Moving his head closer, he stares intently into my eyes as if he's trying to communicate with my soul.

"It's a special day for us, Victoria, and I don't want you thinking that I'm taking it for granted. I hope you know I recognize this is a big step for us. I really care about you and I've been dreaming of this day for a very long time." He moves his lips just above mine, barely touching. I can feel his warm breath on my mouth, and I notice he smells very sweet. I can't help but get lost in the sensation of the heat on my lips. He slowly moves his finger down my neck and over my collar bone, moving out toward my right shoulder, where he softly yet firmly holds my shoulder. It sends a chill all over me. I can feel my nipples pebbling beneath the fabric of my corset, begging to be released from the constricting lace. He speaks softly, in practically a whisper, "I can't wait until the dance is over and I can show you *all* the ways I intend to ravish your delectable body."

I knew in that very moment I had wasted months looking for Mr. Perfect because he was standing in my living room.

Chapter Six

That Feeling When Opening A Present, Revealing The Mystery Inside...

Jack —2002: University of Richmond

I decide to go to my parents' estate and pick up the Aston Martin. Since the little secret about my identity has been revealed, it doesn't make any sense to drive my six-year-old Honda Accord on such a special date. When I arrive at Victoria's apartment, I practically convulse when I see the way her dress clings to her body. I would have preferred to skip the Spring Fling entirely and proceed on to the next stage of the evening, but I figure that would be a total dick move. The problem is going to be getting through the night watching all the other guys gawking at her tight body without getting into a fight. I know my parents will be in attendance as alumni benefactors, so I have to represent the family well.

I decide to take Victoria to The Jefferson Hotel's signature restaurant, Lemaire, for dinner. She seems surprised to witness the maître d's recognition of me, as well as my behavior while fine dining.

Lemaire is hardly the school's cafeteria. Sometimes I surprise myself at how well I can transition between acting like a struggling college student and multi-millionaire. There really is an art to ordering at a five-star restaurant. It's second nature to me since my family enjoys them so often.

We enjoy a fabulous dinner, and then make our way to the grand ballroom. Everyone looks forward to Spring Fling so there is no short supply of beautifully dressed women and penguin suits galore. Of course, with Victoria on my arm, we notice many heads turned our way. I was expecting the guys to break their necks, but I wasn't expecting the noticeable turned heads and whispers amongst the women. I first think it's my imagination, but I quickly realize Victoria sees it, too, and the scathing looks she returns, almost has me chuckling.

The University President appears at the podium and gives a few words, but I inwardly cringe when my parents suddenly appear beside him. The moment I have been dreading so much since college began is upon me. My public anonymity is about to end. Everyone will know who I am and treat me differently. My heart begins to race and I suddenly feel so fucking hot in this damned tux. I can't hear anything being said and the scene before me seems to play out in slow motion. I begin feeling so weak I could almost pass out. I watch my parents move to the podium and the audience begins clapping. The sounds around me sound so distant and garbled. I begin to notice faces turned to look at me. Some have smiles. Some are openly shocked with open mouths. Some of the women who whispered while staring at us before have smirks plastered on their faces, like cats about to pounce on canaries. The sudden attention makes me incredibly uncomfortable, and there isn't anything I can do about it. Mom begins speaking, and I can tell she is scanning the crowd to connect with me. When our eyes meet, she smiles brightly and lovingly. I truly adore my mother, but I don't want to be called upon in front of everyone. She seems to notice my reservations, and with a slight nod, she finishes her speech, announcing a new educational endowment gift from our family to the University. Everyone claps and the University's President beams with delight. Well, why wouldn't he be happy to receive a ten million dollar contribution? The strange part occurs when Victoria gasps loudly and twists her neck sharply to look at me at the mention of an educational scholarship endowment. It is an odd moment, one I can't really explain. Soon after, my parents clear the stage and the music resumes.

I hardly notice the pull and tug on my arm, but the gentle lips on my cheek pull me from my thoughts. Victoria. Her warm breath pulls me from my revelry. I turn to look in her eyes and find a genuine sincerity there. "Care to dance?" I somehow mumble.

With sweetness in her eyes, she says, "I'd love to. I thought I'd lost you there for a moment."

Nodding at her, "I think I lost *myself* for a moment, to tell you the truth."

We dance and dance and dance. It feels so natural to hold her in my arms. Her body pressing against mine feels so good. "I can't wait until I have you all to myself," I whisper into her ear. She nuzzles her face into the crook of my neck, like a puzzle piece that perfectly fits. So perfectly right. So mine.

On the side of the room, I notice my parents waiting. I know they must want to speak with me and decide I should indulge them, considering my mom spared me the public introduction. I pull back from Victoria and thoughtfully look into her eyes, "I want to introduce you to my parents. Okay?"

Surprised at my words, "Oh, um, sure, but I, ah…I am rather nervous to meet them I must say."

"Don't be nervous. Look, my mother is a kind woman. She'll love you. Father is a great man and I aspire to be just like him. It's important to me that you meet them." I move closer to her and gently give her a quick peck on the lips. "Don't be nervous."

As I lead Victoria from the dance floor and walk toward my parents, I notice Victoria changes subtlely. She smiles a little too forcibly and stands a little taller. There's almost an air about her that I notice in a split second then it's gone. I'm sure it's just nerves. Having just watched my parents give the University a huge sum of money, it must be a little intimidating.

"Mother. Father. I have the pleasure to introduce to you, my dear friend, Miss Victoria Winfield."

I watch my parents carefully for their responses. I have never brought a girl home to meet them before so this can go either way, really. My mother responds kindly, but the raised eyebrow of her left eye and slightly raised outer lips are not the warm reception I was hoping for. She immediately extends her hand to greet Victoria. It would be very poor etiquette to openly ignore her and my mother's deep southern heritage is engrained against it. "My dear, Miss Winfield, oh how nice it is to make your acquaintance."

"So nice to meet you, too, Mrs. Loving." She then turns to my father and sweetly smiles, "And Mr. Loving what a generous gift you have made to the University! The school is so lucky to have your family as benefactors."

"Well, we love the University of Richmond deeply. It is our joint alma mater and we met here while students, so we consider this home. We support as many initiatives as possible." Mother turns to me, places her hand on my elbow with genuine love, and smiles big, "We are incredibly proud that Jack decided to continue the family tradition."

"I love it here, as well. I'm just thrilled that Victoria made UR her home. Otherwise, we might not have met."

Mother's eyes narrow slightly and I know she is teeming with thoughts and questions but would never choose this occasion to voice them. She gives us each a questioning glance and with a final smile says, "Well, so nice to meet you, Victoria. It has been a long evening and I'm ready to retire." She turns to Father and bends her arm around his elbow, "Dear, are you ready to call it a night?"

Father looks lovingly in her eyes and smiles, "Yes, my love. All of this dancing has made this old man realize he's not in his twenties any longer." He extends a hand to Victoria and kindly speaks, "So nice to make your acquaintance, Miss Winfield. Perhaps we shall meet again." He turns to take Mother's hand, "Son, we hope you enjoy the rest of your evening."

An impossible to contain chuckle leaves my lips, "Oh, I'm sure I will". I reach my hand to the small of Victoria's back and firmly press my fingertips against her.

"Jack, dear, please call me tomorrow. I have a matter to discuss with you, okay?" I nod and she gives me the look that says 'I have questions for you, buddy' and they exit the ballroom.

As I watch their departing figures, I lean close to Victoria's ear. "How about we leave as well? I think I've used up all the restraint I had left." I slowly move the tip of my tongue to the shell of her ear, kissing her earlobe.

With a quiet moan and obvious shiver, she wraps her arm around mine and begins moving us to exit. "I thought you'd never ask!"

I reserved a beautiful suite at The Jefferson. I prearranged a spring flower bouquet, selection of fruits and delectable sweets, and a bottle of wine. In hopes that Victoria would spend the night, I took the liberty of ordering breakfast from room service. So many of my lonely nights have included dreams of this night and I want it to be perfect. Granted, now she knows I am wealthy, it allows me to openly spoil her. It comes from a good place inside me, though. I really like this girl. I might even be falling in love with her. Watching someone from afar for almost a year has slowly churned these feelings inside me. The chills that run up my spine when she is around are intoxicating and only make me crave her more. Finally, she has taken a more serious notice of me. It was rather coincidental, her discovery of my family, but I cannot allow myself to focus on that too much. No, tonight, I make my dreams come true as well as making it a special night for Victoria's first time.

"Oh, Jack! This suite is breathtaking! I cannot believe you went to all this trouble."

"No trouble, sweetheart." I release her hand, turning her to me. Looking deeply into her eyes, I place my hands on each cheek and gently move in, giving her a soft kiss. I pull away, taking a moment to just look into her eyes before my lips move back in with a firmer touch. My tongue traces the crease of her lips, tasting her sweetness. The small moans leaving her throat tell me she is enjoying herself. I wrap my arms around her shoulders, pulling her torso close to mine. Her nails move up the back of my jacket, yet I feel the strength of them as if they were scratching my bare skin. I try to refrain from pressing my erection into her abdomen, but it's so difficult not to. I'm hard as steel and my cock is begging to be freed from its constriction; touching her has been on my mind constantly for months. We hold on to one another so tightly, and our breaths become fast and desperate as we hungrily eat at one another.

I pull away slightly, holding her face in my hands. "You are incredibly beautiful and I want you so badly."

Panting loudly, she says, "I want you, too. Please, Jack, make love to me."

"It would be my pleasure." I take a slight step back and remove my tuxedo jacket, throwing it on the closest wingback chair. "I want to undress you. I want to slowly remove everything until the artwork of your sculptured body is revealed to me."

She nods slightly and smiles the most alluring smile. I turn her away from me and slowly unzip her dress down to the top of her ass. It is then that I get my first glimpse of her bare skin. I can't seem to help my desperate need to run my thumb along the path the zipper has just taken. Her skin is warm, almost glistening. The bare flesh of her back robs my breath away. I close my eyes and take a stabilizing breath before placing my hands on her shoulders to turn her, facing me. I want to make time, stand still, and enjoy the sight about to be before me. Once she turns around, I slowly open my eyes and force them to look straight ahead to her face. I can see so many different things in this moment: fear, lust, and something I can't quite identify.

I suddenly realize I have a huge responsibility to get this right, for her. She's a virgin. What? I still cannot seem to wrap my head around that idea, but it's a major gift to me nonetheless. First and foremost, I am a gentleman and I will never take advantage of any woman. "Victoria, I need to be absolutely sure this is what you want. We can stop right now. We can stay the night, just holding each other and nothing else." We both stand there looking at one another. I study her eyes closely for signs of reservations or regret and find none.

"I want you, Jack. I trust you and want you to be my first." She crosses her arms over her chest, grabbing at the fabric over her shoulders. Without looking away, she reveals one shoulder at a time while still covering her breasts. The slight swoosh of air from the heavy fabric falling away and pooling around her hips is as refreshing as a cool breeze on a Richmond afternoon.

I slowly tear my eyes from her face, and inch-by-inch make a mental record of this moment, seeing her nakedness for the first time. All I can see is the small amount of black lace at the underside of her strapless bra. I gently place my hands on each of hers, removing them from her chest. Her breasts are heavy within her bra. Their swells spilling over the top. Judging from what I learned in my live nude class, her décolletage is perfect. My breath can't help but hitch as I lightly run my index finger along the tops of both breasts. The rise and swell of her chest grows more pronounced with her heavier breaths. I place my hand around her hips and gently push the dress away from her. The remaining half of her body is revealed to me so beautifully, yet I ache to see, taste, and touch her most intimate spaces still shrouded in mystery. I help her step away from the fabric surrounding her ankles and swiftly pick her up in my arms, walking her over to the bed, laying her down as close to the middle as I can reach. I run my thumb across her bottom lip and move in to gently kiss her. "Don't move, beautiful." After releasing her, I stand tall and slowly gaze at her body from head to toe. Sexy. Just so fucking sexy.

I swiftly move about the room lighting the candles I had prearranged. I pick up her dress lying in the floor; reminding me this was a fun night of dancing, yet seeing our bodies move skin-to-skin is what I desire most. I adjust the lights in the suite, hoping to make her more comfortable. Of course, I need and desperately want to see her body, but women can be rather reserved about their nakedness and I want her entirely relaxed with me. It's finally happening. I'm about to make her mine.

At the bedside, I kick off my shoes and socks followed by my watch and cufflinks. Victoria is watching every move I make and there is something thrilling building in me unexpectedly. It's like stalking prey, but at this moment, I'm struck fiercely not knowing which of us is the hunter. I remove my tie followed slowly by my shirt. Being a dedicated athlete, I work out religiously. Body image is not a problem for me. My trousers are the last to leave me as I crawl next to her.

We hungrily attack one another as if we're desperate for each other's air. All of the waiting and prolonged events of the evening have made my horniness explode like a rocket. I grind my pelvis into her and can feel her warmth through her panties and my boxers. Kissing her deeply, I delve into the back of her mouth as far as I can reach. My tongue leaves her lips as I lick her neck, along her chin, and up to her earlobe. She tastes slightly salty, invariably from our evening of dancing mixed with our new found lust. Facing her, I move to straddle her legs, sitting on my heels. As I look down at her, she is gasping for air. Placing my hands around her long neck, I gently squeeze. "Feel me, Vickie," I whisper. She stays silent and stares back at me with rapt attention. Spreading my fingers wide, I move them down to her swells and firmly squeeze my hands around her breasts covered with lace. "Feel me, like I feel you when my fingers touch your bare skin." Moving my hands to the back clasp of her bra, I quickly pull it away. My eyes dart to her bare breasts, exposing their fullness and pebbled tips of her hardened nipples. I place my hands on her warm mounds and struggle to catch all of her breasts in my grasp. Her areolas are large, yet perfect. Nipples that are small, yet perfectly suckable. "Feel my mouth as I devour you." Moving my tongue over her nipples, I firmly massage her breasts. Licking and gently sucking. Ever so carefully, I nibble them between my teeth until they are fully engorged and standing upright. Her skin fills with chill bumps, reminding me of braille. She moans and with hooded eyes begins to rock her pelvis into me.

"That feels so good, Jack. Please don't stop!"

With a full mouth, I mimic a vibrated response, "No, never". She is so responsive to my touch. Her hips move harder up into me. Can it be possible she can orgasm this way? Deciding to spend attention on her bountiful tits, I lead them to feel their way to pleasure. I harshly whisper to her, "Baby, go with the feeling and concentrate hard. Bear down on your pelvic muscles and try and come for me". With vigor, I suck her nipples and massage her chest. She begins to thrash her pelvis and I use my legs to trap her. She pushes up into me and her moans become louder, louder, and her breathing more strained. I watch her face closely, and when I see the almost-missed clinch, I suck on one nipple and with my fingertips pinch the other nipple…hard. She violently thrusts her pelvis upward into me, and with a scream, bellows out her orgasm, gasping for much-needed air.

"Oh god! Jack, oh fuck! Shit! That was…I don't know what that was? I've never felt something so intense in my life!" She looks at me, quite bewildered, seeking answers to what just happened to her.

"Baby, apparently you just had your first orgasm using nipple stimulation. Judging by your reaction, I'd say you enjoyed it." I smirk at her and move in to quickly kiss the tip of her nose.

"Don't make fun of me! That was incredible. I've never…well, I mean, I um…oh never mind."

"No way, Victoria. We *will* talk about our lovemaking. So don't clam up on me." I give her a moment to open up, but I can see this may need some prodding. "O-kay, let me try and help you a little. I assume you have orgasms through self-stimulation, *right?*" Her eyes widen to golf balls and her jaw drops. Silence. Total silence. "Don't go shy on me."

"Well, yeah I guess so. Sure, I masturbate if that's what you really want to know. Geesh!"

"Actually, yes that is *exactly* what I wanted to hear. Do you routinely use a vibrator or use your fingers?"

Suddenly, she sits up in bed and with an appalled look says, "Jack Loving!! What kind of question is that? You should never ask a lady a question like that. Are you out of your ever loving mind?"

Oh no. This could go bad real quick if I don't explain—fast! I quickly move to pin her back down beneath me. My mouth presses to hers and she resists, but I forcibly move my tongue to the crease in her lips. I lick at her furiously and begin to grind myself into her. She resists at first, but her body overrides her and she begins to submit. *Damn. She totally went limp and gave her full submission. Could it possibly be that she might go for my innermost hidden desires? Without much resistance or hesitation, she sure as hell let me lead her. Damn, that's fucking hot as hell!*

I pull away from her only after I know she won't move away. I kiss her gently on her lips and lightly give a peck to her nose. "I think we need to have a very serious conversation. I'm going to tell you a few things. You're going to listen and then I'm going to continue to ravish your sexy fucking body until the sun rises. Then, we'll have breakfast, at which time we will have a more serious conversation about where we go from here. Okay?"

She gives me the deer in the headlights look but nods nonetheless. "Okay."

"First of all, you need to know I've been attracted to you all damn year. You've practically ignored me, but that's okay, I will forgive you." I smile at her and give her a quick peck and she looks a little sad. "Anyway, I love sex. You need to know that about me. Yeah, you probably think 'oh yeah I already know you dumb jocks only think about sex' but it's much more than that for me. It's hard to explain, but I am like a student in search of knowledge. I want to know everything there is to know about technique, positions, timing, everything! The female body is like a piece of artwork to me. I want to know how it moves and how it aches. Most importantly, I want to know how it purrs." I can't help but give her a cheeky smile and she returns a small giggle. "I asked you about masturbation because it's totally natural and shouldn't be something that makes you ashamed. It feels good! I admit, I jerk off quite a bit, especially these past months because a certain girl had me tied in knots all the time!"

"Oh, come on, that's not true. I didn't do anything on purpose to you to be mean."

"I know you didn't, but Vickie, you have to know how fucking sexy you are." I begin to run my fingertips over her breasts and her bare nipples begin to tighten and swell in response. Oh, dear god, help me. This girl is going to fucking drive my dick crazy. I take a deep breath and try to begin again. "Look, what I'm trying to say is sex is really about communication. The better the communication, the better the sex. You're a virgin and I'm just really beginning to appreciate what an enormous gift that is to a man like me. I want to know everything about your body if you give me the chance. Let me teach you what I've learned. I want to show you lots of ways to achieve orgasm. Nipple stimulation is just one of many, I assure you." I watch her carefully and begin to notice there's something churning in that brain of hers. "Talk to me, baby. What are you thinking right at this moment?"

She hesitates, and with questioning eyes, opens and closes her mouth twice before speaking. "How many women have you been with exactly?"

"Oh, damn, you're probably thinking I'm some man-whore or something, aren't you?"

"Well, the thought *did* cross my mind, I'm sorry to say."

"No, that's understandable. I'm definitely not a virgin but far from being a man-whore. I had an older girlfriend that I kept secret from my family while in high school. We began dating when I was sixteen and she was twen-.... Oh, never mind, it's not important."

"The hell it's not. You know my history and you began to say something. Please, trust me enough to finish it." Her kind eyes are imploring me.

"Please don't judge me or her when I say she was twenty-two when we first met. I was a hormonal teenager and she was beautiful. Having had some personal struggles going on in my life, the girls my own age did nothing for me. We dated up until middle of my freshman year at UR. The subject of my age didn't come up when we first became involved. Physically, I was always huge for my age so she didn't know I was a minor. Truly, she didn't know. She was very free spirited and open to new experiences. I became enraptured with knowing *everything* I could about sex, just to please her. Eventually, it was more about my need to experience life, and we became more daring you could say. She devastated me when she moved to California and that was the end. However, I continued to learn as much as I could...*the internet*. Victoria, I know what you're thinking!

Plus, my college classes on sexuality. I've chased you all junior year; I've been celibate since I decided to pursue you. I had a few flings in between, but I'm no man-whore, I assure you."

"Thanks so much for being so open and honest with me."

"Absolutely no problem. I want honesty from you, too." I look down at her and can't help but become breathless with her beauty. Even though we paused for a sexual history reality check, I need to taste her. Suddenly, more desperately now than ever, I kiss her firmly, pull back, and look into her eyes once more. I feel my cock begin to swell and push my pelvis into her abdomen. Material? What the fuck? Damn it all to hell; I have yet to see her most private of spaces. The barbarian in me needs to smell and taste her, now! Climbing off of her, I lower my face to her neck. Slowly, I lick and suck all around her neck and ears. Using the tip of my tongue, I run it down her chest and between her breasts, careful to not touch her anywhere else on her body. As I swallow and remoisten my tongue, I lick at her, leaving a wet trail in my path. Traveling down her flat belly, I circle her belly button and move to her outer hip bone. When she feels my quick nip, her body flexes. Pressing my face firmly in her side, she's overcome with shudders and quivers. I trace the route along the top of her sexy black panties to the other hip and just as she tightens in preparation for the assault on her side, I blow cold air through my lips and she relaxes. Just then, I move in with a nip and breathe warm air over her and she flinches uncontrollably.

Looking up into her eyes, I wait for her to open them. When she finally does, her questioning baby blues seek what? She is so visibly ready to feel what comes next. I can almost smell her need as it assaults my nose through her panties. Placing my fingers on each hip, I slowly begin to pull them down. As they lower, I am in a trance, hardly able to breathe and almost forgetting to move. The Super Bowl, World Series, and the Stanley Cup have nothing on this moment. God, how I have daydreamed and beat off 'til practically raw, thinking of this. I want to see her. I'm desperate to taste her and run my tongue through her folds. I don't understand why I'm being such a pussy. "Close the fucking deal" is what Stephen would say, closely followed by "what the fucking hell is wrong with you?" I don't know. I just...I just...

"Jack, what's wrong? Is something wrong?" she says with marked panic in her voice.

"Oh, *nothing* is wrong. Absolutely nothing! Everything is *right*. I just want to enjoy and savor every moment." A rush of heat suddenly envelopes me, and I'm taken aback with the knowledge that I've never felt like this before. Quite honestly, I'm scared as hell. I'm overwhelmed with emotion that somehow this girl will bring big changes to my life. So why do I have a nagging voice telling me to RUN?

I look down and seem to concentrate on the swirls and weaves within the lace pattern of her panties, making a mental snapshot in my mind. This is it. The moment is now. I lower the lace to expose a finely manicured, narrow strip of blonde hair just above the finest lips I've ever seen. Fuck. I just might explode like a petulant teenager right here. I can smell her and unconsciously lick my lips, over and over, as I lean down and make contact with just the tip of my tongue. Her smell fills my nostrils and my cock aches for its turn. I push deeper in with my tongue from the top of the slit down. Using my thumbs, I peel the lips back like a Christmas present to reveal the prize inside. Her clit. Her entrance. Fuuccckkkk! It's maddening because I want them both at the same time. Starting at her clit I swirl my tongue around it several times, intentionally avoiding going over it. Moving down, I find an opening in the flesh. The glory hole. I delve deeper and taste as far inside as my tongue will travel. She squirms and moans, so I know my playful fun is enjoyed by her. The taste buds on my tongue are covered with the thickness of her arousal—her body's essence—filling my mouth and overwhelming my senses.

After I have licked her thoroughly and playfully slow, I pull away, looking up at her. She has such a contented look on her face. "Victoria, I want you to do something for me." She lifts her head slightly, regarding me with her full attention. I reach for her right hand and place it over her pussy. "I want you to show me how you pleasure yourself when you're alone."

With a look of shock, she shakes her head timidly no. "Please don't ask me to do that."

"Baby, I plan to ask a lot of you. We just discussed –this—how natural it is—not to mention, fucking hot as hell. Please. Show me how you rub yourself when no one is watching." I push her fingers down against her clit and press my fingers firmly over hers. *Damn, please do this for me.*

Chapter Seven

The Gift Of My "V" Card...

Victoria —2002: University of Richmond

can't believe I'm about to do this in front of him. This night has been so unexpected. In fact, everything in my world is off its axis since learning Jack is the man I have been seeking as my life partner and my family's savior.

I begin to rub small circles over and around my clit. His face is practically buried in my crotch. Deciding to give this a try, I close my eyes and focus on relaxing. Finding I need to tune out the idea that I'm giving him an up close ticket to my solo performance, is unsettling. My clit begins to swell and I move my left hand up to my breasts, tweaking my nipples and playing with them. I begin to feel that tingly sensation in my core, releasing an uncontrollable moan of desire. As I imagine my own sexy fantasies, I'm deep in thought when I suddenly feel slick warmth entering my personal core. The feeling is so incredibly intense. Jack is shoving his tongue deep in my pussy while I stroke deliberate circles over my clit. Building fast, I really don't want it to end. This feels so damn good! Suddenly, I feel Jack move his fingertips up to my nipples and he pinches—hard!

"I'm going to come, Jack! I feel it, it's almost there...oh please, please don't stop. Jack! Jack!" Then all I see is a burst of light behind my eyes. My orgasm rips through me at warp speed. It just seems to keep building in intensity and I ride the wave. "Oh god, that was totally incredible. I've never come so hard in my life!" I can barely speak because my breaths are short but my mind is reeling and I want him to know how it felt.

"Well, the ride is far from over, baby. Your orgasms are just beginning. The count is 2-0, with no end in sight." Shifting his body, he submerges first one, then two of his fingers in his mouth, withdrawing them slowly. Then he buries his index finger, palm side facing up, slowly inside my pussy. "Baby, your pussy is so tight. I'm going to love spreading your walls open. Open just for me." Moving his head down to my clit, he gently sucks it between his lips. It's so sensitive, I almost jump clear off the bed but he braces me back down. He quietly chuckles to himself. "Hmm, I love it. That, my dear, is the aftershock of a *real* orgasm and it can't be faked. It feels so good when you quiver on my finger." I'm not totally sure why he's saying this, but I guess it will be clear soon enough. Sucking my clit continuously between his lips, I feel pressure being applied inside my channel with his finger. He speaks up to me, "When you feel you're close, I want you to bear down against my finger." Then he attacks my clit with laser-focused attention while stroking my front wall. Suddenly, I'm building again, but it's TOTALLY different this time. I'm in full arousal: my breasts, my clit, my pus-...oh wait! My god, I'm about to h-h-have a..."FUCK! FUCK!" The overwhelming, all-consuming, thought-stealing orgasm is upon me. My body writhes with excitement. My mouth is so dry I feel cotton balls must be present. I can hardly catch a breath, especially when my heart is beating from my chest.

Jack removes his finger and climbs up my body, kissing me as he journeys north to my neck and traces the shell of my outer ear. Whispering softly, he says, "Did you enjoy your first ever g-spot orgasm?" I still can't seem to speak so I plaster the largest smile on my face I possibly can. "You tasted amazing. Want a sample?" He places his index finger on my bottom lip and moves inward toward my tongue, leaving me frozen with an unusual taste I've never experienced before. Suddenly, I jerk away, bashful when I process I'm tasting my own juices. "Don't move away. You taste the best, I assure you. Wars have been fought, men have most assuredly broken their own will to sample sweet juices like these. I'm too selfish to let you have all of it, that's why I'm just sharing a little bit." He smirks then he pops his finger the rest of the way in his mouth, eyes rolling back and softly moaning. Yes, he's satisfied indeed.

He winks at me, leans to my lips, and kisses me thoroughly. "I can taste you on your lips. Can you taste yourself on my tongue?" I almost pass out from the filthy words he speaks and the warmness traveling through me as he grinds into me. "Put your hand around my dick. I want to feel you against me." I run my fingernails down his back and over his ass. Reaching inside his boxers, I grab him firmly and squeeze. "Yeah, that feels good."

Nuzzling my neck, he kisses me passionately, deeply, and with so much skill it's overwhelming how inflamed I get from just his kisses. Lifting away from me, he removes his boxers and reaches for a silver condom packet. He aligns his body perfectly with mine after sheathing himself. Placing his hand behind my knee, he lifts it to a bent position. Spreading me wide, he lowers himself between my legs. I can feel the cool chill at my opening caused by the lubricant he applied on us both. He begins softly kissing me and the look on his face, quite serious. "Victoria, this may be very uncomfortable for you at first. I promise you, however, that it *will* get better. If I go too slowly, it will hurt more. So, because I want to cause you as little pain as necessary, I'm going to force through the barrier quickly. Once in, I'll still give you time to acclimate. When you're ready, I will move again. It's best to move as quickly as possible, though, okay? Are you with me?"

In this moment, I realize I have found the most kind-hearted, considerate man I've ever known. Instead of being a Neanderthal like most men probably would be, he is being gentle and sweet even though he plans to hurt me for all the right reasons. How could I be so lucky? All of my dreams just might come true.

"I know it will hurt. Just go ahead. Please don't stop. I want to feel you inside me." It's hard, however, to imagine how in the hell he will ever fit inside me. He's huge!

"You remind me of a lily. So beautiful with strong lines and striking colors yet they are incredibly delicate to touch. You're mine now, Vickie, and I just might need to keep you forever." He leans down and gives me the gentlest of kisses on my lips, leaving me breathless and blown away. "I want you to take a deep breath when you're ready and hold it, okay, beautiful?" I nod my understanding and mentally prepare myself for incredible pain.

Nodding my head that I'm ready, I grab his shoulders tightly and Jack pulls away from me pressing into my opening with his cock. Suddenly, he pushes hard, very hard, and the sheer pain ripping through my body absolutely, unequivocally is the sharpest, most intense pain I've ever experienced. He grunts loudly, followed by "Holy fuck, you're tight!" My legs close around him and I flinch awkwardly. My body can't seem to help its desire to retreat, but it can't because this is a natural part of life. Jack studies my face closely and I can see he's very concerned. "Are you okay?" *No, I'm not,* I say to myself. This fucking hurts. I can't breathe. I'm afraid to move—afraid it will undoubtedly hurt worse. I can't be totally honest because he might stop, and I need him to continue, so I just stare at him, willing him to be still. "Victoria, talk to me. I need to know how you're doing."

Realizing I need to say something, I whisper, "I'm fine, it just hurts."

He watches me seriously and breathes outward, "I really need to move in you. Your pussy is like a vise, squeezing my dick so hard it fucking hurts. Are you ready?"

I nod my head solemnly.

"Big breath in and please relax. Let me love you, baby…" and he pulls almost out before slamming back inside me. "FUCK! FUCK!" His body is so rigid above me and the look of pain on his face is undeniable as well. "Ready?" He looks at me lovingly before I nod to continue. His hips pull back once more before he takes another stroke followed by another. The pain is letting up, but the burning sensation is so sharp that it's hard to think about his pleasure. He slowly strokes in and out of me, careful to be as considerate as possible. His kindness as a lover is absolutely remarkable. He is so considerate, and obviously his true character is being revealed to me in these moments. The pleasure appearing on his face is accompanied by his sexy moans and grunts. "I'm sorry, but I can't hold on any longer, sweetheart. You're so tight around my dick. You're sucking the come right out of my nuts." He increases his pace carefully, and with a roar his hips go still, deep inside me. His pelvis is ground so tightly against me and, even though, the burn is so intense it's oddly pleasurable at the same time.

"You're mine now, Vickie. Only mine." The burning intensity in his eyes tells me he is very serious. Then he smiles down at me with love in his eyes.

It's hard for me to speak clearly so I tighten my arms around his neck and he crashes his mouth against mine, kissing me deeply. The tingles that cover my body feel incredibly good. I pull back and can't help but offer a happy and contented smile. Life is about to change in a big way. In this moment, I feel incredibly loved by this man. *How can I be so lucky?* I ask myself yet again. Life is not just good, life is suddenly great!

Jack and I spent most every minute together in the days following Spring Fling. Jack was extremely cautious about "overuse." He just kept telling me that I needed to have time to heal completely. He gave me so much oral sex you'd think I'd have died of exhaustion. I was so happy and totally fulfilled. The man knows how to eat pussy! The problem was he wouldn't let me touch him for fear that we'd have intercourse. "I'm fine, sweetheart. You have no idea how much I get out of pleasing you."

About a week later, following a night of fantastic orgasms, I'd decided enough was enough. I wanted my mouth on him. I decide it's my turn to give him some pleasure. After devouring a full southern breakfast, I push him to his back on the bed, admiring his hard, tight body. How I long to run my tongue all over his chest. I can't believe I didn't notice just how remarkably sexy Jack is. Sad to say, but I ignored him because he couldn't help daddy and I had to follow the plan.

Slowly, I remove his boxers and the most magnificent cock is before me. I didn't get to fully inspect him the first night, but it's long and thick with a purplish head. Lowering my mouth to him, I timidly lick it. He is quite the man, and taking him in will be a challenge, but I'm excited to comply. Licking my lips eagerly, I grab him at the base and begin lowering my mouth on him. I'm intrigued and excited with the taste of his pre-come on my tongue. I begin to work him up and down taking more with each stroke. He places his hands on my head, directing me and massaging my scalp. His moans and hooded eyes are proof that he's enjoying my warmth. "That's right, baby. Suck me good." It suddenly occurs to me that I can't appear too experienced. I am supposed to be untouched. My movements slow down and I concentrate on filling my mouth with him, firmly sucking on the up-stroke, and paying close attention to the large vein on the underside of his cock directly on my tongue. I actually enjoy giving blow jobs so my mouth just takes over, having a mind of its own.

"Fuck, baby, your mouth is magical. You really have a talent for giving head. I'm a very lucky man." I let out a moan and the vibration causes him to grip my hair tighter and stiffen his legs. "Feels so good!" The expression on his face is pure delight. He holds his breath, momentarily rolling his eyes in the back of his head when I suck harder and begin using my hand to stroke near the base of him. "Victoria, I'm not going to come in your mouth, okay, baby? I want you to release me when I say so and stroke my cock hard, up and down, when I tell you to." I nod my understanding and moan deeply so he can feel it throughout his shaft. I press hard with my tongue and suck as tightly as I can when he yells out loudly, "Now! Make me come for you, baby!" And I do exactly what he asks. His hips thrash, his abdomen tightens, and a sheen of sweat covers his body. Holding his cock in my fist, I stroke him, up and down, while using my other hand to gently massage his balls. The first ribbon of thick white cum propels from his body across the bed, followed by two more. My fingers become wet with his warmth, lubricating his shaft even more.

I know I can't appear too talented, but he gives directions really well, so I'll just say I'm an attentive student. Besides, he does make me feel so good all the time, which only makes me want to return the favor. Bottom line, I have to capture his heart and what better way than to convince his manhood that he can't live without me?

Chapter Eight

Girls' Night!... Gone Awry

Lizzie

Sniff, sniff. "I just don't know what else to do. I've tried everything and nothing works. He just doesn't love me anymore. I'm convinced of it. No matter what I try, he's more interested in everything and everyone but me."

"I don't think the problem is you, Marianne. You're gorgeous. You just need to spice things up a little. Couples can become monotonous over time and you need to try new things. You two have been married twenty years. Derek loves you! Look, I know it may be a little embarrassing for me to tell you specific things to try, but I'd like to. Okay?"

"I'm definitely willing. All of our friends talk openly about how you give the best bedroom advice. Bring it on, girlie, please!!" The desperation on her face compels me to do what I can. Somehow, I can help all my friends but can't do shit for my own marriage. At least some of my friends might have a chance at getting some good loving tonight.

"Okay, this is what I want you to do…"

Next week…

The girls and I meet for our weekly get together at The Boathouse. No matter what's going on in our lives, we normally try to take time out for each other. Since my financial circumstances have changed, the girls generally pay for drinks. I'm blessed to have wonderful friends. After a few glasses of wine, the conversation normally always turns to sex: good sex, bad sex, naughty sex, unusual location sex, etc. Loose lips always lead to surprising new information about each other.

"Lizzie, you're a life saver. You really need to be a sex therapist. I tried out the things you suggested and let's just say, I burned in a good way Monday morning!" Marianne exclaims with a wicked laugh.

"Ohh, tell all! What good bits did our sweet Lizzie impart? Please, please do tell!" Jenny laughs aloud.

The rest of the table joins in with cheers of support for Marianne and Derek. Not wanting to repeat our private discussion, I stay silent.

Marianne looks a little timid, but after a deep breath, she finds her courage. "Well, the first thing I did was take a trip to the local sex shop. I had no idea what was available these days. It was quite shocking really." The snickers and giggling, as well as the bright knowing eyes of our friends, surround us. It reminds me of being a little girl and giggling about our first loves. "I spent almost two hours in there talking with the sales clerks and laughing with other women. It was crazy, really! At one point, I looked up and counted eleven vibrators out of the packages spread out on the table. They actually had me test the strength of the vibrations on my inner arm. It was hysterical! Who knew, right? Apparently that's how you get a feel for what it's going to feel like on your…oh, you know!!"

"Oh, I *do* know. I love going in there and coming home with a surprise or three for my hubby," Jenny giggles.

"I just don't know if I'd have the courage to go there alone. Besides, I have one vibrator and that's all I need. BOB never complains!" Janice announces to the giggling women.

"I can't believe you stayed there two hours, Marianne. What in the world kept you busy that long?" Jenny inquires.

"I wanted to buy several vibrating dildos and other, uh… oh, I mean… oh my god, I can't believe I'm admitting this. I bought a vibrating butt plug!" The women are stunned into silence and begin to roar with laughter. It's then that Marianne looks a little worse for wear.

I decide I should intervene since I got my friend in this trouble. "Why snicker? These items are tremendous fun. If you haven't massaged your husband's prostate with a vibrating dildo, he doesn't know the fun he's missing out on. And you haven't gained the pleasure that ensues when controlling your man's orgasm. It's a big turn on. For him and you. More importantly, Marianne, did you enjoy the new experiences with your husband?"

A huge smile crosses her face, "If having fucktastic sex twice a day for the last seven days qualifies as enjoying my new experiences, then hell-to-the-YES!! I feel like I'm twenty-one again. My only question now is an important one. Lizzie, what's your next recommendation, because the bar is seriously high?"

I burst out into laughter. "Oh, I have plenty more ideas to share."

After spending an amazing evening out with my friends, I come home. I always feel guilty walking through the door after a few hours away. The only reason I'm able to get away at all is because my elderly neighbor graciously watches the kids for a few hours and then puts them to bed for me. Of course, my friends paying my way helps, too. I immediately notice the kitchen looks the same after I made dinner for everyone. Gee, even the leftovers are still out. I make my way to give the kids a kiss. No matter how old, they sleep like precious angels. Walking down the hall and into my room, I'm shocked at the sight before me.

Jeremy is laid half across the bed. His pants are off, boxers on. His shirt is unbuttoned and shoes and socks nearby. The smell immediately fills my nostrils. Vomit. Everywhere. Liquor bottles strewn across the bed are mostly empty. Even as horrid as the scene before me, it doesn't compare to the pain that rips through my heart when I see my grandmother's wooden puzzle jewelry box empty and upside down in the corner. Pain slices through me so fiercely I suddenly can't breathe. My mouth is completely dry. My legs surely have cement blocks attached because they're so heavy they can't move. I suddenly hear the shrillest sound ever, and I have no idea where it's coming from until I suddenly realize it's me. I'm screaming. I'm screaming loudly. I'm screaming so loudly and Jeremy continues to lay motionless. I can almost see myself hovering over the room looking down upon us in an out-of-body experience. Reality is quickly making sense to me. Jeremy pawned my inheritance. He drank away my precious jewelry. More importantly, the rent money I was saving which is due on Monday is gone. I kept it in the hidden compartment that only opens once the wooden slides were pulled in the secret way. I had to hide my valuables so he wouldn't find it and waste it on booze. But he did find it. Now, we have no money. I should just kick him out, but the truth is he has nowhere to go. I see separate bedrooms in our future, at minimum. Visions of the Richmond Sheriff serving another eviction notice fill my mind. *What will I do now? What the FUCK will I do now?*

Chapter Nine

Present Day: The Life Of A Millionaire Wife...

Victoria

I wake early, shower quickly, and consult my day planner for the day's events. Wow, another day overbooked without a clone in sight. While serving on the Board of Directors for four charities takes up a lot of my time, I still make the time to take care of myself. As a married woman in one of Richmond's most philanthropic families, it comes with the expectation to make charity work my full-time job. Even after ten years of marriage, I have to work triple hard to be accepted among the blue-bloods in this town. To stay sane, I pamper myself. Some would say excessively so, but I deserve it. Being a wealthy woman allows me many, many perks. Besides, I have to look good for Jack, so the way I look at it, he's the one benefitting by having a drop dead gorgeous wife.

My days always include a two-hour workout, physical pampering of some sort like massage, manicure, pedicure, or hair appointments.

Occasionally, I meet my best friend, Cathy, for a tennis match. Without exception, I make a daily stop at the club for social hour and coffee. Many of my philanthropic duties are held there as well. There may be many powerful and wealthy men that enjoy membership, but behind every good man is his philanthropic wife who truly makes the decisions about which worthwhile charity should receive our fortune.

"Well hello, Victoria. So nice to see you again, dear."

With fake smile firmly plastered, I reply, "Nice to see you as well, Mrs. Collins. Beautiful day, isn't it?"

"It truly is. Your ears must be burning because Mrs. Loving and I were just discussing the Children's Hospital Christmas Gala. She's proudly announced Jack has agreed to MC the event this year. The committee is thrilled!"

Standing in shock, I quickly think of something kind to say to the old bag. *Dammit, Jack! Why didn't you tell me?* "That is truly great news, isn't it? He has such a way of convincing Richmonders to part with their wealth when it's for a good cause, doesn't he?" *Including giving far too much of his own away,* I quip to myself.

An odd look crosses her face and she quickly recovers. "So can we look forward to your help again as well?"

"Absolutely. Our family is firmly committed to the children in our area. Please excuse me, but I must run along." I know it sounds admittedly selfish, but this is one charity Jack does *not* need to be involved with. He and I agreed long ago that I would handle all the donations. Mainly due to his busy schedule; however, my interests are to control the lavish amounts he has historically given. Children's Hospital is a weakness for him and he loses his ever-loving mind! Seriously, the endowment he set up took ten percent of our fortune and it still makes me hyperventilate when I think about giving so much away. *Don't worry, Mrs. Collins, I will definitely be helping if for no other reason than to control my husband by reining in his free-flowing heart! o other reason than to control my husband by reining in his free-flowing heart!*

Chapter Ten

The Interview...

Lizzie

I spend the next day perusing the Richmond Times Dispatch classifieds section. I need money fast. I need a good job with excellent money, pronto, or my children will be homeless again. I heard a friend mention Craigslist as a source for classifieds. Nothing really fits my skill set, though. As the hours go by I am becoming more panicked. I run my fingers through my hair, desperately pulling. Somehow the pain leaves me more grounded. Shit, I'm fucked. I mumble outwardly to no one, in particular, "I failed, Mommy. Should have become that strong independent woman you begged me to be."

Suddenly, I find an ad obviously misplaced in the wrong section. Or maybe it was intentional, who knows. It reads, *"Need money fast? Make up to $1,000 a day providing escort services. Totally legal. Beautiful and interesting people strongly encouraged to apply. Call (804) 777-7777 today."* Well, that sparked my interest instantly. It says it's legal so maybe it is. I call and speak to a Ms. Martin who seems well-refined and knowledgeable. She explains that her clients often need dates for high profile events. They are expected to be graceful, able to hold conversation easily, well-groomed, prompt, courteous, and most importantly, they respect their privacy so confidentiality is a must. I question her repeatedly about the sex issue. She assures me I will not be required to have any physical relations. However, if I want to, that's *my* choice. Still feeling uneasy about how I can earn so much money, she explains there is a base fee I would earn and if the client is happy he may tip. He may tip very well. I explain I'm a married woman but have a desperate need for money, immediately. She asks to meet me in person to check my physical appearance. I agree. So, today's the day— a physical inspection of sorts. *Gee, just what I'm looking forward to.*

I pull up to a nondescript building sandwiched between two other well-known buildings on Main Street. Other than the street number and outside door buzzer above the building, you'd have no idea it was even occupied. After pressing the buzzer, I wait. I happen to notice a small pen size camera off to the top. *Hmmm, that's interesting.* Obviously, security is taken seriously here. Just then, I hear a noise followed by an unlocking sound coming from the door. I immediately have this weird moment of dread, but I push open the door anyway.

Walking in cautiously, I first notice the sounds of classical music. I'm somehow calmed. The second thing I notice is the strong smell of roses. Just then, I hear a distant voice calling, "Oh Lizzieeeeee….come back here, dear. I'm in my office, sweetheart."

I walk toward the back, paying attention to the extensive, and some might say gaudy, artwork lining the walls. The paintings are everywhere in thick gold frames. I notice the brushstrokes, leading me to the conclusion that someone is quite the collector of oils. The pale yellow walls open up into what can only be described as a cross between a French boudoir and a whore-house sitting room. Assuming what I would know of whore houses which I certainly would not know anything of these matters. The pink walls and decor exude femininity. On every available surface of space, long stemmed roses of every color dominate the room.

"You've noticed the roses I see. They are a gift from my dear Henry. He just adores me and refreshes them every other day. He says as long as he breathes air, I shall only breathe the sweetest of things to remind me how special I am. He's a dear, really. So sweet."

"Is Henry your husband?" I ask.

With obvious shock, she says, "Good god, no. He's someone else's husband, but he prefers my company to hers. Supposedly, she's a total nag and they have a sexless marriage. That's what *he* claims, at least." Her wicked snicker tells me she is unaffected that a married man is emotionally attached to her.

"Your office is, ah...how should I put it? Eccentric?"

With a big belly laugh, she replies, "Sweetheart, it's downright highbrow for sure, but they were all gifts from admirers throughout the years. I may not want to look at them in my home, but here at work it classes the space up. When you're entertaining men with money, they don't want trailer-trash tchotchkes. When they come here, it sets the pace of things. They know I provide them with quality escorts."

Just as quickly, her invasive eyes look me over from head-to-toe. Twice. After a few moments, she speaks, "You are quite beautiful, Lizzie. Your figure and obvious sex appeal will be quite marketable. What is your availability?"

"Well, almost anytime. I'll be honest, I'm in desperate need of funds so I will make myself available."

"That sounds good. What does your husband think about you providing escort services?"

"I honestly haven't told him. He's struggling with alcohol consumption these days due to a long term job loss, so that's why I'm here today. My family needs an income fast. As bad as it may sound, I don't really care what he thinks. My kids need a roof over their heads."

"So, you have children? What ages and how many?"

"My daughter is thirteen and my son is eight."

With serious eyes, she asks, "How do you plan to balance your duties with your children? Because I can tell you the first time you have a conflict and leave me in the lurch or embarrass a client, you're finished. You need to know that."

With as much sincerity as I can muster, I try to explain, "I can appreciate your position. Please know I have a circle of friends that understand my plight. There will be backups to my backups. I promise you. You have my word. I need an income. Please believe me when I say I'm desperate and I will need work far more than you'll ever need me."

Squinting her all-knowing eyes, she stares at me—trying to decide if I'm truthful or if I'll cause her trouble. "Okay, but couple of things to remember. First, you never discuss clients. Never. Second, you behave professionally at all times. While at events, let the client lead the conversation. Never become intoxicated, ever! One drink maximum. No exceptions to this rule. Never socialize in your home because this can lead to big problems. So DON'T DO IT! Never, and I mean NEVER use drugs. I will ask that you submit to initial drug screening and periodic screenings thereafter. You will need appropriate attire specific to the event. I will assist you with selecting your garments if you have concerns. In fact, until we become more comfortable with one another, I will probably have you text me a picture of your outfit prior to the event to ensure I feel it is appropriate. Also, another note about confidentiality: you may overhear business-related information. Sometimes it can be strategic or proprietary. When this occurs, you must ignore it. If you repeat anything that gets back to anyone, especially competitors, you and I will be in significant trouble. We're talking lawsuits and most important to me is the damage to my professional reputation. My clients use me because they know we're solid. They can let their hair down, so to speak. You don't want to cross me, Lizzie. I'm dead serious."

The look on her face means she is, in fact, deadly serious and I better not fuck things up for her. Well, I don't intend to, so we're good. "I have an instant drug test I'd like you to take. Run along to the ladies', will you, dear? The test kits are in the second drawer on the left side of the vanity. Bring it to me when you're done."

Well, this wasn't what I expected for my list of things to do today. Nevertheless, eyes forward. Need money. Fast. When I enter the restroom, I think I've entered a room out of Versailles. Smatterings of gold flourishes are everywhere. Pure opulence is the only way to describe it. Anyone walking down Main Street would shit a brick if they knew how much money adorned the walls and fixtures of this nondescript building.

I take the test quickly and return to her office. She's on the phone, so I decide to linger in the hallway. I can't help but overhear my name and my ears tune in. "She is quite beautiful, isn't she? The picture I sent to you was obviously taken without proper attire for your event. I'll make sure she's adequately groomed. I have a good feeling about her, Mark. She's eager, classy, and refined. You will approve, I'm sure." After a moment, she ends the call, explaining she'll be in touch soon.

"How about tomorrow night, Lizzie? There is a fundraiser to benefit the Richmond Children's Museum at six p.m. It's being held at the Richmond Marriott on Broad Street. Mark Chesney requires accompaniment. He is a very polite gentleman, single, and forty-five years old. He's an investment banker and previous ladies have swooned after events with him. He's quite the catch, but remember you're doing a job. That's it."

Standing before her, it suddenly occurs to me how real this is about to become. I'm about to go out on a real date with someone. What if my old life collides with my new one? If I'm attending functions, I may run into someone I know. Shit! Well, it's either do this or my children may not eat so I can't worry about being seen. I try to gather my thoughts quickly and respond to her as coherently as possible without sounding like a total ditz. "I'm absolutely available." I try to carefully pass her the urine sample, guessing she will be grossed out or something. She meets me with a gloved hand, and moments later announces the test results. "You're good to go." Somehow just hearing that gives me instant relief, even though I have no reasons to fear the contrary. "Go home and send me pictures of yourself dressed in cocktail attire. I need three options within the next three hours." Wow, this is really happening. My first step toward independence, but literally, this job determines whether my children will eat or possibly become homeless. Everything is on the line for my family so any uneasiness I may feel, I have to forget it. Plenty of women have had to take jobs they didn't want for the betterment of their children. I'm absolutely no different. I'm not better, or worse. It's my new reality. "Oh, and Lizzie? Mark is an excellent customer. If you act unprofessionally, I will know about it." Suddenly, I'm walked out the nondescript door and onto the cracked sidewalk of Main Street. Somehow it's like leaving a fairytale and walking into the inner city. I can't help but be startled.

I decide to confide in my good friend, Jenny, about my new job. She can't stand Jeremy and has known us a very long time. She's seen the good and the bad in the Macintyre household, warts and all. Knowing she will help me with the kids is a massive load off my mind.

After texting the pictures to Ms. Martin, we agree on the appropriate attire. She's rather controlling, but I'm hoping in time she will trust my judgment more.

Everything is confirmed: location, time, wardrobe, hairstyle, attitude, and confidentiality. The client and Ms. Martin are so focused on Mr. Chesney's possible blowback. The problem is, I haven't stopped to consider my own repercussions.

Chapter Eleven

And So It Begins...

Lizzie

After utilizing the very convenient valet parking, I'm scheduled to meet him in the swanky hotel bar. Luckily, we've seen one another's pictures, so it shouldn't be too difficult to find him. I arrive and immediately spot him. Wow! I'm suddenly breathless. This man is gorgeous. Even though he's considerably older than me, I find him incredibly sexy and all he's doing is sitting there drinking an amber-colored beverage. I approach him timidly. My feet feel like they have cement blocks attached. Almost as if he senses me, he turns and our eyes lock on one another.

"Are you Lizzie?" he asks me cautiously but with a smirk.

"I am. Mr. Chesney?" I smile in return.

"You are quite exquisite. Ms. Martin didn't adequately prepare me for how strikingly beautiful you are."

"Oh, you're too kind, Mr. Chesney."

"No, Lizzie. Too kind is the senior Mr. Chesney. Please, call me Mark."

With a smirk, I return, "I'm told your kind reputation is quite based, in fact, Mark."

"Ah, well then we shall revisit that question at the conclusion of tonight's festivities." We both share a chuckle and a smile and I instantly know I am in the presence of a genuinely nice man.

"Tonight's event benefits Richmond's Children's Museum. It is a cause I generally support heavily. Thus, I am a platinum level patron. I mention this to you, not as an opportunity to brag, but because my presence can sometimes draw quite excessive attention from other benefactors. I wouldn't want you to think I was ignoring you."

"Mark, I certainly understand that my presence here is to support you. Whether that means as a girl on your arm, standing in silence in a pretty dress or as a participant debating the benefits of nature versus nurture, I'm here for you." We continue to chat about the most random topics and I quickly realize Mark is a fascinating person. Not only is he easy on the eyes, but he's quite intelligent. We share similar backgrounds, both enjoy giving back to our communities, especially children's charities, and love outdoor sports. He's even an Orioles fan, which is a no-brainer in my book.

"Where have you been all my life, Lizzie?"

"I've been here the whole time. Plus, raising my two beautiful children." He glances down at my left hand and gives me a questioning look. "I'm married. It's complicated. My priority right now is my children and supporting them the best way I can."

His eyebrows move upwards as if he is studying me carefully and he nods. Then he shoots me one of his panty melting smiles and I feel like I'll be reduced to a puddle any moment now.

"Well then, shall we join the benefit, Lizzie?" he asks with a full bow, raised hand, and megawatt smile.

"I'd be delighted to join you, Mark." I accept his hand happily and feel a little bereft when it moves away. Suddenly, my lower back tingles when his fingertips press there and begin to guide me away.

We approach the grand ballroom and I can hear the sounds of a string orchestra and an audible sigh pushes past my lips. "They play beautifully!"

"Ah, yes. The Richmond Philharmonic is donating their talents this evening. We are truly lucky to have quality musicians in Richmond. Do you play, Lizzie?"

With a downward, shy smile, I reply, "No, I could only wish to play at their level. I dabble, really."

Once we fully enter the room, Mark is truly under siege. It seems everyone wants face-time with the handsome Mr. Chesney. I don't fail to notice women are giving me very pointed, rather odd looks. Suddenly, I have an overwhelming sense of panic as I ponder if it's Mark they are interested in or if it's me. Lizzie, the married woman. Lizzie, the ex-country club member. Lizzie, the poor displaced, homeless mother who has no financial help from her alcoholic, deadbeat, out-of-work husband. Why did it never dawn on me that I might run into my former privileged, Richmondites while escorting these men? I feel my throat begin to close. My face is turning multiple shades of red, I'm sure. At that exact moment, I look across the room and see my worst nightmare, Cindy Hall. *Damn.* She was particularly a catty bitch to me when our lives began falling apart. I know if she sees me this will not turn out well for me, and especially Mark.

I don't realize I am gasping for air and a very concerned Mark is speaking to me in quiet, comforting tones in my ear. "My darling, are you unwell? What might I do? You look as though you're about to pass out." Suddenly, I feel him leading me out of the ballroom quickly. I don't even remember moving my feet, but somehow I'm outside on a balcony overlooking Broad Street.

"Lizzie, take deep breaths. You'll probably be okay, but let's try deep breathing, shall we?" And here we are. A very surreal experience. Less than one hour into my first assignment and I know I will surely be fired. How mortifying and stupid of me not to anticipate this social failure? Yet this handsome, attentive man, who doesn't know me at all, has left his major charity function to attend to me. A perfect stranger.

"Mr. Chesney, I'm so sorry for my public behavior. I feel very ashamed and embarrassed right now. I'll gather myself together and leave since I know I've caused you so much trouble."

"Are you finished, Lizzie?" With a raised eyebrow, he patiently waits for my nodded response. "Good. You will do no such thing. I'm quite enchanted with you, sweetheart. Anyone with half a brain would recognize a panic attack when they saw one and you most definitely panicked in there. May I ask what happened to cause this?"

I just stare at him. I don't know what to say, but the comforting way he holds me feels really good. At this point, I know I have nothing to lose because this will be my last assignment so I may as well be honest.

"I saw someone across the room and I *did* panic because I knew if she saw me with you, she might embarrass me, but I didn't want it to affect you."

"Lizzie, I highly doubt that, but please explain why you believe that to be true."

"As I stated, my first priority is my children. My husband has some serious challenges he's dealing with and it has caused our family to downsize our lifestyle." With caring eyes, he strokes my hand, and for some reason I just want to speak freely. "My husband is among the ranks of the long-term unemployed. We went from our dream home and country club life to being essentially homeless. He struggles with alcohol addiction to numb his pain and feelings of worthlessness. I decided to take charge of my life, which has led me to tonight. The woman I saw, Cindy Hall, knows of our misfortunes and definitely would have called me out in front of you."

He harrumphed a disgruntled sound of displeasure and shook his head slightly. I can feel the waves rolling off of him. *I need to leave this place. Now! This was a huge mistake.* I move to stand up quickly and feel five tightly wound, warm fingers grab my wrist and pull me back. With a startling voice, he asks, "Where are you going?"

"This was a mistake. I sincerely apologize. Mr. Chesney, I must be leaving now."

Mark stands before me, placing both hands loosely on my face. He leans down and places the lightest most exquisite kiss directly on my lips. Pulling back, I begin to feel the cool air as it crosses my now damp lips. "Please don't leave. I've enjoyed getting to know you these last few hours. I read people really well. It's a habit, really. Something tells me you and I will become friends, Lizzie." He moves my hands together and squeezes his on top. "Make you a deal. You let me have the remainder of our evening together and I promise to field any and all questions from opportunistic old bags. Deal?" He gives me the most delightful smile, and for some reason, I truly trust him. There is a genuine quality to Mark. I feel very safe in his care and he makes me believe everything will be okay. He begins moving us in the direction of the ballroom before I can even answer.

"I wouldn't want my troubles to interfere with the Museum. The fundraiser is such a worthy cause."

"You're right, it is. That's why I need you here. You're obviously passionate about children's issues. Are you not?"

"I am." I pause, just staring at his beautiful face as we continue to walk in the ballroom."

"Oh, and Lizzie, darling?"

"Yes?"

"Please don't leave my side. I want to be able to stare at those delectable lips of yours." He smirks and winks.

We're immediately swarmed with people wishing to have his attention. It seems everyone has a project they want him to fund or a committee that needs a co-chair. I notice he keeps my hand firmly wrapped in the bend of his elbow. He often taps my wrist lightly, stroking up and down my fingers. He tries to move through conversations quickly and I'm aware of kind tactics he uses to avoid the more aggressive personalities. After inserting myself into a conversation regarding the crime statistics for the Richmond region, I immediately regret my unrequested input. However, he just smiles at me and comments his pleasure that I am up on such details. I soon realize I am participating fully in all of his discussions. He invites my input and even begins introducing me as his business consultant.

The moment I have been dreading all night occurs when Cindy Hall suddenly appears at my side with a snarky attitude and disapproving eyes on my wardrobe. "Well, Lizzie, it's such a surprise to see you at a fundraiser of all things. I wasn't aware you had the means to support our projects any longer."

Mark suddenly turned our bodies to the side with his more directly in her line of eyesight. "I'm not sure we've met. Surely you don't have a Board of Directors position at the Children's Museum?"

"Oh, it is very nice to finally meet you, Mr. Chesney. The leadership and financial backing you've provided over the last five years has been second to none. May I call you Mark?" she says brightly with a fake smile.

"I'm not familiar with your work here, Mrs.—"

"Oh, it's Ms. actually. My name is Cindy Hall, but please call me Cindy—"

Mark continues to talk over her, "Lizzie here will be consulting with me. She'll be my eyes and ears regarding my next endowment to the Museum." It was impossible to hear my sudden intake of breath gasping at that little bombshell. "So, I look forward to hearing good reports." He begins to step us aside, but suddenly looks back, and in an almost impossible whisper to hear, states firmly, "Ms. Hall, I expect complete professionalism and confidentiality from you with regard to Lizzie. If that will be a challenge for you, I'm sure the BOD will be happy to comply with my need to expel you." *Oh shit!* The look on her face, when she turns to look at me, can only be explained as 'oh bitch, it's on now.' And with that parting jab, he shuffles us away to the dance floor.

We dance to all genres and decades of music. I especially enjoy *Moon River, At Last,* and the more current and upbeat Pharrell Williams, *Happy.* Before I realize it, we've danced for an hour straight with no breaks. I am a sweaty mess, but I'm having fun.

On the last song of the evening, Mark pulls me incredibly close. I feel so alive and the friction against my sensitized breasts is overwhelming. His large hands holding me close at the small of my back occasionally include wandering fingers along the top of my ass. He bends low to rest his head along my neck. I can feel him inhale deep breaths, taking in the combination of Calvin Klein and undoubtedly sweaty scent specific to me.

I sway to the music and his unquestionable dance skills. It feels really great and totally comfortable. This man, whom I didn't know before tonight, has an intoxicating, dominant personality. Something about the way he's led me throughout the night, on and off the dance floor, I just know it to be true. If I were a single woman, I undoubtedly would jump at the chance to sleep with him. I have a strong sense it just might be earth shattering. As the song nears the end, I feel his warm tongue begin to lick the shaft of my neck. It's as if my legs give way and my body melts in his arms. He moves his lips to my ear and whispers, "The music has unfairly quit us, Birdie."

I try to regain my composure, looking at him questioningly. "Birdie?"

With a knowing look, he simply states, "My dear sweetheart, we Orioles fans have to stick together."

"Ah! Yes, we do." I can't help but enjoy the beautiful look on his face. Even covered in sweat, I am absolutely smitten.

After a few rounds of quick conversations, he leads us away. "Did you utilize valet this evening?"

"I did."

He moves us to a quiet corner and begins speaking in hushed tones. "Lizzie, I really enjoyed your company this evening."

I can't help but smile and suddenly become shy that the evening is ending. "You are the perfect gentleman, Mr. Chesney."

He takes a huge intake of breath and looks deeply in my eyes. "There are times I am definitely *not* a gentleman. For example, it would be most inappropriate for a gentleman to say to you something like—ah, let me see." He appears to ponder deeply for the right words. Leaning into me, my body quivers and shakes from his warm breath as it spreads across the folds of my ear. "How about this: my tongue still holds the beads of sweat that I licked from that tasty neck of yours. Every time you bent forward this evening, I was surely there to sneak a peek at your bosom. It was a travesty that your nipples were covered, but I could feel them against my chest as we danced. It took all of my control not to grind my hardened cock into you, begging for some contact with your tight body. You're a beautiful woman, my dear. If you were free, I'd take you upstairs, lay you down, and fuck you 'til the only name that ever left your lips was mine. I wouldn't stop until first light of dawn, leaving you quaking in my aftershocks." He leans in and licks me long and slow down my neck and my legs suddenly collapse from the shock of his erotic words. "But, I sense you're not ready to go there with me. I will be thinking of you long after we part, sweetheart. Please know it."

With those shocking words, I can't speak if I had to. My body sways in response to his frankness. He leans in and firmly presses his lips to mine. My mouth seems to beg him, leaning into his lips, demanding his tongue to pass through but frustratingly, it refuses. I have trouble keeping up with the conflicted thoughts running quickly through my mind, but I know he's right. I'm not ready. Much too quickly, he pulls away. The oddly bereft feeling I suddenly experience leaves my brain in an uncertain fog of emotions. I gather my wits when I realize he has led me to the valet toward the certain end of our time together.

Once my car arrives, I have this overwhelming feeling of regret. For what, I can't say exactly. This is only a job. A way to keep my family sheltered. I am not a cheater. He waves the valet away, opening my door for me. "Drive carefully, Lizzie. I fully intend to be in touch soon. You're a talented woman and I'd appreciate your assistance with my Museum endowment."

Pushing through the fog in my brain, I'd nearly forgotten his words to Cindy. "I didn't realize you were serious."

"Quite serious. You'll come to realize I have good insight about people. I want us to continue our acquaintance because you're a smart woman and I'm not a stupid man. It will benefit me enormously to have you in my corner. Thank you for a lovely evening, my dear." With that, he closes the door and stands there, smiling affectionately at me through the glass. I drive away thinking, *What the fuck just happened?*

Chapter Twelve

An Unexpected Blessing...

Lizzie

"It added two and one-half inches! Not two inches, mind you. Two and one-half! It felt amazing!" Marianne exclaims.

"I've never heard of anything like that in my life! Lizzie, how do you know about all this stuff?" Janice questions.

"I've heard about it. I'm not saying I've used it, but I'm not saying I haven't, either. My lips are totally sealed." Jenny smirks and we all laugh in unison.

"Oh, I don't know. I guess I just enjoy perusing the aisles of my neighborhood sex shop—or three!"

"Well, tell me again. What is it exactly?" Janice is so flustered. She has already finished her third glass of wine and now she's working on number four. Our weekly girls' night out at The Boathouse always includes great conversation. More often than not, the conversation leads to great sex talk and recommendations from yours truly.

Trying to catch my breath from laughing with these girls is often a challenge. "Well, it's easier to explain its benefits. It's a silicone sleeve that is placed over a man's penis, or if you don't have one readily available…" I bust out laughing, along with everyone else because it's so hard to keep a straight face around these cackling hens, I swear. "You can also place it over a dildo. This sleeve comes in various textures. You can get them ribbed, plain, or with little bumps/nips all over. The little bumps create their own pleasure, but I digress. Anyway…"

"Oh, don't digress, I want to know all about the nips!" Marianne says a little too loudly, and I suddenly notice the table near us has four guys who are very engrossed in our hysterical conversation.

"Sorry, really I am. Anyway, this sleeve is considered an extender to your man's dick. If he's seven inches now, he's nine. If he's ten inches, get ready for surgery because now he's in the foot club."

"Oh, no…he was approaching that when he was seven, Lizzie because my sleeve is two and one-half inches. Don't deny me my half-inch, girlfriend!" Marianne announces across the bar. Now the table of guys is busting out laughing since they are hanging on our every word.

"Bless your heart, I'd never do that to you." Shaking my head, I laugh at these crazy girls I love so much. They grant me the comic relief I desperately need to get me through until I see them again. "It gets better, though!" Noticing I have their full attention, I continue, "There are other benefits to these sleeves. Even if your man is blessed with length, he may still be a quick trigger. These provide a solution." I smile broadly, and everyone is hanging on my every syllable, even the table of four guys who has casually stood up and moved in our direction to hear a little better. "These sleeves come in various thicknesses and include a built-in cock ring. They help to desensitize his cock so he won't come too fast. Obviously, if he is wearing it, he's in the moment and will stay interested because he's watching your motions and listening to your sounds of ecstasy. So, unless there is a medical issue, he shouldn't lose his erection."

They all look at me like I've found the cure for cancer. Damn, I'd bet there is a run on penile sleeves at the adult bookstore tomorrow. I glance at the guys and they look just as thrilled until they notice I've caught their reactions and suddenly they're macho, shaking heads and "Oh no, not me" expressions dominate their faces.

"You want to know what I think the best benefit is about these sleeves?" Their eyes widen, patiently waiting. "Has anyone seen the rabbit ears that come on certain vibrators?"

"Hell yeah! The two pieces on top of the vibrator resembling bunny ears that go around your clit when it's inserted inside of you, right?" Jenny guesses excitedly.

"Absolutely correct. There are some sleeves that come with the bunny ears and they include a silver bullet for maximum chance of clitoral orgasm. Some include vibration patterns. So if a regular, steady buzz gets you off, then good. If you need a pulsing pattern, you got that covered, too. No longer, one-size fit all, ladies. We have options!

"It's heaven, really…these silicone sleeves are a guaranteed orgasm. Think about it like this…use it alone or with a partner. It has pleasurable nips along the shaft which really feel good going in and out. It will outlast your partner even if he comes because chances are it will make the sex last longer since he's desensitized. In this case, size really doesn't matter because you can make up for the penile length if that's really important to you. Marianne's sleeve was two and one-half inches, but they go even higher. You can set the vibration to match your body's needs and another benefit: some have a semen collector in the base of the unit. Easy clean up. My only suggestion, have plenty of lube available."

I'm staring at everyone and their mouths are dropped open and then I notice we are surrounded by a sea of people who have moved in, listening to our conversation. *Oh my goodness, when did that happen?* I'm a little embarrassed so many people have been listening to my intimate sexual aid conversation. Suddenly, everyone starts drilling me with questions. "What brand did you buy? How much does it cost? What's the biggest one you've found? What store has the best selection? What works best, nips or ribs? (Shouted from the back)…Can you put it in the dishwasher?" *Whoa…what the fuck? Where did that question come from?*

Two days later, Ms. Martin summons me to her office. I was stricken with panic to the point I almost bailed. She's intimidating to say the least and I don't want to experience her wrath.

"Ah, Lizzie! You came. I must speak with you right away." Following behind her to the ostentatious office, I don't bother to sit in case I need to make a quick and hasty exit. "Sit, my dear. You look positively shaken. Whatever is the matter?"

"Oh, nothing." I sit on the chair's edge very gingerly. Notably, the chair closest to the exit.

"Mark raved about the event. He couldn't say enough positive things about you. He believes you have quite the poise and professionalism needed to escort him to future events. In fact, he wants me to politely cancel event dates with some of my other ladies in favor of you. He mentioned you will be working on his endowment to the Children's Museum. I have to be honest with you, Lizzie. Mark is a close friend of mine. I don't have many true friends in my life and those that are, I protect fiercely. He is a very private person with regard to his business affairs. You must have made quite the impression on him."

I stand there with my jaw open. Here I was, ready to be yelled at for having a panic attack, and she's giving me praise. *Well shit! All that worry for nothing.* My blood pressure fights to regulate while I take slow, deep breaths. "Mr. Chesney is a kind man with whom I enjoy spending time. We have similar interests and conversation flows evenly between us."

"Ah, yes it would appear so. Just know where I stand when it comes to Mark. Don't hurt him or lead him on, Lizzie." An uncomfortable silence extends between us. I'm assuming she's being a loyal friend. In that case, I understand her motives. "I have a check for you. There is something extra in there as well that Mark messengered over this morning. I will text you the future event details this afternoon. Please send me your wardrobe options by midday tomorrow."

Leaving her office, I can barely contain my excitement. Something personal from Mark! I can't wait to reach my car. Inside the manila envelope are two envelopes, one thicker than the other. The smaller envelope is my paycheck from Ms. Martin. No surprise there. The second envelope is larger. I open it and find a letter and another sealed envelope. The linen paper embossed with the name of Mr. Mark Chesney in a very masculine formal font adorns the letterhead. My excitement grows noticing his beautiful handwriting.

Mr. Mark Chesney

My Dearest Birdie,

You must know the time we spent together has dominated my thoughts. Not only do you possess poise, beauty, and passion for our combined causes, but you're incredibly intelligent. I've selfishly decided I need to be around you so your smarts may rub off on me.

I appreciate your current situation, and please know I shall always respect your wishes, even if two cold showers will become a permanent nighttime routine for me. Being in your company was incredibly thrilling for me and not soon forgotten.

Please accept this token as my gift to you to be used any way you see fit to support your wonderful children. They are truly blessed to have you in their lives.

With warm regards,
~M

I can't help but feel the warmest of feelings in the pit of my stomach. The slight chill on my cheek causes me to discover a stream of tears I didn't know I was leaking. To hear praise like this is very overwhelming. Jeremy used to utter supporting comments to me all the time and I forgot how much I miss hearing them. Nowadays, he doesn't ever seem to notice anything anymore.

I carefully open the thick envelope and my jaw drops down in shock. "Shit!" I mutter to no one but myself. The envelope is full of cash. I flip through quickly and notice all one hundred dollar bills. I immediately count it and find five thousand dollars. Relief. That is the emotion that dominates my thoughts. I mentally calculate rent, electricity, food, and insurance. Since we are so far behind on our bills, I breathe a huge sigh of relief because now I have enough. I can bring everything current! Then… I'm overwhelmed with a different feeling. Dirtiness. Why would he give me so much money? I can't accept this, can I? What would Jeremy think I did to receive so much money? I know Ms. Martin said Mark may tip me, but this is extravagant, to say the least. I desperately need this money. In my heart, I know I didn't commit a crime since I didn't have sex with anyone. Ahh, dammit! I guess I will just hold on to it while I decide what's best to do.

Anyone walking by my car would wonder what is wrong with me. Tears flow down my cheeks. I'm on the verge of hyperventilating from the relief and happiness I'm feeling. I won't have to worry about eviction notices if I decide to keep it. My children can sleep in comfort tonight. I am content, for now at least. I have options and it has been a while since that were true.

I drive home, conscientiously noticing the gas gauge always nearing empty since I normally can't afford to fill it. My ever-present fear of being stranded is soothed when the gauge reads one-fourth filled. Pulling into our apartment's lot, I notice the building manager walking away from my door. My body is overwhelmed with dread because he only makes an appearance while in search of late rental fees. Of course, it would be too much to hope he would show up to complete the various repair work orders that I requested months ago. Besides, who needs hot water, right? Deciding that I do not have the strength and patience to engage with him, I deliberately hold back in my car. Eventually, when he is out of sight, I approach my door and notice a rolled up paper attached to the doorknob with a rubber band.

These papers are practically glued to the doorknob because the band is twisted about a hundred times in anger, I'm sure. My heart races as I remove the paper and read:

Mr. Jeremy Macintyre
Mrs. Elizabeth Macintyre

> **Your rent payment is seriously delinquent. We will be forced to proceed with eviction proceedings if full payment is not received within three (3) business days. No personal checks; only cash, certified funds, or money order will be accepted.**
> **It is our fervent hope that you settle your account immediately.**

Building Management

Well, I guess my decision on whether or not to keep the money has just been made for me. I just hope this doesn't backfire in my face. At least I can fill my gas tank for the first time in forever.

Chapter Thirteen

Just Another Guilty Soul...

Jack

"Patricia, can you please bring me the Sawyer file?"

"Yes, sir. Right away."

The criminal case I'm working on now has consumed my time for the last six months. My client is providing witness testimony for the prosecution before a secret Grand Jury, in exchange for no jail time for his contributory actions.

Some cases really get to me and this one is the worst in recent memory. My client drove the getaway car following the murder of an entire family, including three children under ten years of age. I'm never immune to the uneasy feelings in my core that my client will walk away with probation. He is a true criminal who has confessed multiple crimes to me, many of which are unknown to law enforcement. No matter what he may be guilty of, he has a constitutional right to an adequate defense. Enter yours truly, at an expensive hourly rate, I might add. It never bothers me to charge inflated prices to the clients who have committed the most heinous crimes. Because I am one of Richmond's best criminal defense attorneys, he will not serve the lengthy incarceration he deserves. Every time I look at the crime scene photos, I become more unsettled with my role in helping him. There are days when I am sickened to look in the mirror even though I know I'm just doing my job.

When I went to law school, I knew I wanted to practice criminal law. Domestic, torts, contracts, etc., none of that bullshit did anything to excite me. My undergraduate degree in Criminal Justice – Law Enforcement, was solely because of my childhood dream. I wanted to become a police officer for as long as I can remember. Sometimes, a few of us have our career paths determined before birth. The baby, His Royal Highness, Prince George of England comes to mind. Whereas I'll never rule a kingdom, I am one of those few unfortunate individuals having strong family commitments controlling my future. Not able to follow my dreams like other people may seem strange to some but when you are from a family with extreme wealth, many life decisions are made for you. I try to ignore the bitterness that invariably seeps up. Besides, most people do not have empathy for the wealthy so the "pitiful me" words of woe do not often leave my lips to others. My frustrations have to stay quiet but deep down I'm mad as hell that I am forced to live my life serving others and can't even pick the career that I truly want. The situation is fucked up, plain and simple.

My mother's family was seriously wealthy. They invested heavily in real estate and somehow managed to strike it rich farming. The real increase in earnings came during my mother's control of the finances. A business major at University of Richmond, she is a very smart lady. The profitability in her portfolio and by extension, my trust fund, is nothing short of brilliant investing. Instead of using her wealth for her own extravagance, she has made it her life's work to epitomize southern philanthropy in a very modern way. The kind sweetness conveyed in her Virginian drawl, along with her charming disposition, often masks the bulldog within. Don't underestimate her. And don't steal, lie, or cheat her, let alone harm me—her precious only living child—because she just might cut your tongue out.

Coming into a philanthropic family, I had to participate in the family decisions when I turned eighteen. Near this time, I began school at UR. My mother explained, as gently as she could, that my very existence was so crucial to the very charities we support, that voluntarily entering into a violent career was NOT going to happen. Once I really delved into the specifics of our finances, I understood it, but deep down have never really accepted it.

I thought by being a criminal defense attorney I could keep my feet in the arena. Problem is, I'm totally disgusted with the system. It protects the offenders and I despise taking on guilty clients. So many attorneys, like my well-known father, can separate it. "Everyone is entitled to a defense regardless of guilt or innocence," he has preached to me over the years. I know that! I love this country and all it stands for, but when I have a client get a slap on the wrist when I know what he *really* did, I can never seem to rest well at night.

Following a knock on the door, my assistant says, "Jack, the file you requested?"

"Yes, thanks so much, Patricia. Oh, Patricia?"

"Yes, sir?

"Can you get Detective Wallace on the phone for me, please?"

"Sure. Right away, sir."

Before I can open the file, Patricia's voice over my intercom relays, "Jack, Detective Wallace is on line two."

"Appreciate it, Patricia."

"Detective Wallace, thank you for speaking with me. I have some questions about the immunity agreement as well as the plan you have to keep my client safe while wearing the wire…"

We speak for quite a while and come up with a plan I feel is a safe one for my client. I request to be present in the surveillance van while the action takes place. Inside, I'm brimming with excitement! Due to strict confidentiality, I cannot tell anyone about the logistics of the meet. When I learn the first attempt will be this evening, I cringe because Victoria and I have plans. Plans I promised not to cancel, again. *Fuck! Why does it have to be tonight?* She will be majorly pissed and I can't tell her the truth. I know this will not go over well. At all.

I decide to call and get it over with because her wrath is no fun.

"Hello?"

"Hey, Vickie. How's your day today?" I ask sweetly. I'm met with a pause, a very *long* pause. "Vickie, are you there?"

"Yes, Jack. I'm here, but I get the sense that I will not like this conversation, will I?"

I take a long, deep breathing sigh. "Ah, no sweetheart. No, you probably won't."

"Dammit, Jack! You're canceling on me, AGAIN!"

Feeling like a total asshole because this really is becoming a habit, I decide to offer my sincerest apologies. "Baby, sweet Vickie, I'm not doing this on purpose. I've had something come up and I can't get out of it. I'm extremely sorry and realize that you are absolutely right to be pissed with me. I'll make it up to you. I promise."

"Don't Vickie me! You think you can make it all better with endearments, but not this time, Jack. I've had these tickets for three weeks. You swore you'd take me!"

She's exactly right. I did swear I wouldn't cancel. I'm such a dick. I could probably call Detective Wallace and send a junior attorney in my place, but I'm invigorated to go on this one. The safe confines of the office walls are closing in on me. I'm dying to see some real action.

Realizing I need to bring her emotions down, I decide to entice her with a guaranteed plan to divert her angry attention. In a hushed voice, I whisper, "Baby, take Cathy with you tonight. I'm sorry I've missed so many of our dates lately. I promise to try and do better. And Vickie?"

"What!" she bites back.

"Two things: one, I know you're irate with me right now and that's understandable but… let it go by the time I get home. And two, I expect you to remember who's in charge. That means naked, in position, and ready when I walk through our bedroom suite."

She momentarily pauses sighing deeply and quivers her response, "Y-yes Jack."

"I love you, Vickie."

"I love you, too, Jack-ass!" she says, dragging the last part out. I chuckle, knowing I had it coming yet I'll thoroughly enjoy punishing her ass later for the jab.

Now, time to get changed into comfortable clothes and get ready for some excitement!

Chapter Fourteen

Unexpected Flames Burning Bright...

Jack

Thrilling. No, more like so fucking intense at times, I can't breathe. That's how I feel just listening in from base command to the exchange with my client and the intended target Detective Wallace was hoping to get evidence on. Just knowing at any moment guns could be drawn is majorly fucking scary, but my adrenaline is pumping so hard I love every minute of it. I have to keep reminding myself of why I'm here. It's so hard because I want to be on the good guys' team. Really badly…..Fuuckkk, I HATE this!

During the course of the night, new evidence came to light on a totally separate investigation. It's not unusual for things like this to happen; crime begets crime, after all. The downside or upside depending on how you look at it is there will be more undercover opportunities for my client. Inherently, this would be very risky for him, but a fucking great opportunity for me to be up close to the action! Selfish thinking, I know.

The meet lasts a little longer than expected, so I decide to run to a nearby Starbucks for a quick coffee to-go. As I approach the register, I notice a woman ordering in front of me. Weirdly, from behind, there is something familiar about her then it hits me cold. *That* voice. I wait patiently for her to turn around and when she does, I feel all the blood drain from my face. My jaw is locked helplessly open. The familiarity mirrored in her eyes confirms she is who I believe her to be. *No, this can't be right, can it? Is she really standing before me?*

She attempts to speak and it's obvious she is struggling as much as me. I'm incredibly relieved when she stutters out a greeting, "J-jaackk?" All I can do is nod slowly up and down. I barely register the Starbucks employee requesting my drink order. A hand held up in her direction is all I can manage in response. "Oh my goodness. Jack!" Suddenly, she throws her arms around my neck tightly and squeezes. "I cannot believe I ran into you! It's really you, Jack!"

Finally forcing my clouded brain to absorb this moment and actually use my mouth for something purposeful other than drooling, I grant her the biggest smile my face can manage. I quickly order my coffee so I can give her my full attention.

"Erin, I'm honestly in shock. I thought you lived in California now?"

"I moved back here about a year ago. This is so crazy, Jack. I've honestly been thinking a lot about you lately and suddenly you're right here in front of me. Totally surreal moment I'm having."

"You're not the only one. Look, do you have a few minutes to sit down and chat?"

"God, I'm glad you asked. I'd *love* to catch up! I'll grab a table while you wait for your order."

I hadn't realized how desperately I needed these precious few moments to collect myself, but I surely do. *Fuck! Erin is here. Erin is right here in fucking Starbucks.* I have so many emotions that have been locked away for something like twelve to fourteen years, and I can't even think clearly. So many memories begin to rush through my mind. This woman was my first for so many things. First person to have intercourse with. First love. First person to introduce me to kinky sex and, my-oh-my, she was *fucktastic* in bed. Also, first woman to break my heart. Erin was special. I loved her. A lot.

Trying to process the sea of emotions flowing through my mind, I walk to the table and join her. Still not quite processing the current events, I know I need to snap out of it or risk looking totally stupid.

"Erin, please talk to me. Tell me what brought you back and what you've been doing since returning home. I still can't believe I'm sitting here with you."

"Me, neither. I moved back here after a pretty bad breakup. I decided that I rather missed the wholesome south and took a huge gamble. I packed everything in a U-Haul, closed my bank account, quit my job, and drove cross-country. That was almost a year ago now. It was the craziest and possibly most dangerous thing a single woman could do. I took my time along the way visiting different places. It was a healing experience, really. The California lifestyle was a little too free-spirited for me."

My eyes surely bulged from my eye sockets, but I couldn't hold back a smirk. "Too free spirit, *for you*? That doesn't compute Erin."

"Yes, yes. I know. It's really different on the West Coast, Jack. Living in the American south is like living in a foreign country compared to California. I'm happy to be back. I truly am." She smiles hugely at me. Closely evaluating my reaction, she asks, "Jack, please tell me, are you married? Do you have a family? Where do you work?"

"I'm married ten years to my wife, Victoria. We met in college, my junior year at UR. We have twins, a boy, and a girl, who are eight years old."

"Twins! That's so cool to have twins."

"Yes. We think so, too. They're great kids. I really love being a parent."

"So, tell me, did you end up being a lawyer?"

"I did. I practice criminal law with Loving & Loving. I'm, of course, in partnership with my father in our downtown Richmond offices." She gives me an unhappy inquisitive look. "What?"

Looking a bit hesitant, I watch her expectantly, silently encouraging her to continue. "I guess I hoped you would eventually stand up to your father and join the police department like you'd always wanted to do."

Wow. In a matter of minutes, so many feelings have flooded back to me. Erin was always so supportive of my pursuits. I forgot about that. I can't help but look away from her disappointed eyes. "Unfortunately, Erin, I have had to accept my life plan was decided long before I ever argued with alternative choices. Practicing criminal law allows me to dip my toes in the water occasionally. That's what I was doing tonight, actually, but I'm really not supposed to be telling you that. I don't know why I just did, to tell you the truth." I smile back, unable to ignore the beautiful woman before me who could always convince me to bare my soul.

Well, fuck me running. This has been a most unexpected trip to Starbucks. Never in a million years did I expect to spend my day like I have just spent it. All of these emotions and memories have flooded my brain about the times Erin and I shared.

Damn…the sex. Some of the best sex of my *life* was with this woman. Always so open to new things and new places. She seemed to have an outdoor fetish because we constantly had sex outside, always at the risk of getting caught. The woman was the fiend of every man's dreams. Never did she make excuses or put off having sex. Her needs were *every* day, sometimes *multiple* times a day.

Because I was so young and inexperienced, I quickly realized I needed an education, and quick, or I would risk losing her. That's the reason I began my quest to become an expert in the sack. I wanted to dazzle her so she would have a reason to keep coming back to me, as shallow as that sounds. I was far from stupid and the idea of a sexy "older" woman is what led me around by my dick. I thought it was a brilliant plan, actually. And guess what? It worked for two fantastic years. We had AMAZING sex! Her openness made me so comfortable to say anything. If there was a fantasy, we did it. She never mocked me; she encouraged me. She was definitely my teacher when our relationship began. Since I was so obsessed with learning new ways to get us both off, my relationship with her is what led me to be comfortable enough to pursue the type of sexually fulfilling lifestyle Victoria and I have today.

She's aged, as we all have, but even though she is older she's still sexy as fuck. It's hard not to get distracted merely by her presence. I guess when you run into an ex-girlfriend whom you haven't seen in a very long time—one you cared about deeply—it's normal to be tongue tied. Especially when the feelings lingered for a long time because you felt like you never really had closure.

"Jack, are you still with me?" She gently taps me on the arm and I suddenly feel a zing tear through my limb.

"Oh, I'm so sorry. I just got lost there for a moment." Embarrassed to be caught daydreaming, I pause to just take a moment of time to enjoy the woman before me and the memories we had. Her brown, shoulder length hair is shorter than I remember. Her body is just as tight and sweet as it ever was. It's obvious that she takes care of herself and works out. What really gets to me is her voice. The cool rasp is so unusual. It's what makes her such a great singer. As much as I love it, I resent it as well. It's what took her to California. Took her away from me. "Are you still singing, Erin?"

She turns her head and looks out the window, clearly deep in thought. Her contemplative eyes are heavy with burden and possible sadness. It's a look that concerns me, and my deeply hidden, long-time affection for her begs to know the cause of it.

"Not so much anymore," she whispers to the window, almost as if she is seeking answers from the pane of glass.

"What happened when you went to California? Did you get the record contract you wanted so badly?"

"Umm…let's just say my career has hit some serious highs and some serious lows. I *did* get a record deal and made an album I was very proud of. The music business is a tough, tough business, Jack. There are a lot of shady people working in it. As much as I love to sing, I want to survive and be happy. Sometimes, you can't have both."

"That sounds very ominous. I'm guessing this bad breakup didn't help matters?"

Looking very sad and hurt, she replies, "Not. At. All." It bothers me to see her looking so forlorn and empty. "Sometimes, I wish I had just stayed here. Life was so good back then. We were so good. I just felt like you needed to grow and experience life and I certainly needed to try and make a go of the music biz."

I study her face carefully and believe I see regret. It's the same regret I had when she left me all those years ago. My heart ached for her for a very, very long time. "It killed me when you left, Erin. You taught me so much about life." She lets out a huge laugh and her face turns ten shades of red. "Yes, you definitely taught me a lot about THAT, for sure." We both share nervous giggles, hardly able to look one another in the eye. "I do understand why you needed to leave."

"I told myself that because you were so much younger, you needed to enjoy the fun of college and all the new experiences. I'm sorry I was so cold to you. It's painful to admit, but I can tell you now that it was totally a front. I knew I needed to try and make a clean break, but I missed you so damn much. You were really mad and thought I was a cold bitch, but the truth was I didn't fare well emotionally when I left you. It was years before I considered a real relationship. No one compared to you then or since if you want the truth. Additionally, I probably shouldn't tell you this because you're married and all, but I had hoped to run into you just to see how you were doing. Truthfully, I guess I've missed your friendship the most."

Damn. She is so right. We were really good together. Our friendship, in addition to our fantastic sex, was very fulfilling. I smile back knowingly, shaking my head in agreement. "Where do you live?"

"I have a condo at Rocketts Landing," her eyes beam with sudden joy. "I love it so much since they revitalized the area, and the neighbors are great."

Not wanting to lose touch with Erin, I boldly pick up her cell from the table and text myself. "There, now you have my number and we won't lose touch again."

She reaches over and grabs my hand, holding it between the two of hers. "I really hope not, Jack. I have truly missed you, and reconnecting with you has been the highlight of my day for sure."

I feel so lost in her eyes and my arm tingles all the way up from her touch. Suddenly, I'm a little taken with guilt that Victoria probably wouldn't appreciate me holding hands with another woman. Just as I'm about to pull away I hear "Jack?" from somewhere behind me. I turn around to find Victoria and Cathy standing there and Victoria's trained eyes are straight on our joined hands. Reflexively, I pull my hand away from Erin's delicate touch as if I'm being burned. *Smooth, Jack. Like that didn't look guilty enough as it was.*

I stand quickly, reaching for her, "Victoria? What are you doing here?"

"What am I doing here? Um, I think I should be asking that question." If looks could kill, I'd certainly be dead considering the look of wrath on her face, not to mention the revulsion on Cathy's face as well. Jeez, this doesn't look good at all.

"Oh, yes, I think I should explain." The quiver in my voice doesn't hide my discomfort at all! "Victoria, please meet Erin Hughes." Looking back to the lady of the moment and motioning to my wife, "Erin, please meet my wife, Victoria Winfield Loving." The look on Victoria's face is statue still, white as a sheet. She looks totally stunned in her silence. There's no doubt she has connected the dots of my ex all the way to the image of our hands gently embraced. *Fuck.*

"Nice to meet you, Victoria," Erin comments warmly and reaches her hand out to shake hands.

Victoria looks down at her extended hand, undoubtedly recalling the moments prior. Her face is so cold and uninviting. She refuses the return gesture and Erin pulls her hand back quickly.

I lean my face in closely to Victoria and whisper, "Don't be rude." She looks up at me, taking in a breath, and after a long dramatic pause, quips in Erin's direction, "Regards to you as well, Ms. Hughes. I must apologize; I wasn't expecting to find my husband here in Starbucks late at night, holding hands with another woman. How convenient for me to know he's meeting with the ex-lover who broke his heart so long ago."

"Victoria!" I grit my teeth in anger.

Looking extremely chastised and uncomfortable with the scene before her, Erin responds, "No, it's really okay, Jack. She's right. I'm very sorry. Please know, Mrs. Loving, this was totally unplanned. We happened upon one another in pure, random luck as we stood in the line getting coffee. I just moved back here last year, so we were catching up. That's all it was." She looks at me with definite regret in her eyes and a soft smile on her face. "It was so nice to see you again." Erin takes a lingering look in our direction. "Goodbye, Jack," she says to me. Even though she looks down quickly, she can't hide the tears beginning to form in her eyes or the slight quiver in her voice as she turns to walk away. It's in this moment I feel a severe, sharp pain go through my heart. It's like I'm back in 2000 and the love of my life is walking out the door and all I can do is watch.

Suddenly, I'm filled with anger. I pull my eyes from Erin's departing figure and turn to face Cathy. "Please excuse us, but my *wife* and I have matters to discuss." I grab her by the hand and begin to pull her out the door. I faintly hear her departing comments to Cathy about touching base tomorrow. Now on a mission, we need away from prying eyes. My wife and I have *plans*.

Once arriving at my car, I open her door and slam it behind her. I'm so filled with contempt for her rudeness that all I can see is red. I ignore her pleas for discussion the entire drive home.

After parking my beloved Camaro—a red convertible with black racing stripes—in our garage, I walk around to her side, opening her door. Always the gentleman 'til the bitter end; however, I'm seething and not uttering a peep to her. "Jack, I know you're angry, but you have to see it from my perspective. I walked up and found my husband holding hands with a beautiful woman."

Focused on my mission and having no patience whatsoever, I refuse to acknowledge her words. "Go upstairs, now. It's time—get yourself in position. You *only* have five minutes. Go." I bite out my words like I'm not playing one fucking second longer and judging by the look on her face, she fucking well knows it.

I need to think clearly. I tell myself to calm down. *Get a whiskey. A double. Breathe. Fuck!* This is testing every bit of patience and control I have. Erin is actually back, and I spoke with her. Erin is back, and she looks amazing. Erin is back, and she was filled with regret. Erin is back, and I know without a doubt that I could have been balls deep within the hour if I'd wanted to. Erin is back, and Victoria acted like a fucking bitch to her. Erin is *back*.

I'll have to take time later to process how I truly feel about our conversation. But that's on the agenda for tomorrow. Because now, now I have to get some things straight with my dear wife.

After our varied appetite for sex, we've come up with our own way to satisfy our interests. Sometimes we are romantic, soft and sweet. Other times, we are hard and fast. Occasionally, we delve into our modified version of BDSM that works just for us. I need control most of the time, but I find enjoyment in giving the reins to her as well. Most often, she wants me to lead our intimate moments so it never really causes conflict.

There are specific times, like tonight, when she is so blatantly out of line that the Dom/sub relationship is unquestionably in play. Within the BDSM community, brats are defined as submissives who are outright defiant to goad play or attention. In an effort to get my attention, Victoria was deliberately rude to Erin out of jealousy. In the past, when I prepared her in advance for an encounter, she would become very excited in anticipation of what was to come.

Tonight, she had a range of emotions from anger, learning I wasn't coming, to lust, knowing what was in store for her later. She spent hours steadily more horny with no relief considering she was with her friend Cathy and I do not allow her to self-stimulate. When she stumbled onto our moment and witnessed our closeness, she perceived a threat to her lustful thoughts. Most people would think it was about the anger of her husband spending time with an ex. No, that's not the case at all. I know my wife very well and she was in full sub mode, modeling bratty behavior. Her vicious stab about Erin breaking my heart was really a statement begging me to pick her instead. My words, which are her trigger, were like a recording on repeat: *get in position.* She knows when I'm in Dom mode, don't fuck around. The problem is, that's what makes her act out because she craves it.

I move quickly to our master suite located in the left wing of our mansion. I find her on her knees beside the bed, head bowed, naked except for her bra and panties. She won't speak because she knows the rules.

I walk and stand before her, looking down, not saying a word. I move to my closet and change into some workout shorts. Upon return, she hasn't moved an inch. "Do you enjoy being a brat, Victoria?"

I just barely catch the hopeful sigh in her throat that she carefully attempts to mask, proving she quite favored her behavior. "No, Sir."

"Do you feel it is appropriate to raise your voice and yell at me in a public setting?"

"No, Sir."

"Detail your day's transgressions."

She sighs deeply and bends her head closer to her lap. "I was very rude to Miss Hughes. I spoke to her about matters that came before me that had nothing to do with me. It was not right that I mentioned you were hurt by her actions."

"Is that all?"

"No, Sir. I did raise my voice at you when you whispered first to me. I should not have done that."

"I'm losing patience. And?"

"Sir? I am unaware what I have failed to mention. I was rude in how I spoke to both of you. You are my husband and I trust you. I should know better."

"How quickly you forget about your outburst today when I notified you I couldn't accompany you this evening."

"Oh, yes! So sorry, Sir. You are correct. I did not conduct myself well when I learned you had to cancel. I called you Jack-..."

"Yes, you did. I was most unhappy by your disrespect then and this evening." I decide to pace the room, deep in thought. Not only to calm myself but allow her time to build her anxiety. Having decided the appropriate punishment, I once again stand before her. "Have I ever given you reason to doubt me, Victoria?"

"No, Sir. You are a wonderful husband."

"I do really try to be everything you can possibly need. I have never been unfaithful to you, Victoria."

"Thank you, Sir. I believe that and love you very much."

"You came upon a situation and assumed the worst, didn't you?"

"Yes, Sir. I'm sorry for that. I-I just didn't like her. I know what she did to you and when I saw the love in her eyes, I was very angry and I lashed about because I hurt for you that she caused you pain. She was selfish."

"Oh, dear Victoria. I appreciate you were concerned for me, but that was a conversation for private discussion, not public consumption."

"You are correct, Sir."

"It hasn't escaped me that you had hours of sexual tension building in anticipation of our play tonight. Even though you haven't clearly admitted it, you thought she would replace you in our bed tonight. I don't enjoy your vicious, bratty behavior, Victoria. Stop doing it to get a rise out of me."

"Yes sir, I was actually thinking about tonight when I walked through the coffee shop's doors. When I saw your hands touching, all I could see was her hands all over your body and suddenly I was so jealous. I apologize, Sir, because I know you will always do what is best for us."

"I will take your intentions into consideration." I stare into her eyes, making sure I have her full attention. Finally, I breathe deeply, "You will safe word if you need to, correct?"

"Absolutely and thank you, Sir."

"Move to the center of the bed." She promptly lies on her back and I attach her arms to the cuffs on the headboard. "Don't move." Deciding we both need some additional cooling down and contemplation, I decide a short workout in our home gym is just the ticket. Without a word, I walk out.

Victoria

When I went into the coffee shop and saw Jack sitting at a table with a beautiful woman, I was immediately confused. But when I saw her holding his hand, I wanted to grab the bitch by her hair and cram my fist down her throat. Over the years, I've had to fend off many opportunistic women who see my beautiful husband and decide they want him. When a man has money, he is sought after, non-stop. Everyone knows he is a multi-millionaire many times over. Publications predict he could be a billionaire when his parents pass away and he inherits their assets. It's really hard to say in reality because Sarah and Jack, Sr., have given away quite a bit over the years to many charitable causes. Much more than I would have given away, for sure. In any event, I have to constantly be on guard, fending off the money hungry bitches.

What made me rude and catty tonight, was when I discovered the twat holding my husband's hand was none other than the holier-than-thou, Erin Hughes. Jack was sucked in by her and haunted by her memory. He has always had a look in his eyes of severe hurt when speaking of her and I'm incredibly jealous. Not only because she holds a piece of his heart, but because he was so infatuated with her sexual prowess and "older woman" free spirit. She set him on the path that has made him a god in bed today. So, I guess I should be thanking her. The man can fuck. No kidding or exaggerating. Just when I think he can't blow my mind any further, he comes up with some refreshing new way and I realize I'm lucky to be experiencing this ride with him. Regardless, I couldn't seem to shut my mouth when I knew who she was. Instantly, I didn't like her and wanted her away from my husband. So, if it means I get some punishment, it's worth it. Jack is right about my bratty behavior. It was too easy to put Erin in her place, and yes, I was horny as shit. So I pushed the limits of proper public decorum knowing he would rush to take me home and screw my brains out. *Checkmate; I win, Miss Hughes.*

I can generally sense from my husband his moods and how that relates to our sexual experiences. Telling me earlier this evening to get *into position*, is our code for a more formalized style of play. I love our sex life but particularly crave it when he expects me to be submissive. Most people might think it's demeaning, but I love not having to make decisions. The truth is, I'm naturally submissive, so it works for us. I can give myself over to my husband who will make the best decision for both of us. Besides, the beast he turns into while in this zone is a huge turn-on.

Lying on our bed with my wrists bound has given me time to reflect on the day. Being left alone, unable to leave our bed, is all part of my husband's plan and the beginnings of my punishment. About an hour later, Jack returns. Sweat covers his magnificent body. The veins in his neck and arms bulge from his skin. His hairline is wet and he is only slightly out of breath. This tells me he ran on the treadmill very hard. He always does while in deep contemplation. I am immediately jealous, knowing any extra gym time was because he was thinking of Erin.

Jack walks to the bathroom without uttering a single word and returns quickly after showering. I have a fleeting sense of disappointment that I won't be tasting his salty skin on my tongue. I'm suddenly engulfed with the clean smell permeating from him and I'm drawn to him like a moth to a flame.

Jack walks to me and begins fondling my breasts with his hands. He knows the exact amount of pressure to give my nipples since they seem to have a straight connection to my clit. This knowledge has always thrilled and empowered him to control and play my body like an instrument. Having incredibly sensitive breasts affords me the greatest orgasms, but I fear their resulting deliciousness will wait.

Today, as punishment, he keeps my orgasm at bay. Just when I think I might climb high enough, he refuses all touch knowing how much I crave it. My body moves toward him, begging for skin-to-skin contact, but considering the restraints, I don't move far. "Please," I desperately beg. He resumes his light touching; my body delirious from his incredible nipple tweaks and pinches. After bringing me to the edge then ceasing all contact three times, he moves his torture lower. With no end in sight, I'm breathless and my skin sings with electricity. "Oh, please. I can't take anymore, Jack! I want to come so badly."

His index finger travels a straight line down my core to my lips. He teases and flicks around as if he is amusing himself greatly. Deliberately avoiding my clit, he works a single finger just inside a few inches. "You're wet for me, I see."

"I am, that's very true."

"Do you want to come, sweetheart?"

"Oh yes!" I enthusiastically answer. Probably too enthusiastically.

"Hmmm. That's what I know, dear, but you can't always get what you want." He removes the finger and goes back to diddling along my lips, still avoiding my clit. *Damn frustrating man!* "For example, I wanted you to listen to me this evening and be nice. You didn't do it." He returns the single finger and turns his wrist, focusing on the front wall of my vagina. That's the precise moment I know I'm really in for it. This could go one of two ways and the dreaded option is orgasm denial, if he's still really upset with my disrespect, is at the forefront of my mind.

He begins to rub that glorious g-spot in a way only he knows how to control all my pleasure. I'm a slave to his movements and he knows it. I'm powerless to just lay here and hope he has mercy on me. My eyes are locked on his, afraid to blink, hoping he hears my unspoken pleas.

The rubbing intensifies and I quickly build toward orgasm. The power and fierceness in his expression controls everything in me—my breath, my eye movements, my dry mouth, the paralysis in my muscles. He owns me, and then…he takes it away. He removes his hand and I immediately lose the growing unreachable orgasm I crave so desperately. Uncontrollable whimpers leave my mouth as I grab the sheets, desperately clawing to get the feeling back. My body's unconscious need for friction of any kind is overpowering, but the feeling doesn't return.

I'm struck so severely on my over-sensitized skin when his index finger glides across my fingers on my left hand. He then moves slowly down my wrist and forearm to the base of my elbow. He draws random circles, adjusting finger pressure, along the inside of my arm leading to my shoulders and across my collar bone, left to right. I'm in a dreamlike state where my skin is on fire, enjoying his identical pattern of touch down my right arm. Everywhere his finger lands reminds me of the handheld sparklers from Fourth of July firework celebrations.

His touch glides down my core, repeating the path to my lips and his devilish diddling at my expense. He brings me close a second time and stops again. I'm breathing hard and pulling on my restraints as hard as I can. "Please stop. Oh, please let me come. I want to so badly." I know if play ever gets out of hand, I can always use my safe word to end the madness, but he plays my body like a violin. He's building my pleasure and the master knows how to get the best out of me, so I let him. I always let him.

The third time, he follows the path the exact same way. When his finger enters me, he rubs the front wall and I can feel the familiar feeling building. My body uncontrollably stiffens and I'm afraid to move. Afraid that he might stop again. Afraid because the explosive orgasm building inside me will most assuredly be too much. I just know it will.

As I carefully and cautiously enjoy the climb, he suddenly changes everything with his pattern. He adds a second finger and a thumb to my clit while pinching my very sensitized nipple. Hard. Leaning over, he says quietly, "Now, Victoria," before he sucks hard on my other nipple and I'm in a glorious state of euphoria. I scream out loudly, over and over, so many indiscernible words and sounds. I don't care whether or not I appear odd or sound strange because the way he pulls the intense throbbing vibration from my core is addictive. Using his body to hold me down is the only thing keeping me from jolting upwards with my hips. The feeling ripping through my body is indescribable. My eyes roll back, I'm almost hyperventilating, and my limbs begin to feel like Jell-O. It's a mind fuck because the denial, which at the time was torturous, to say the least, is what sets my body on fire by the building sensations over and over in my pussy. It's the perfect recipe for an unforgettable release and a testament to his limitless sexual talents.

My mind is still in a lust-filled fog, but I vaguely register "Umm… that was fun to watch, my sweet, but I'm not done with you." Crawling up my body, he is totally naked and straddles me under my shoulders. His cock is fully erect as he slowly strokes it above my face. He pushes it down and rubs the underside across my lips. I open my mouth and my tongue desperately reaches to lick around the engorged head. Smacking my lips with his cock only once, he apparently decides to inflict further punishment by taking it away from my seeking mouth. "You want my dick, baby?"

I moan deeply, "Yes, please I want to taste you."

He grips my chin somewhat forcefully and holds it open while burying himself deeply in my throat. "That's right. Suck me, baby." Stroking slowly once, then twice, and on the third time he picks up his pace. I cover my teeth as best I can. He tilts my head back, allowing his cock to slide down my throat easily. Many years of practice have allowed me to curb my gag reflex so he knows he can stroke deeply.

Grabbing my head on either side of my face, he maintains a steady rhythm. I know he is enjoying my oral talents given the intense moans coming from him.

"Bite me, baby. Just the way you know I like it."

I uncover my teeth and begin to softly nibble using my back molars. Biting is something most men avoid, but Jack is not most men and knows that when done correctly, it's very enjoyable. When he is in a deep state of arousal, nibbling followed by stronger bites is enough to almost send him over the edge. Pain and pleasure are often separated by a very fine line.

I calculatingly moan loudly, and the vibration along with the well timed bites sends him just to the point of no return. "Fuck!"

He lets go of my head and moves down my body. I know what's coming and the anticipation is almost too much to bear. I pull on my restraints, knowing it's a lost cause. My body's need for friction is intense due to the sudden loss of his heat. Pulling my legs up, he presses his large hands on the undersides of my thighs and rolls me up and over. Looming largely over my "pretzel" self, he plunges sharply and deeply into me with no warning. He knows he can expect me to be drenching wet from our play. His deep strokes make me feel ripped apart in the most delightful way. Holding me up, he pushes with the tops of his thighs and uses one hand to pinch my nipple hard and the other hand moves down to furiously rub my budded clitoris. This feeling of complete fullness sends my brain to this weird space of almost floating. I quickly build with very little effort and soon I am nearing that place that makes me lose all reason. The complete and total sensuality of this moment has me fulfilling all my erogenous zones so, so sweetly.

"I'm coming! I'm coming!"

He cuts me a harsh eye and pinches harder. My orgasm, which was nearing its conclusion, either begins anew or a different one takes its place because I am soon climbing that exquisite mountain again.

Totally breathless and stiff limbed, I freeze and allow all the fantastic waves to run through my body and just feel. Once it has run its beautiful course, I am left completely bone-tired and exhausted.

He smirks at me, grinning a half upturned smile along with a devious post-orgasmic rub along my still sensitive clit, "Next time, it's 'I'm coming, *Sir*'!"

Chapter Fifteen

Moving On From Broken Hearts...

Jack

The next day I head to work, trying desperately to focus. I have court this afternoon and I'm supposed to be preparing, but my mind invariably wanders to my unexpected coffee companion last evening. Erin is back. I really cannot believe it. The chances of running into her ever again seemed so slim. Besides, Richmond, Virginia is hardly the music epicenter of the U.S even though we do have some pretty cool Indy bands. I really hate the way we left things. She seemed to dislike the sudden way we separated at my wife's arrival, too. I decide I must reach out to her again.

I call my firm's private detective, explaining my need to find a personal associate. Since I know approximately when she returned and where she is living, it takes just under an hour to get the information I need. Not able to concentrate a moment longer, I head out to find her.

Stopping by a local florist, I decide on a peace lily—the largest one in the store. I have some amends to make, I fear. It seems apropos considering I'd like some type of future relationship with Erin that's peaceful for everyone.

Having the best PI in Richmond on speed dial is a huge perk, I must admit. I guess it's one of the benefits of the mega rich. He gave me her vehicle and apartment information. Rounding the corner, her fully restored 1969 cherry red Camaro with black stripes comes into view. I cannot believe she still has it, after all, these years. It doesn't take a psychic to put together my love of Camaros and why. I quickly become annoyed that she drove cross country in a classic. *What would she do if she was broken down? Damn frustrating female!*

Walking to her door, I'm suddenly nervous and second-guessing my decision to come here. Ambushing her, giant plant in hand, is probably not my best decision of the day. Staring at the brass door knocker for some type of guiding wisdom obviously doesn't help me out at all. So after a solid three to five minutes staring at the bright shiny object, I lift my trembling hand and knock. And knock and knock some more. *Fuck, she's not even home.* Exhaling deeply, why I do not know, I decide to leave the mini-forest at her door. I strangely feel lighter and depressed at the same time. Not that seeing her face, which is what I really need, isn't going to help me focus in court this afternoon. At least the card I included will let her know I'm thinking of her.

I walk away and almost reach my car when I hear, "Jack?"

Turning around, I see Erin coming down the sidewalk dressed in running gear, complete with iPod and earbuds. Her brown hair is pulled back in a ponytail and the skintight pink shirt fits her body like a glove, accentuating her generous breasts. I can't seem to control my wandering eyes down her beautifully fit body, especially when I notice the impression of her nipples which seem to harden before my eyes. I shake my head slightly, trying to regain my uncooperative composure.

Erin meets my eyes with one upturned eyebrow and a small smirk. She caught me spying. Then again, she always did.

A smile forms on her beautifully heart-shaped face. "You're here. How did you find me?"

Feeling a little embarrassed for tracking her down, I can't help fidgeting, moving my legs side to side, and look down, shaking my head. "Ah… I, ah, didn't like the way we left things last night." I pause, looking upward to her eyes for some clue what she might be thinking.

Her eyes move to my feet and my hands clenching in obvious nervousness. Sensing my discomfort, she walks slowly into me and places her hand over both of mine and squeezes, "I understand." We stare into one other's eyes for a few moments and I swallow hard. So many memories flood back in the span of these seconds, I feel almost dizzy. "Come inside, Jack."

I beg my brain to fire signals to my legs to get moving and finally they respond. Following behind her, I almost trip like the dumbass I feel when I see her sexy ass bound by her second skin running pants. They're so tight that the obvious lack of panty lines has my cock stirring. Shaking my head, I tell myself to calm the fuck down and get my thoughts out of the gutter. I almost don't hear her sigh and the subsequent, "Aww, Jack. You didn't need to bring me a plant!"

"It's a house-warming of sorts. You know, to welcome you back to Richmond."

We move into the apartment and it's nice, *really* nice. The space is bright and open with tall ceilings. You can see everything in these warehouse style lofts. It's really a comfortable space and nothing like the formal, cold, "don't touch" that I always feel in my own home.

"Well, thank you very much. I have just the perfect spot. Have a seat, please." Moving toward the full length wall of windows, she places it on the perfectly sized table.

I move to the seating area and wait for her to sit first, years of engrained manners taking over. I decide to sit in the chair a comfortable distance opposite her on the sofa. We both look at each other and say nothing. Our eyes taking each other in and surveying one another, looking for the mystery of our past years after having been separated so long. Slight physical changes catch my notice. Only a slight mar of aging crosses her face, but what I really notice is the hardness of her body. She obviously has a workout obsession now, considering her abs and ass of steel. Her arms rival some men and my mouth waters. I also notice a tattoo on her abdomen, but I can't quite figure it out as it disappears in her shorts. I try not to be obvious by looking at it but now my curiosity is extremely piqued.

"Erin, I probably need to explain dropping in on you." I look away from her eyes, unable to concentrate. "I was so off-guard running into you. Last night, I couldn't sleep, and all morning when I should have been prepping for a case, I just couldn't concentrate. Even now, sitting here with you, I'm so twisted in knots."

With kind and caring eyes, she replies, "Hey, it's okay. I totally understand. It was a big shock for me, too. I took it out on the pavement just now for the same reasons. It affected me to see you, too."

"It's been so long and I'm a married man, Erin, but it's almost as if I'm taken back to that day. I was heartbroken and pretty much frozen for a very long time. I loved you so much. You were everything and we had so many good times." I can't help but smirk when our sexual escapades become fast moving images quickly moving through my thoughts.

She swallows hard, looking down at her clinched hands. "I don't want to interfere with your marriage, Jack. I would never do that to another woman."

I nod solemnly back to her. "Nor would I ask that of you. My marriage may not be the best, but I take my vows seriously."

We sit there just staring at one another. Neither of us knows what to say yet it is written all over our faces. Regret. Regret for what we lost. Regret for what we could have had. This woman-owned the space that allowed me to breathe. And when she left, she foreclosed on the lease of my happiness.

"I would have waited for you."

"That's not fair, Jack. Not fair to you or me, but *especially* you. You were so young and you needed to enjoy college and build a career."

"You always thought too much about our ages. You're incredibly naïve if you think I didn't have the maturity to take care of you."

"I didn't want to use you, Jack! Everyone else saw you as a meal ticket. I didn't! I loved you, too, but you were eighteen fucking years old!"

"I know my money wasn't important to you; that's one of the things that made you special. Your honesty and integrity were so refreshing. I gotta tell you that you are honestly the only woman I dated who didn't have dollar signs in her eyes when she looked at me. I've had lots of experience looking at those eyes and yours never did. That genuine care for another person, excluding the fringe benefits, is so rare, Erin. You really don't know what it's like. A man like me is hounded by vultures all the time! It's exhausting constantly being picked at by them! Even as a married man, I'm approached routinely with offers of guilt-free sex."

"I imagine so. I truly do. Music is my life. I may not have always been quite as successful as I planned or hoped to be, but I always knew I needed my own identity. Listen, Jack, you are an incredible guy. You're smart, giving, and any woman would be lucky to be with you. You want true honesty?"

"Of course I want honesty. Nothing less."

"Okay, here goes." She closes her eyes tightly, summoning up courage. I can read her face like a book. "I feared that I would eventually get swallowed up in your world and then who would I be? What about my music dreams? My identity?"

I look at her in confusion. "What are you talking about? I *always* supported you. I always thought you had tremendous talent. You're not making sense, E." Without thinking, her nickname rolls off my tongue, surprising us both.

"Your family's money, Jack. Your mom is an incredible lady. She does so much for this community. She will probably never get her full due for all the ways she supports people in need."

"Yes, my mom is an iconic woman—the best female role model I could have ever had. But what the fuck does that have to do with you?"

"Think about it, honey. Look at your mom's work. Think about your wife's work. It all goes back to the money. You never had a choice—you were predestined, that's why you're not a cop. It would have never worked because it would have been expected that my job was your various charities. Never my music. I would have *never* stood a chance in your world. How could I considering *you* never did? You're a lawyer, not a cop. You didn't stand up and you would have resented me if I did."

I sit back in the chair, hoping to disappear in the cushion. I am blown away. I can't breathe and feel dizzy. Realization hits me like a ton of bricks. That's why I lost her. That's why she didn't stay even when I offered to pay for making the fucking album myself! I told her I'd find a way to help her, and I would have, but she didn't believe me. She didn't fucking believe me. My money caused the demise of our relationship. It has taken so much from me! When will it ever end? Why can't I just be a normal guy with normal problems? I know my family does a lot of good in this world, but selfishly, I'm resentful that my love life takes a backseat to being a good samaritan.

I stare at her, my mouth dry and my vocal cords paralyzed. Finally, voice cracking against my will, "Oh, Erin, you just didn't get it.

I would have walked through fire for you. When we were together, you made me strong. Your music dream was my dream, too. You didn't see that, did you? When you love someone, you sacrifice to make them happy." Suddenly needing space from her, I swallow hard and move to the full-length windows overlooking the James River. "You were everything. You taught me so much about life, in general. You set me on the path to my sexual freedom and identity that I have today." I can't help but stand a little straighter and a little stronger. Turning around with heat in my eyes, I continue, "The boy you fucked at eighteen is most definitely not the man who fucks his wife today. It could have been you. *You*, E."

Hearing whimpers as I move toward her, I see tracks of tears streaming down her face. I stand before her, reaching out my hands and pulling her up to me. "Glad you're back. I really am. I hope we can be friends on some level. Please call me if you need anything; I genuinely mean it." I grab her face carefully between my hands and take a moment to memorize all her features. Her beauty still has the ability to make me weak-kneed.

Whispering softly, I tell her, "You will always own a part of my heart, Erin." She inhales loudly and I lean in, softly laying a kiss on her lips. It takes more control than I ever thought possible to refrain from running my tongue between hers, forcing them open. But I don't do it, much to the dismay of my instantaneously stirring cock. I pull back, suddenly finding it difficult to breathe, and stare deeply into her eyes, conveying my own feelings of a future that never happened. A future that would have been amazing. I'm heartbroken, and the pain shooting through my gut is almost enough to bring me to my knees. "Goodbye, Erin." I release her, willing my legs to move me to walk away and praying for the courage to not look back at her. I have to do the right thing—for her, my wife, my children. I leave her. I do the right thing for everyone else. I always do.

Chapter Sixteen

Sometimes You Have To Take The Bull By The Horns...

Victoria

I notice for the next several weeks that Jack is irritable, short-tempered, and snips at the kids, which he never does. Asking him what's wrong all the time yields no answers. The truth is, I can feel it, though: he's pulling away. Ever since he saw Erin, he's a changed man. His sex drive has practically disappeared and no matter what I do to entice him, he always claims to be busy. His home office is his home away from home these days. Gone is the man who consumes my body practically every day. I'm really worried.

"Okay Mom, I understand. I'll make the transfer today. You can do what you need to do, but you have to stop pressuring me, and you *have* to stop calling when Jack's home. I don't want him hearing these calls, okay?"

"Fine, but see that it's done. Your father needs this money right away. The distributors are pressuring him, and by extension pressuring me. Got it?"

"Yes, ma'am, I got it!" I slam the phone back in the cradle with barely contained strength. No matter what I do, it's never enough for them.

I pull out my smartphone and check my notes to find out exactly how much I've transferred this year. "Holy fuck!" I mumble to no one, in particular. This can't be right, but my notes are meticulous so I know it is. I've sent them $1.37 million this calendar year alone. *Shit!* I have to find a way to tell Daddy I can't keep doing this. Jack will divorce me if he finds out I'm sending money to him. Again. He stumbled onto it a few years ago totally by accident and told me never to do it again. Since that time, I've had to cover my tracks really well. Thank goodness I greased a few palms along the way to keep these transfers buried or I'd be fucked. He doesn't understand the responsibility I feel to help my family, especially when I have so much. I know how he feels, though because Daddy is always a total shit to him, and, in particular, me. I'm a Daddy's girl, though. Through and through.

Tonight is Project Take Back Jack! Besides, I'm his wife and I know every one of his sexual vices. It's time to recharge my husband's batteries.

When the driveway alarm sounds, I know he has come home from work late again—no surprise there. I sent him a text earlier that I was concerned about the bathroom floor buckling due to leaky pipes. Random, I know, but all men get concerned about structural defects that suddenly appear in their homes. Besides, I couldn't take the chance that he'd head straight to his home office yet again.

Swiftly, I jump into position and wait.

I hear him approach the stairwell and my heart begins to beat rapidly. Jack likes to control our sexual fun, so I don't normally instigate our lovemaking. I begin to breathe quite shallow, wondering if I've made a big mistake.

When the doors open, I try very hard to maintain a neutral expression. I stare at him, saying nothing, watching every move he makes.

"Ah, Victoria?" He looks at me with a very puzzled look on his face.

"Jack."

"What's going on?" he says slowly.

In a sultry and seductive voice, I crawl to the end of the bed, "Sorry for the ruse, darling, but mama's pipes are wet and leaky. Don't you have a B-I-G wrench or something that can help fix me?"

A slow smile appears on his face along with a quiet chuckle. "Baby, daddy has a very big wrench that tightens around most any size pipe. I think I'm the man for the job." His eyebrows lift up in expectation, waiting to see where I'm taking this.

I reach out and yank him to me hard by his tie and he stumbles forward. I run my hands firmly up his chest, pulling his jacket from his shoulders, removing his tie and dress shirt. Staring intently into his eyes, I run one hand slowly down my abdomen and it disappears behind my panties. With my other hand, I put one finger in my mouth and suck in and out, sounding as sloppy as I can make it sound. My eyes roll back in my head and I begin to gyrate my hips in a thrusting fashion and moan deeply. "I'm so wet for you right now, Jack, you know that?"

"Fuck yeah," he says, panting hard.

"Finish stripping for me. You have some heavy labor to do." I watch him as he practically rips his remaining clothes off. He's fighting a serious inner battle. He wants control and I've turned the tables on him, yet he's so turned on, he's curious to see how this plays out. His fingers open and close, not knowing if he should reach for me or not.

"What's your plan here, sweetheart? Is this your idea of topping me?"

"No, Jack. This isn't one of our domination games." I move my hips more intensely and let out a prolonged moan. "The truth? You have seriously neglected me and if you don't make me come soon, I think I just may tie you up myself. It's simple, really. Your wife is horny." I give him a devious smirk, very full of myself indeed.

He slowly takes my body in with his eyes. His excitement is hard to ignore, considering his heavy breathing, nostrils flaring, lips being licked, and hips involuntarily thrusting.

My hand travels down his abdomen, using my fingernails to mark my path. His lengthy cock moves closer to me with the help of his intentional thrusts. Each time he fails to make contact on the first thrust, second thrust, third thrust, I hear his frustrated sigh.

"Eager for my touch, baby?

No words are spoken, just a deep swallow moving his Adam's apple and a slight sheen of sweat that has formed on his skin. He moans deeply and adjusts his legs to run his balls over the top of my thigh, anxious for any skin-to-skin contact.

I know exactly what it feels like to crave his touch and suddenly miss it like crazy. It's like the memories are so fierce, they scorch the landscape of my womanhood, desperate to be experienced again. Since he is always my leader, he doesn't really know what it's like to be at this level of sexual frustration.

It must be very vulnerable for him to desperately grind himself on me in such a way as this. Having full respect for the general rules of submission, he wouldn't dare touch me in this moment. He's watching me intently, playing along with my little game of torture and control.

I run the tips of my fingernails along the head of his cock and he pushes himself into the palm of my hand. I lightly scratch up and down the length of him, causing him to openly shiver and roll his head around his shoulders. It's quite a powerful and heady feeling knowing I'm capable of demanding his full attention. He wants me so badly, but the high I get just knowing I am in control of his pleasure is quite intoxicating. Considering these moments are none other than rare occurrences, the devilish side of me chooses to enjoy them.

"Look at me, Jack." He complies, but I notice it's painful to tear his eyes away from my torturous touch. Holding his attention completely, I press my nails in slightly firmer, up and down, and he attempts to coordinate his movements with mine. I suddenly squeeze him with my fist, working him good, up and down. The connection we have between our eyes is so fucking exhilarating. He feels but he cannot see. Not having control is something he hates. In these moments, he is lost in the passion. I beat his cock as firmly as I can. He thrusts his hips powerfully and moans uncontrollably with how good it makes him feel. When he begins to swell in my fist, his eyes enlarge. He knows, and more importantly, he knows that I know. His orgasm is building quickly.

Still with total eye connection, Jack says, "Stop," and he immediately ceases his movements. He is breathing hard and his chest is heaving for relief. I move my fist to the base of his cock, squeezing hard to prevent ejaculation, quickly followed by a firm tug of his balls away from his body with the same goal. Success. It's heady to have that kind of power, specifically over a man.

Jack stands there, allowing me to have my fun. I know being the cooperative lover is killing him. "Torturous, is it not?"

"Yes. No doubt."

Still breathing hard, I release the firm control on his cock and stroke it gently. Tearing my eyes away from his to look down at it, his cock is absolutely glorious—so full, so thick. I'm truly a lucky woman to receive the benefits it offers deep within me. "You've been ignoring me since Erin returned and I don't like it." Still avoiding eye contact, I need to get this out before I lose my nerve. "She's your Achilles heel and I've always known it—"

"That's not true—," he interrupts but I ignore him.

Feeling very proprietary with a slightly raised and firm voice, I continue, "It is true, but let me finish. I'm your wife and she has interfered in our private life. This is about me taking it back." My gentler strokes turn markedly firmer over his still very erect cock. I take his hand and lead it to my pussy, guiding his fingers through my wet lips. I thrust my hips, burying his fingers inside me. Torture time…over. "You need to focus your attentions on more pressing matters. As I see it, your hands are rather full at the moment." I smirk at him. "Please, fuck me hard, Jack."

He looks at me, jaw dropped, like a deer caught in the headlights. "Yes, ma'am, Mrs. Loving!"

And he does…fuck me hard, that is. I know Erin is responsible for our sudden cold streak in the bedroom. Guess I'll just have to take control more often and turn up the heat.

Chapter Seventeen

The Beginnings Of A True And Loyal Friendship...

Lizzie

"You bought him what?" Jenny asks.

"No, you didn't!" Janice exclaims.

"Seriously? I'm impressed Marianne. You've really become quite the shopper at the adult bookstore, haven't you?" I tease her.

"Yes, I have, actually. I'm no longer shy about going in there, that's for sure. Besides, even if I was, did you know Amazon has over six thousand different sexual aides available for sale?"

"Ah, no...I didn't know that, but it says more about you that you actually do. Anyway, don't try and change the subject, missy. Explain what this is before we get into *why* you gave him the newest item in your ever-growing arsenal of sexual aides," Janice requests.

"Okay, I'll try. It's called an oral male masturbator..."

"No fuckin' way!!!" Jenny interrupts.

"…and it's meant to be used by the guy when he's alone. It simulates a blow job."

"Does it work? I mean, I assume it must *work*, but does it feel the same?" Janice asks.

"Well, it's impossible for her to know if it *works*, Janice since she lacks a dick!" Jenny teases her.

"Touché, bitch! But seriously? What does Derek think about all of this? And we still haven't gotten to the million dollar question of, *why the hell did you buy it in the first place?*" Janice asks impatiently, and then discreetly points out the table of three guys sitting behind us who have become quite interested in our conversation.

"Okay, calm down, ladies, and let me finish. First, to answer *why* I bought it? I have to travel out of town occasionally for work. While in the shop, I saw it one day and thought this would be a pretty cool gag gift, so I bought it. I had to travel unexpectedly this week and discreetly left it on my pillow with a note. Here, I thought you guys would appreciate the humor.

Use often for maximum comfort and relaxation during my absence

"So, the next day when I was in a meeting with my new boss, mind you, my cell phone alerts with a new text message. Before I had a chance to remove the phone from the table, our eyes locked on the picture message of Derek while he was in the midst of 'maximum comfort and relaxation.' I was mortified, but there was nothing I could do. I just grabbed it quickly and changed the subject."

"Oh, shit! How embarrassing for Derek!" Jenny exclaims.

"Well, he doesn't know and I have no intentions of telling him, especially with the welcome home reception I received." We all agree that might be for the best. "I'm not willing to share the picture, but let me just say that what started as a joke turned out to be shockingly satisfying...for both of us."

Everyone looks at one another, confusion on their faces. "Some people find it very gratifying and arousing to watch their partners masturbating while in a vulnerable position," I explain. "I'm sure it was startling for each of you if you've never tried it, but it sounds like both of you may even benefit from more voyeuristic situations in the future. It's still intoxicating—watching another person reach orgasm right in front of you when normally they masturbate alone. It very forbidden, in a way."

"Oh my gawd, Lizzie! You're exactly right and this is why you're the therapist of our little group. I never thought about it like that, but it was fuckin' hawt, girl!" Marianne loudly announces and we all laugh at her. "This masturbator is similar to the sleeve—soft, cylinder shaped, fitting over a cock. Once he's wrapped up tight in there, with lots of lube, of course, it has these pleasure beads, stroking him up and down and giving maximum stimulation. The benefits of battery power allow you to adjust the speed you need to reach orgasm."

"Battery-powered?" a loud, rough voice somewhere behind us calls out. "Somehow, I missed that part. Damn, I wish my wife bought that for me!"

"Yeah, no doubt. I get lonely, too."

"Dumbass. First, you gotta find a wife who *wants* to put up with your sorry ass!"

"Aww, fuck you!"

One hundred, two hundred, three hundred, four hundred, five hundred, twenty dollars and….thirty-six cents. That's all the cash to our names, but at least we have it. I've paid all the rent, utilities, insurance, and groceries and I have money left over. I feel like I'm walking on air right now.

It's a good feeling to know we have a roof over our heads and food in my babies' bellies. This is a new feeling for me and I can't seem to get settled about it. Jeremy has always been the breadwinner for our family. Now, I have this overwhelming responsibility to be the provider and it's scary, to say the least.

The sleaziness I can't seem to shake knowing how I made this money haunts me all the time. Even though I haven't committed a crime, I'm not proud of it. Jeremy has not questioned how we're making ends meet. He's totally oblivious to his surroundings most of the time. He's either missing or passed out drunk across the bed. What kills me is the look on the kids' faces when they see him at his worst. Not a proud moment as a parent.

Ever since he found my hiding place for the rent money, I've had to get creative. I never leave all of it in one place. He would wipe me out if all of it was together. One night, at three o'clock in the morning, he woke me up, making sounds as he trifled through my purse and cosmetics drawer looking for money. He's found some here and there so I have to be careful and move it around diligently.

My sweet neighbor, Mrs. Rawlings, gave me a peace lily house plant. It's rather large and gives the apartment some much needed "green love". There's a plastic barrier protecting the wicker basket, so I've decided to hide my money there, silently praying for the green love to keep our money safe from the man of the house. Pitiful, I know.

After Mark's bonus money, I was able to pay all of my delinquent bills. I'm hoping more bonus money may be on the horizon since I'm scheduled for two more events with him. He was totally serious when he asked if I would help with the Children's Museum project. Apparently, I made an impression on him with my very pointed interrogation of the current fundraising campaign. In hindsight, I should have been fired from the assignment. Ms. Martin would have had a cow if she had seen me swaying from her 'seen not heard' point of view. Considering my abilities within my committee work from my previous comfortable lifestyle, I was perfect for the assignment.

Hearing my phone ringing, I race to answer before they hang up. Seeing Ms. Martin's name on the front, I pick up, "Hello?"

"Yes, dear, it's me. Just confirming your attendance this afternoon. Are you set to wear the outfit we discussed?"

With an eye roll which thankfully she can't see, I respond, "Yes, ma'am. I will arrive at twelve forty-five p.m. for lunch at Lewis Ginter Botanical Gardens, including a strategy meeting to discuss the Children's Museum funding."

"Perfect, Lizzie. I have to say I'm totally perplexed about this arrangement Mark is suggesting between the two of you. Never have I had a client request an escort cross the line into their business affairs. Quite frankly, I don't care for it. If it wasn't Mark asking for this, I'd never agree."

Not knowing exactly how to respond, I take a moment to reflect on Mark's motives. "Mr. Chesney and I seemed to bond over the importance of children's charity work. Not to be rude toward your other escorts, but I wonder if I'm different than them. I traveled in his same social circles, so I just blend in easily. I, myself, have a passion for the work so I greatly appreciate the opportunity."

"Just don't screw it up, Lizzie. My reputation is everything and if you bomb at this, you're making Mark look bad which makes ME look bad. Got it?"

"I understand, Ms. Martin." Then I hear the click of her disconnecting the call. "Well, that's no pressure at all," I quip.

Looking like the fabulous, but not-so-confident person I used to be, I walk into the Robins Tea House at Lewis Ginter. In my former financially comfortable life, I had a membership to the gardens and dearly loved my visits here. The large windows overlook the lake and beautiful Asian Valley garden. I could just get lost in the beauty here. I'll have to remind myself to stay present in the conversations and not the view.

Looking across the room, I see Mark, and as if he senses my presence, he looks up and our eyes connect. He looks a little annoyed and I immediately become concerned, glancing down at my watch. No, I'm not late. Ten minutes early, in fact. Then my attention is pulled to his arm being pulled slightly to get his attention. *Shit. My nemesis, Cindy Hall.* Dammit, I forgot she would pull all the stops to get in on a meeting with the amazingly handsome Mark Chesney. Of course, she would sit her ass right beside him.

I walk to the table, and as if she has carefully prearranged our seating, she quickly pushes people into their seats. Mine is notably at the far end, away from all the major decision makers, and among the handful of personal assistants who are setting up to take novels worth of notes.

Mark is visibly even more annoyed, and when he catches my eye again, I smile kindly and motion with my hands the universal "it's ok" symbol.

We are brought up to speed on the current fundraising initiative and the future projects they hope to fund. Mark is very inquisitive about the specific details of cost and acquisition of materials to build the displays. I'm impressed with his knowledge and willingness to offer incredibly useful information. Mark Chesney is a very intelligent businessman indeed. He's impressed me so much and I'm thrilled and anxious at the prospect of working for him on the endowment.

I listen very carefully to everything and when I feel I have a contribution or suggestion, I add it. I'm pleased my thoughts seem to be well-received and I notice quite a few notes taken down upon my comments.

Toward the end of the meeting, Mark makes a very clear directive that his busy schedule doesn't allow him to be hands-on. "I really appreciate everyone's time today. As you all know, this is personal for me. I want my money to be used for the good of helping Richmond's children. Since my time is limited, I have decided I want a designated individual to make the tough choices regarding funding. I have full faith she will do me proud." Cindy sits up proudly and a smile beams so brightly she could have lit up the downtown skyline. She giggles in a most annoying girly way, mumbling something as she reaches over, gently touching his arm. Mark pulls his arm away and leans in my direction, "Lizzie Macintyre shares my same passion. She will be the Chesney Financial Limited contact that you should all use whenever you would ordinarily need me." Facing Cindy directly, he adds, "That includes signing the checks."

She could have swallowed a kickball, she looks so dizzy in confusion. Then that confusion turns to anger as she turns to me and intentionally rolls her eyes. Wow, jealous much? Mark stands up and walks to my end of the table, "Shall we go, Mrs. Macintyre? I have some funding issues to further discuss with you." Still processing his comments and realizing the importance of what he just publicly announced, I shake the shock away. We give our goodbyes and leave as quickly as we can.

Once outside the Tea House, Mark says, "Lizzie, will you walk the gardens with me?"

It doesn't take much twisting of my arm to convince me. I used to love walking the paths and dreaming my home landscape would look the same. Now, it burns my veins to know I no longer have the precious soil to grow beautiful plants any longer. My heart truly aches for it.

"I love it here. Many of my afternoons were spent here dreaming to have a garden as beautiful as these."

He places my hand in the crook of his elbow and we walk along the paths, quietly reflecting in our own headspace. "You are truly an incredible woman, Lizzie Macintyre."

We walk throughout the rose garden among hundreds of varieties—pink, yellow, red, blue, white, and all combinations in between. We gaze at the butterflies and try to count each new one we discover. They are nature's magnificent painting in motion. I am always mesmerized by their simple elegance. We take in the countless variety of trees, short to tall, stringy to thick limbed. Each one more beautiful than the last.

Taking me from my intensely strong concentration on my surroundings, I notice he has led me to the Children's Garden. I loved bringing my kids here to play and more importantly to learn. The activities abound, but they always seemed to enjoy the water garden and getting wet head to toe.

Feeling totally comfortable and relaxed with Mark, I decide to gather my nerve and seek answers to questions which have been dominating my thoughts recently. "May I ask you some questions, Mark?"

With a pleasant smile on his face, he looks at me kindly, "Of course you may ask, and if I can, I shall answer."

Now I'm hesitant. Really, it's none of my business. I don't want to ruin our walk. I'm so happy just being here today. Sensing my hesitation, he stops us from walking, turning me to face him. "Lizzie?"

Taking a deep breath, I forge ahead, "I don't know anything about your personal life. I was curious why you focus heavily on children's charities?"

Watching something pass over his face which closely resembles pain, he quickly restores his bland expression. "I am not in the habit of discussing my personal life, Lizzie because honestly, it's quite painful."

Instantly, I feel intense guilt and wish I can take it back. I've ruined our friendship, I just know it. "I'm so sorry, Mark. Truly it's not my place as an escort to discuss personal history—"

He quickly interrupts, "Don't, Lizzie. Please—"

"Seriously, I'm very, very sorry." I begin to pull my arm away and he moves his hand over top of mine, clamping it tightly to his side.

"Stop. I want to tell you, but first, this escort designation as you call it, I don't like that term. At least not where *you* are concerned. I realize that technically, the term suits, but in a very short period of time I have accepted you and I will be friends. I don't want to diminish or slight you when I value you differently." My lips tighten between my teeth to make myself stop speaking, his eyes watching my mouth closely. The heat in his face suddenly warms my heart because he isn't angry with me. At least that's something good. "As I said before, there's something about you that leads me to believe you are quite special. No matter what, I strongly believe we shall be in one another's life in some form or fashion. I'm picky about that, by the way."

I chuckle because I quite believe he protects his privacy, and by association, his friendships. "Can I truly trust you, Lizzie Macintyre?"

I'm immediately taken aback. It's hard to understand why, but I have this sudden idea that whatever he tells me will be important. I look deeply into his eyes, willing him to see me clearly and trust my motives. "You can." And in that moment, I decide no matter what he is about to confide in me, I will never betray his confidence.

He looks away from me and takes a shaky breath but holds on to my hand and squeezes, almost willing my strength to pass to him through my touch. "I had a child. My son was almost two years old. My wife suffered with post-partum depression and became an alcoholic. She killed them both when she intentionally drove her car into the river."

I gasp, my mind reeling with this revelation, questioning whether or not I heard him correctly. I'm sure my legs will collapse. My weight falls into his body and I feel it strange that he is the one holding me up. No, it couldn't be. Surely I heard him wrong. I only vaguely recall something in the press, but I've been focused on our problems so I don't remember exact details. Mark's son died. He died because of alcohol. My sadness is laced with rage for lives lost. It isn't fair. Knowing I need to say something, I will my brain through the fog of anger and look at Mark. He looks deep in thought and I know I need to somehow reach him.

"Mark, you have my deepest sympathy. I know you were an incredible father." I squeeze his forearm with my other hand.

Pulling away from my grasp, he takes two steps away, turning his back to me. "No. Not good enough, Lizzie. A parent's job—a father's job—is to protect! I failed! I didn't know she was sneaking around drinking. She hid it well. Afterward, I found hidden bottles of vodka all over the house. It was disgusting. She saw a therapist for post-partum and she convinced me everything was good. I missed all the signs because I was self-absorbed with my work. It was more important to make lots of money for other people rather than work less, spending more quality time with my family and seeing what was right in front of my face."

Not liking the distance he put between us, I move around behind him and approach from the opposite side. Forcing him to look directly at me, the sadness in his eyes breaks my heart. It just hurts so much to watch him relive these events before me. "I can only imagine what you are feeling. Not that it's the same, but I worry all the time for Jeremy. His drinking is so out of hand. He steals lies, anything to get his next drink. I hate it, truly I do."

"At least he's here and you can get him help. Learn from my mistakes. Most importantly, watch out for your kids and never let them ride with him while he's drinking. I would rather be homeless if it meant I could see my son one more time."

We stand there for long minutes, maybe five, maybe twenty, I don't know. Each of us lost in our own thoughts. Analyzing his situation, it makes sense why this handsome and caring man uses so many escorts. He's consumed with grief and has found comfort in paid escorts to satisfy his physical needs. I know he's exactly right about the inherent risks to children having an alcoholic parent. I need to have a conversation with Jeremy very soon.

It suddenly occurs to me the personal connection Mark has to children's charities. His lost son. "You do everything at the Children's Museum to honor your son, don't you?"

He won't look at me. He just keeps staring at all the children playing at the Children's Garden. Several minutes go by and he is totally deep in thought and painfully quiet. I allow him these moments of privacy, knowing when his mind clears he will let me in and respond. "My wife loved the gardens. We would come here when he was just a tiny little thing. She held him close to her heart, always in a sling. Of course, he didn't understand anything she was talking about, but she pointed out all the different flowers, shrubs, rose bushes, and trees. She always knew the scientific names I couldn't begin to pronounce and would talk to him about them, imparting all of her knowledge. I teased her relentlessly and she took it in jest. Even when she was pregnant, she would come here and watch the children playing, daydreaming that our child was the one laughing. As he got older, she let him run around chasing butterflies, touching everything he could. I'll never forget when I thought a bee was about to sting him one day. I jumped up to kill it and she about had a heart attack. She went on to lecture me about the importance of bees pollinating and I was NEVER to kill them. Gosh, I totally forgot about that story until just now. I scoffed at her because he would never remember any of it. She also insisted that we go to the Children's Museum and Maymont Park, too. Insisting he receive culture early on, she demanded it on the weekends. We were very happy and then one day she got drunk and killed my family. When they put them in the ground, they buried my heart right alongside them."

I'm void of thoughts. He is visibly in pain and nothing I can say is going to bring them back. Nothing. The entire time this man stands before me, his heart totally shredded, Jeremy keeps selfishly entering my mind. Now I'm scared I could end up just like Mark, with no family to love.

"Thank you for confiding in me. I know it wasn't easy."

He takes a deep breath, shakes his head as if clearing away unpleasant thoughts, and finally turns to look at me. "You are unique, Lizzie. You're warm, bright, and incredibly sweet. Beautiful as fuck." The heat in his eyes as he licks his lower lip tells me he has switched gears in his brain for sure. "I told you, I am the smart one for demanding you be in my life."

I smile a small smile and look away bashfully. "I'm married, Mark."

"Don't keep reminding me. Ugghh." He shakes his head back and forth, looking disgusted as he's contemplating his next words. He moves in close to me, bending down and whispering close to my ear, "I can almost taste you on my tongue, sweetheart. Just because you're married and that shithead doesn't recognize how amazingly talented you are doesn't mean I can't fantasize about having you in my bed." He quickly leans in and kisses gently where my ear meets my neck and pulls away.

Standing there, I'm left shivering uncontrollably. I'm a mess of short-circuited micro orgasms. *Damn, that felt good. Too good.* I smirk at his inappropriate liberty he's taken and just enjoy the energy surrounding us.

"We have a job to do, Mr. Chesney."

"We do?"

"Oh yes. I need to get to work on your endowment and you need to get your John Hancock ready."

We start walking away from the Children's Garden toward the exit. My arm is once again in the crook of his elbow. A solemn look graces his features. "Lizzie?" I look up at him in answer, "His name was Joshua, but I called him Josh." I don't answer him back; I just squeeze his arm and nod my head.

Chapter Eighteen

Shiny Red Things...

Lizzie

The next month is a whirlwind for me. My personal life is still a mess because I haven't kicked Jeremy out. His constant promises just lead to more pain when they remain unfulfilled. I insist on separate bedrooms because I know he has nowhere to go. I'm heavily involved with the endowment, much to Cindy's regret. I work really well with the BOD members and everyone seems receptive to my ideas. I guess it doesn't hurt that I control the purse strings, so they wouldn't dare go against me. I try not to think of it in that way, though.

Cindy makes my life hell at every turn. Several times, documents mysteriously go missing which contributes to lost deadlines and costs Mark unnecessary money. Of course, I can't prove anything. I don't want to bother Mark with catty bitchiness, so I just persevere.

The mock build-out is complete on a new display we are working on concerning cyber-bullying. I am really proud of it because it was one of my ideas. I feel it's important to get the information out to kids and parents as well.

I'm also working on several park renovations in the urban area of the city. We're installing new equipment and flexible, safe, rubber mulch. Mark doesn't know it yet, but the reopening dedication includes a new name for both parks: Josh's Jungle and Mark's Meadow. A permanent reminder of a father's love for his son.

Things are moving quickly and I'm in heaven with how busy I am these days. Of course, busy means income, especially when Mark Chesney is involved. He insists that I track my hours and via Ms. Martin, pays me an enormous hourly wage. It's ridiculous, really, but I just look at it like any other job.

Tonight is an exception. He needs an escort to a business event. Since this isn't a fundraiser, I'm not free to express my opinions. Ms. Martin made sure to put me in my place on that one. Jenny agreed to come over to sit with the kids until I return home. Thank God for friends.

I'm dressed in an off-the-shoulder black silk dress that feels like it fits me perfectly. Mark sent it to Ms. Martin with a request I wear it for the occasion. Of course, it included shoes that fit and the perfect bag. I have never owned something so decadent. It makes me feel very special, indeed. According to the all-knowing jetsetter, Ms. Martin, the dress cost at least five thousand dollars. I promise myself if I spill food on it, I will never eat again in protest.

Included in the box, I find a smaller rectangular gold box. Instantly, I know it has to be either a necklace or bracelet. I open it and find the most stunning heart-shaped ruby with diamonds surrounding it. Instantly, I want to cry knowing that other than my engagement ring, this is the only jewelry I now own, considering Jeremy pawned everything else to feed his alcohol addiction. As I am removing the necklace, an embossed notecard similar to one I'd seen before falls out:

Mr. Mark Chesney

Dearest Birdie,

Thank you so much for being the kind person you are. You make this world a much better place just by living in it. The work you're doing on the endowment means more to me than you could imagine. This necklace honors your kind heart, and please know countless kids have smiles on their faces because of you.

Yours very truly,
~M

    I can't help the streams of tears flowing down my face. This kind-hearted man who is so special is actually thanking *me*? It is *his* money that's funding these good works. Surely he knows his importance in all this. Right?

    I arrive at valet parking at The Jefferson Hotel. I can't help but cringe thinking about what the valet must think of my vehicle. Moving that idea out of my head quickly, I walk to the hotel bar in search of Mark. Looking across the room, I'm immediately calmed by the sounds of the piano. This luxury hotel is so beautiful and a treasure for the eyes. It has so much history here and I can't help but be a little nostalgic that Mark and I enjoyed Lewis Ginter Botanical Gardens and now we are meeting at Lewis Ginter's dream: a magnificent grand hotel built with Renaissance architecture, among others and considered among the finest examples of Beaus Arts style in existence.

If only these walls could talk. From fires, to closings, to alligators in the marble pools, to the breathtaking staircase widely considered to be the model for the famous movie "Gone with the Wind", I'm sure there are many more stories to be told. Dressed in this dress, feeling very beautiful as I walk through this opulence, I'm breathless. I feel so light as if I don't need legs because I'm floating along.

Suddenly, I feel a firm grip around my waist and warm breath on my neck. "Don't turn around," a faint whisper is all I hear.

I'm frozen in my place. The warmth on my skin radiates over my body making my nipples pebble. The chill bumps travel at warp speed and I suddenly feel weak all over. My body helplessly sways back into the firm chest of this unseen man controlling all of my movements.

"It was worth every single cent to watch you move through the room looking like a fucking goddess. Seeing dozens of swinging dicks with their mouths open all trying to compete with one another to speak to you. If I die right here, it will be okay because my eyes have feasted on the prism that is your beauty. How I long to touch you so badly and to know you are not available to me is torture. You are the epitome of sweetness, my dear Birdie." Then he leans in closer and slowly licks the shell of my ear before setting me free.

I think I just had my first ever orgasm by words alone. I'm scared to move for fear I might fall to the ground, or more embarrassing, the pool of wetness which has collected in my panties just might drip down my legs. I instinctively reach for him, knowing I can't stand alone yet. Breathless, I whisper "Hold me, please."

He pulls me closely to him, my back to his front, and I feel the imprint of his erection at my lower back. I try to remain still even though my body desperately wants to react and push my ass back into him, grinding against his fullness. "You smell so good, sweetheart."

Trying to clear my head, I focus on the cool metal touching the pads of my fingers as I reach for my necklace. "Thank you and thank you for my exquisite wardrobe ensemble."

"Think nothing of it."

I manage to turn around, still caressing my ruby heart. "This was very sweet of you. I don't have many pretty things these days."

He looks at me with his all-knowing eyes and reads my pain like it is branded on my chest. "He's sold your jewelry for booze, hasn't he?"

Shocked that he figured it out so quickly, I can't formulate a response before he interjects with his own solution. "You will receive details by ten a.m. tomorrow with the location of a prepaid safety deposit box. I expect you to move all your valuables there. And before you ask, it will be in your name only. I want you to trust me, Lizzie."

Not really knowing what to say but realizing he is exactly right, I just agree and shake my head. "Thank you, Mark. I appreciate your kindness." He winks at me and gives me a sexy smile that surely gets him every woman he could ever want.

We spend the evening talking and chatting with many of Mark's clients and business associates. When the band begins to play, Mark twirls me onto the dance floor and we don't leave for almost an hour. I explained that I wasn't a great dancer, but he made me feel like one. I laughed and laughed until I thought my side would split. The night has been so much fun!

As we walk toward the exit, Mark side skirts us into a vacant alcove. He pulls my body close to the front of his and moves his lips close to my neck. "I have tremendously enjoyed your company, Lizzie. Thank you."

When he holds me like this, it feels so good. The power he has over my body is undeniable. He gives light kisses around my ear. "Will you kiss me, baby? A good kiss to send me on my way so I can dream well tonight?"

I pull my head back and press my lips to his. His tongue comes out and slowly licks my bottom lip before he gives it a light nip. To take away the sting, he sucks my bottom lip into his mouth and moans deeply. His crotch presses into my abdomen and my body responds and presses back against him. He moves his thigh in between my legs, and using his hands, presses my waist down and against him at the same time. Suddenly, all I feel is tremendous pressure between my legs. I feel hot all over; my body literally feels like it is on fire. He moves his tongue all the way in my mouth and we begin this duel for space and control. He tastes divine and his cologne, which has had a lethal effect on me all night, makes me want to eat him alive.

I grind my crotch against his thigh like a rutting fool, but I can't seem to control it. I'm so overwhelmed with my own insatiability I can't think clearly. It's been practically forever since Jeremy and I made love and my body is dying for release.

"God, Lizzie, your pussy is so hot against my thigh. I can practically feel the wetness through our clothes."

"Mmmm, I need—"

"What do you need, baby? Tell me what you need and I sure as fuck will give it to you."

Indecision is written all over my face, I'm sure because he noticeably hesitates and doesn't move us to the next level. "Birdie, I want you so fucking bad but I don't think you're ready for everything I can give you."

I stare at him in disbelief, not knowing what to say, but at the same time my body continues to betray me, having a mind of its own. Not once did my alcoholic husband enter my mind tonight. I fear I have held on to my marriage for all the wrong reasons. Love, noticeably absent.

"Okay, as much as I desperately want to taste you and feel you, I won't." I begin to breathe harder, almost begging for him to finish. "Settle down, sweet one. I'm not letting you go yet." He kisses me harder and situates his thigh upward between my legs while firmly grasping my hips and forcefully gyrating my hips in a fluid movement, up/down, back/in against his hardened thigh. The feeling is maddening and unlike anything I've ever experienced. I build quickly, too quickly for what is normal for me. My clit is so sensitive, and with his mouth kissing me so passionately, I'm on the precipice. Just on the edge of it, just needing a little more contact, if I can just grind a little harder if just, if only… oh… ahhh… suddenly, my right nipple is pinched through my dress, between his thumb and forefinger and… white lights. Millions of blinding white lights as my body explodes in the most passionate, longest lasting orgasm I have ever experienced. He swallows my loud moans with his mouth firmly pressed against mine. My body turns into a wet noodle as my legs go out from under me and thank goodness he's coordinated enough to hold me up. Wow! That felt freaking fantastic. As my body tries to come back inside itself, Mark, the ever present gentleman, pushes my dress down, securing it in a presentable fashion.

"Feel better?" He smirks at me.

Shaking my head at him, I respond, "You have no idea." I look around at my surroundings and suddenly become very insecure about the lack of privacy and my loss of control around this man.

"No one saw a thing. I was sure of it." Looking up at him, I totally believe him. I'm not sure why, but I really believe he has my best interests at heart.

It occurs to me when I look down at the unmistakably large, as in extra-large, tent at the front of his trousers, that he is very much in need himself. I become rather embarrassed for even noticing. He grabs my face between his hands and speaks quietly. "Birdie, do not worry about me. I can take a cold shower. You have given me tremendous memories to work with." He snorts and smiles that devilish smile of his. "Seriously, I wanted to give you this. I know it's important for you because of your husband, that's why I never touched your skin directly. I pinched your nipple through your bra just to get you off. Don't take my decision as weakness, however. I'm barely holding on because I'd rather carry you upstairs and fuck you 'til you come three more times and I match you just as many."

"Well, shit."

"Yeah. That's right." A wolfish smile claims his beautiful face. "I'll let your imagination run wild with you on that one. Just a hint, however, whatever you think you know about me, it's SO much more and better." He chuckles loudly. The damn man has no shame in his varied sexual talents.

"You need to make some life decisions and I won't push you there. I just want to enjoy your company. More importantly, I want your friendship. I told you you're special, and one way or another, I want you in my life. I selfishly wanted the image of you coming apart in my mind. I got that. I told you long ago, I'm no gentleman. I'm a prick for wanting anything I can get from you." He then leans in and gives me the sweetest kiss on the lips. I open my eyes and find him staring at me. He smiles, vulnerability on display, and pulls away because I caught him.

Moving away from the alcove, I reach down and double check my clothes, pulling them into their proper place. I look at him the entire time and never see the shrewd assessing eyes coming around the corner when I make the worst joke of all time to him, "So, did you get your money's worth?"

He stands stock still, neither of us knowing what to say. Surely the eyes that travel up and down my body had caught us nearly in the act, or at minimum are suspicious. Cindy "catty bitch" Hall stands before us, putting it all together. I'm about to spill my guts and ask for a million favors when suddenly Mark speaks up, "Ms. Hall, what a pleasant surprise. If you will excuse us, I'm walking Mrs. Macintyre to the valet." Then he quickly shuffles us away. Not saying a word to me, my mind works furiously, preparing to beg for his forgiveness.

Once my car has arrived, we turn to one another. "Lizzie, thank you for a most memorable evening. I look forward to next time.

Shocked by his warm remarks, I stumble out, "Oh sure. Yes, it was lovely. Thank you."

He reaches down and kisses my cheek lightly. "Don't let old bags worry you, Lizzie, because, in the end, they're just old miserable bags. Move along now and buckle up. Be safe." Once he shuts my door, he watches intently while I buckle up. I can't help but watch in my rearview mirror that he stands watching my car as I drive away.

I wear a big satisfied smile on my face the entire way home. The next morning at precisely ten o'clock, I receive a call from Ms. Martin summoning me to her office.

Handing me an envelope, she states, "Your check and gifts from your favorite, albeit *only*, client."

In the car, I frantically rip it open and begin counting the hundred dollar bills totaling three thousand dollars. Three thousand dollars! That's a lot of money and my excitement cannot be contained. I opened the other envelope containing the now familiar embossed notecard:

Mr. Mark Chesney

Dearest Birdie,

I sincerely enjoyed our night together. You are incredibly special and I won't forget our fun anytime soon. I don't think I will ever see another black dress and not immediately think of you.

Visit the bank manager at Wells Fargo on Broad Street, TODAY. I have prepaid a two year rental for your safe deposit box. Use it!

See you soon, dear.

Yours very truly,
~M

With my beautiful necklace around my neck, off to the bank I go.

Chapter Nineteen

You Won't Find Answers Looking In A Bottle...

Lizzie

"'m in a meeting with two new clients. Suddenly, there is a buzzing sound. It's faint, mind you, but it's clearly a buzzing vibration. They look at each other the first time and just ignore it. I knew IMMEDIATELY what it was, but there was no fucking way I was telling *anyone* where it was coming from."

"So what happened? If it wasn't coming from the three cell phones lying on the table, they knew it was coming from somewhere, right?" Janice asks.

"Oh, trust me, they knew and what drew their attention was the fact we were sitting in hard plastic chairs. I became so embarrassed. You have no idea how embarrassing it was to be wearing a clitoral vibrator controlled by text messaging. Derek had no clue I was with a client and he just kept sending message after message to me, thinking it was funny! Every single message he sent would make a vibrating sound. Now think about that for a moment. It vibrates directly on my clit because you wear it like you wear panties. It's strapped to me. I'm sitting in a hard plastic chair and my client sitting next to me keeps hearing it go on and off. After it happened a few times, and the client across from me asked if I had a phone in my pocket, I about choked because he nearly guessed it, or at least it was too close to the truth for my comfort level."

"Oh my gosh Marianne, that is so damn funny. You and Derek have so much fun together. I think it's great how you have decided to keep things fresh after twenty years of marriage," Jenny laughs.

"Oh, honey, my story is not over. There's more. The client beside me noticed how uncomfortable I got after the phone in the pocket question, and all I can say is he must be one in a million that happens to know about these devices. He got so red in the face looking down at my crotch, even though he was really trying hard not to. He busted out laughing, practically rolling out of his chair. I wanted to slap him, and if I didn't need his account so bad, I would have!"

Confused about why she tortured herself with the constant buzzing, I say "I bet you got so mad at Derek when you saw him. I don't understand why you didn't just excuse yourself to go to the ladies room and take it off?"

"That's the best part of the story. You see, Derek and I have been experimenting a little with the whole Dom/sub lifestyle. Granted, we are by no means actively practicing, we're just enjoying playing with a few aspects of it. Well, I don't know if you've ever heard of being collared before…."

I immediately choke on my wine and spit a very unladylike mouthful of forty-dollar-a-bottle wine across the table. Drawing everyone's attention, Jenny asks, "Dear God, Lizzie, what in the world has you so rattled?" As I am gasping for air and flailing my arms around to try and get a deep breath, she says, "Are you going to live, Lizzie?"

"I don't really know." Trying to avoid passing out, I croak, "Did you just say collared? Do you even really know what that means, Marianne?"

"Well, granted we are just experimenting and I know what we're doing isn't the same as what others do who live that lifestyle full time. We're just playing around, really. The problem is, he put a lock on the back which prevented me from taking it off. Therefore, that thing gave me bursts of vibrations every time he texted me and I couldn't do anything about it. The agony was that it wasn't strong enough to cause an orgasm, just enough to send me to the edge… ALL FUCKING DAY! I was on the edge of an orgasm for ten hours. Ten hours, Lizzie!"

Oh my goodness! I cannot believe he did that to her. Using it that way is more like erotic punishment rather than erotic pleasure. "Oh, Marianne, we need to talk privately, honey."

"Trust me, I got my revenge. I went home and told him the whole story. Then, I lay on the bed and masturbated *twice* right in front of him. Then I took a hot bath and went to bed. I wouldn't give him any attention that night and haven't had sex with him all week. Now, he has a case of blue balls and I don't feel guilty about it."

"Shit, Marianne, I cannot wait to hear what y'all have planned next!" Janice says excitedly. At this rate, Derek and Marianne will try every new fetish and toy they can possibly get their hands on.

My stack of cash at the bank is steadily growing thanks to the dashing Mark Chesney. I really feel like a professional business person. I'm learning a lot and meeting many new people. His confidence in me has encouraged me to reach new levels and I feel like a completely new person.

I manage the endowment full-time and only occasionally work as an escort for Mark. We haven't had any more personal moments similar to the alcove at The Jefferson. I think, in a weird way, he wanted to remind me I'm a woman with needs and not to forget it. It really does bother me because I'm technically married, even though I feel like my marriage ended long ago. I just continue to get up every day and provide for my children the best way I know how. As long as I can provide a roof and food for them, I feel like I'm doing a good job. I try to avoid the hard self-judgment that sometimes seeps into my psyche. Without Mark and Ms. Martin, I'd be homeless. That's a fact.

What has really surprised me most of all is the amazing friendship Mark and I have formed. We've bonded over alcoholic spouses and our support for children's charities. In fact, we've discussed possible new endowments with other needy child charities.

When I lost all the fringe benefits Jeremy's job provided, I was devastated. However, what really sent me, spiraling was the loss of my husband. He is not the same man I married. I've tried to hold on to our family for the sake of our kids, but now that I can provide a living for us, I'm considering my options.

Walking into our apartment from my mid-day walk, I find Jeremy rifling through my things like he's on a mission. My clothes are off the hangers and thrown on the floor. My clothes from the dresser drawers are scattered about. He's moving about the room quickly and doesn't even know I've returned home.

"Jeremy, what the hell are you doing?" He pauses long enough to look at me then keeps on searching for god knows what. "Jeremy, stop!"

"Need money, Liz!"

"Why? For booze? I'm not giving you money for alcohol."

"I know you have some. You're obviously working somewhere. I just need twenty bucks, babe, that's all!"

"You know, that's the first time you've even acknowledged that I have a job. Normally you're passed out in a stupor. There's no money here, Jeremy, so stop ripping my clothes apart!"

He turns and slowly walks to me, staring very intently into my eyes. Fear begins to rise within me and I feel the hair on my neck stand up. Standing directly before me, he reaches out and begins to slowly rub his hand up and down my arm. His head lowers and he gives me a gentle kiss on the lips before pulling away. "Liz, baby. I'm sorry I haven't been the husband you needed me to be. I hate myself more than you could ever imagine." He hangs his head low and all the love I still feel for this man bubbles to the surface. "Forgive me?"

"Jeremy, you have to stop drinking. It's not going to help you find a job and it's killing our relationship. The kids are being denied the fatherly figure they richly deserve."

"I know all that!" He pulls away and paces the room, holding his head in his hand. "I don't need you nagging at me all the time! This isn't easy for me. I've lost EVERYTHING!" he roars at me.

"I understand. I truly get it, but you can't find answers in booze. Liquor doesn't talk back, trust me, I've sure asked plenty of your empty bottles as I've chucked them in the trash!"

"Just… please, just once more, give me twenty bucks. I'll stop, I promise." His shaking hands reach out to me, begging for understanding.

"Don't you find it interesting that you haven't even asked how I have enough to pay all of our bills? You don't even care to know where I'm working, do you?" His eyes flash with understanding and he momentarily is taken aback, possibly concerned with how I can accomplish the feat.

"Please, Liz, just this once have mercy on my stupid self. Give me the fucking money!"

"I can't, Jeremy. I literally cannot give you money because I don't have any here. Even if I did, the answer is no. Sorry, but you're killing yourself. No, I won't do it."

"Bitch!"

"You need to leave and don't come back. I mean it." I quickly move through the apartment and out the door. A string of profanity follows me. Great, now the neighbors have something to talk about.

Not knowing where to go, I drive around in circles. Somehow, I end up at the non-descript building on Main Street. I don't have a clue why, but for some reason a magnet pulled me here. Looking up into the pencil sized security camera, I request entrance.

"Well, this is a surprise. What brings my smartest escort to see me today?" Suddenly, concern replaces the big smile on her face. "Don't tell me you're quitting!"

"No, nothing like that. Believe me, this job is the only stable thing in my life right now. I need you much more than you need me."

"So why the long face? What's wrong, Lizzie?"

"Oh, Ms. Martin, I'm afraid my children will hate me. I just kicked my alcoholic husband out on his ass while he's obviously in the middle of withdrawal. I don't know when it's truly time to accept that divorce is inevitable. My heart says forever, but my brain says it was over a long time ago. Somehow, after driving around in circles, you were like a beacon lighting the way and I ended up here."

"Honey, I've been married three times. I know all about it." She stands up and walks to her refrigerated wine cabinet built seamlessly into the wall. It always amazes me how cabinetry can be hidden in plain sight. She opens a bottle of wine, pours each of us a hefty serving, and pronounces, "Start from the beginning, child."

And I do. I tell her every single detail including all the sexual details—good, bad, and indifferent. After four hours, I feel better to at least get it out there. I've made a close friend during this conversation. She shared some of her colorful history with me, too. "Remember

Henry? The man who spoils me that I told you about?" I nod in acknowledgment. "He keeps asking me to marry him. He claims he's moving on from his marriage and he wants us to retire to his villa in France."

My face surely registers my shock, "Are you serious? Are you going?"

"He claims he's serious but I just don't know. Three failed marriages tend to leave a girl skeptical about the blessed union."

I watch her closely and there seems to be honest emotion in her face when she speaks of him. "You'll make the right decision. You're a tough lady."

"I just have so many responsibilities here with my business. People rely on me and I enjoy it."

I smirk at her. "Yeah, they rely on you alright."

She laughs a huge outward belly laugh. "Hey, it's made you a tidy sum, hasn't it?"

"Undoubtedly. If I hadn't answered your ad that day, I'd likely be homeless."

"You're a smart girl, Lizzie Macintyre. You have a real head for the business world. Mark raves to me all the time about how talented you are. He trusts you and let me tell you, that's a rarity because I don't have any girls or guys servicing clients in a purely professional capacity the way you do. I'm proud of you."

I let her compliment sink in and allow myself a moment of happiness as I listen to it. Then suddenly it occurs to me, "You have male escorts?"

She scoffs, "Well of course, and let me tell you, their bonuses are fantastic! Old gray haired ladies tip well when they've been made to feel young again. It's not just male-female connections I make, either. It *is* 2014, Mrs. Macintyre. I get requests from seventy-year-old ladies wanting to have their first female experiences. You'd be surprised the number of ladies who are married to the same man their whole lives and never felt an attraction for their husbands because they prefer women. There was a lady just last week who had her first orgasm…ever. She was married fifty years until her husband died. Then she called me to make an arrangement with a female escort. She tipped her ten thousand dollars for an entire weekend and claimed it was the best money she ever spent."

I sit there slack jawed not believing what I've heard or what to be shocked about the most. Damn, seventy years with no orgasms? That's too much to wrap my brain around.

"It goes the reverse as well. However, the men aren't nearly as noble. I have had clients come in after their wives pass on and request male escorts. Sometimes, they feel like they are somehow cheating on their spouse, but it doesn't apply if it's the same gender." She shakes her head as if trying to make sense out of it just as I am trying to do. "I just make the connections and leave it up to the escorts to figure it all out."

I reflect on her comments and immediately feel bad that I was originally surprised by it. "Thanks for your advice, Ms. Martin. I will consider everything you said."

"No, I should be thanking *you*. Today has given me the opportunity to get to know you better and it's been enlightening. It is *I* who have much to consider."

I'm not sure what she means by her last comment or why she has things to consider but in any case, I feel better and that is a very good thing.

Chapter Twenty

Unusual Requests...

Jack

Each day at work, I feel more robotic than the next. New client + criminal act = get off scot-free because I'm good at my job. With each closed case, I lose a little more of myself. I pretty much hate my job. My caseload is off the charts because everyone wants a lawyer with a great track record. That's me. Dad praises me all the time and has been reducing his caseload the closer to retirement he gets. I'm happy for him because there is a light at the end of the wretched tunnel. My light, however, is miles ahead and I can't even see a glimmer it's so far away.

My phone buzzes, "Yes, Patricia?"

"Your mother is calling, sir. Shall I put her through?"

I immediately try to think of ways to avoid her call and feel horrible about it. "Yes, please. Thank you."

Taking a deep breath, I answer the pending call, "Hello, Mother. How are you today?"

"I'm splendid, sweetheart. How are my grandbabies?"

"Busy, busy these days with their activities. What can I do for you?"

"I'm calling to remind you of our Trust Account meeting. It's set for Friday at eleven a.m. We are having lunch catered."

"I do remember, but thanks for the reminder. I'll tell Victoria to be available as well."

There is a long pause and I eventually turn to look at the phone as if willing her response to come and it doesn't. "Mom? Did you hear me?'

"Ah, yes, dear, I did hear you. Um, Jack would you be agreeable to Victoria sitting this one out?"

My eyebrows pinch together in confusion because Mother has never made this type of request before. I made it extremely clear when Victoria and I married that I considered her an equal partner in my inheritance and would be just as involved with decision making as me.

"Mother, what's going on? Why are you requesting this?"

She stutters a bit before saying, "The new CPA firm I hired has some questions. It's probably nothing, but they've asked to have a closed, private meeting with the primary beneficiaries of the Trust only—you and me."

I'm immediately on guard because that almost insinuates impropriety and there has never been any. "Mom, I don't like excluding Victoria no matter what they ask for. I don't keep details of my Trust from her and she could potentially be in charge of it anyway, especially if something were to happen to the two of us."

"I understand that fully, Jack, but as the new CPA firm we are under contract with them for five years. You know we make a change every five years to eliminate any possibility of impropriety, so I need you to abide by their request. We don't need any negative audits or issuance of a Manager's Letter. Okay, dear?"

I completely trust my Mother's financial judgment. She is truly a whiz, but it just seems wrong to keep this from Victoria. I know this has nothing to do with her so I concede. "Yes, ma'am. If you feel this is best to keep good relations I will go along with it, but for the record, I really hate it."

"Thank you, dear. Also, before I forget! We need to meet to discuss the Children's Hospital Christmas Gala. Everyone on the committee is thrilled you've agreed to MC again this year. They were frightened we'd end up with Scott Harrison and his drunken wife. Anyway, that meeting is in two weeks, so busy, busy times my dear."

"Yes, it appears so. Love you, Mother. I'm due in Court."

"No problem. Kiss the kiddos!"

I disconnect and can't help but be in deep thought about this auditor meeting. What possibly do they want to meet with us privately about? Mom knows how I feel about Victoria, and the fact she is supporting their position seems very strange to me. I'm concerned there is something she isn't telling me.

Chapter Twenty-one

Totally Off Balance...

Jack

Tonight, Victoria and I are attending the Crime Solvers Ball. It's a wonderful fundraising opportunity for the surrounding communities. Each year, a different locality is chosen to host and this year it's Prince George, Virginia. The chosen theme, "Prince George: The County of Royalty", is an obvious play on its name and early relations with England. Since the birth of England's youngest heir to the throne, baby Prince George, son of William and Kate, the world is entranced with this beautiful baby boy. Some might say the lore of Princess Diana has extended to her offspring—being attractive didn't hurt, I'm sure. Several years ago, Rolls-Royce opened a massive state of the art manufacturing plant in the county. Having the British company in the county sends a significant message to the business community that Virginia is open for business in the manufacturing sector. The Crime Solvers Ball gives the community and business leaders the opportunity to let their hair down and just have fun for the night, raising money to support initiatives in the process.

Ever since I received the call from Mom today, I've been a little off-kilter. I can't put my finger on it, but I just have this impending feeling of doom and I really hate it.

Walking downstairs to wait for Victoria, I decide to check in with Ingrid. "Hello, Ingrid. How are things around here lately? I've been so busy I haven't had time to check in with you."

She takes a deep breath as if contemplating her words carefully, and replies in her thick German accent, "You know me, Mr. Loving, I keep things running in tip top shape."

"Oh, I know you do and I have little doubt in your abilities." I smile warmly at her and notice she seems to want to say something else. "What is it, Ingrid? I sense you want to say something."

She purses her lips and I see her throat swallow deeply. "I'm not sure I should say. I'm an old woman, Mr. Loving, and it's really not my business."

I narrow my eyes, considering how firmly I should press her. I look toward the spiral staircase that dominates our home and realize I don't hear Victoria coming. "Ingrid, you've been with my family since I lived at home with my parents. I consider you family, you know that. I trust you implicitly and more importantly, you are wise. If you have a concern, then I probably should be concerned as well. You're my eyes and ears, Ingrid. I trust you to keep me informed. Always." I raise my eyebrows at her as if to say, 'your loyalty is to me.'

"Several matters are concerning me, actually." I nod at her to continue. "The children's nanny is most unhappy. The demands on her are, at times, extreme in my view."

I contemplate what she could be referring to and immediately conclude this has Victoria written all over it. "Okay, Ingrid. I appreciate your candidness and will speak with the nanny directly. What else do I need to know?"

She looks very uncomfortable. I can tell she is really struggling with whether or not to confide in me. "Mrs. Loving has visitors who on occasion—"

"On occasion, what?"

She blows out deeply and shakes her head, "Mr. Loving, Mrs. Loving's mother calls a lot and has visited some. I was not eavesdropping but Mrs. Winfield yells, loudly."

"What was she yelling about?"

"I can't say, but Mrs. Loving was very distressed and demanded I not tell you this information, but I feel very uncomfortable keeping secrets from you, especially after what occurred previously."

Knowing full well that she was referring to my public blowup about Victoria's father, I requested Ingrid tell me if they visited my home. Quite frankly, I don't trust either one of them. I never have.

"You were absolutely correct to tell me. Rest assured this is between you and me only. You have my word." Just then, I hear the unmistakable sound of heels on the stairs.

Looking very relieved, Ingrid says, "Thank you, Sir." Once Victoria arrives in the foyer, she adds, "Please have a safe and pleasant evening."

"Thank you, Ingrid. Drive safely yourself."

On the way to the Ball, I'm quietly contemplative. Several odd situations have been thrown my way today. I don't like surprises, at all.

"Jack, you didn't say anything about how I'm dressed. I planned this outfit for a week. You could have at least acknowledged how I look."

I look at Victoria, give a quick once over, and say, "You're absolutely correct. My apologies. You look stunning tonight, as usual. I'm a very lucky man."

She smirks at me. "I can't seem to keep your attention lately. It's been ages since you fucked me properly."

"Trust me, I know. My blue balls are pissed as hell."

She returns her attention to the road in front of her and I see a frown marking her face. "Have you spoken with Erin lately?"

I quickly glance over at her while still trying to drive safely, "No, it's been weeks since I spoke to her."

"Well, don't look so disappointed. Damn, Jack. At least you could pretend not to miss her."

"I don't miss her. What are you talking about?"

"You know exactly what I'm talking about. The love of your life is back and you miss her. I can read it all over your face. Just don't insult me by pretending it isn't true!"

I grip the steering wheel fiercely, trying to calm down. "What the hell is wrong with you, Vickie? We've been married for ten fucking years!"

"Yeah, ten years of pent up sexual frustration for 'Miss Fucks-A-Lot.'"

"Are you shitting me? Get over your jealousy of her. She had her chance with me and walked away. What makes you think she wants me now?"

"Oh, I don't know? Maybe she has a thing for millionaire trust fund babies? What I think is interesting is that you said, 'what makes you think *she* wants *me* now.' Why didn't you say, 'what makes you think you would want *her*?'"

I take a deep breath and try very hard to calm myself down. This is going nowhere. Victoria doesn't understand my money is the reason I lost Erin in the first place. It's the reason why I lose a lot of things, like my free will to pick the career I want."

"Drop it. Right fucking now. I don't want to hear another fucking word about Erin!"

She sits beside me, looking out the front windshield, fuming. We both are furious. When we arrive at the valet stand, I know it before the car even stops. I'm going to need to tip him well, very well.

She throws the car door open, not allowing him to open it for her. The door hits him in the hand, obviously hurting him because I see him shake his hand in an attempt to shake the pain away. I mutter obscenities quietly and when I walk around to him, I palm him a hundred dollar bill. "Hey, sorry, man." He gives a chin lift in the universal sign of bro love. Victoria said nothing to the guy which left me seething.

We put on our fake, we're-so-happy smiles and greet as many people as we can. Suddenly, I see my good friend, Mark Chesney across the room. I make a beeline in his direction, needing to breathe some friendly, not-so-hostile air. He sees me and I notice him bending down, whispering in a very attractive woman's ear.

As I get to him, we embrace in an affectionate display of male tap-each-other-on-the-back love. I really like Mark. More importantly, I respect him. He's a smart investment banker, owning his own business, and I have worked with him professionally several times on my funding of various charities. He's older than me, but we socialize well. We have a lot in common since he also attended UR, and as an alumnus, financially supports many of the school scholarships my family supports.

Additionally, he knows my parents very well. He's shared that he appreciates Mom's savvy business mind and has told me many times that Richmond owes her its undying love for the thousands of programs she has funded throughout the years. I guess I always knew Mom was a special person, but when other people in the financial world are in awe of her sound financial investment decisions, it leaves me inspired to make just as big an impact as she has on our community.

"It's so good to see you again, Mark. I haven't been to the club recently to play racquetball so I haven't seen you in forever."

He smiles largely at me, too, "I know. It's been way too long since I kicked your ass."

"Hey, we need to get together so I can at least get the chance to earn some of my money back. You're lethal on the court, dude."

He smirks at me and chuckles. "I'll go easy on you." He motions toward the gorgeous woman on his arm, "Jack Loving, may I introduce to you the lovely Ms. Lizzie Macintyre."

I'm suddenly very dry-mouthed and feel like my thoughts are scattered as I look at this beauty in front of me. When I tentatively reach out my hand to her and finally make contact, it's like a zap of current flows through my hand. I've never been so affected by meeting someone before. She has to be just as affected because her eyes look down to our joined hands and I can almost read her mind when she questions what she feels, too. Bizarre, totally fucking bizarre.

I can't seem to pull my hand away and I know at some point very soon, it's going to look really odd that I'm still hanging on to her. I notice her other hand moves across her chest covering her heart. My eyes are drawn there and I suddenly notice the impression of her nipples through her dress. My eyes are glued on her breasts and I feel like a total douche. This is so inappropriate but something magnetic is happening and I don't want to pull away.

I look up to her mouth and see her biting her lower lip between her teeth, and when we make eye contact, she swallows deeply and raises her chin slightly in an effort to get more air. I search my memory, wondering if we've met before. Oddly, I feel like I've seen her face but I do not believe we've been formally introduced.

"Ah, Jack? Do you want to let her hand go today or next week?"

Feeling totally embarrassed, I pull my hand away like she's on fire and burning me. What the hell is wrong with me? My emotions are every-fucking-where today. I timidly take a peek at her again, "Sorry."

Looking at Mark, I joke, "So what in the world did you have to do to convince this gorgeous woman to go out with you?"

A quick knowing look passes between the two of them and then it's gone. Mark laughs and she giggles the sweetest sound. "Lizzie and I work together on my endowment project with the Children's Museum of Richmond. Trust me, it is I who benefit from our association. Lizzie runs a tight ship and I trust her implicitly." That's odd. I just used that exact word with Ingrid just a short while ago. It's good to know Mark has a loyal connection and I'm oddly jealous because I don't know this woman.

With raised eyebrows, I turn to her, "Oh really? My family has a particular interest in the Children's Museum. We make it a point to support their initiatives in every way possible. In fact, you may know my mother, Sarah Loving? She's on the BOD."

A look of understanding crosses her face. "Absolutely! I just love Mrs. Loving. She's always been so nice to me. Even when I—", she abruptly stops speaking.

"Even when you, what?"

She looks at Mark and shakes her head, looking down, "Oh nothing. I really respect your mother. She has had some amazing ideas for the museum and she's very hands-on."

A big smile crosses my face, "That's my mom. She's a great lady." I continue looking at her and can't shake the feeling I've seen her before. "Have we met prior to tonight, Lizzie?"

With a bright megawatt smile, she says, "We haven't formally met, but I have seen you before at the Country Club of Virginia."

A little too chipper, I say, "Oh, so you're a member?"

A look of sadness crosses her face and she looks away from me, avoiding eye contact. "No. Not anymore."

Mark interrupts, "So, Jack, how's Victoria doing?"

"She's fine. She's here, in fact. These days she stays busy with her charity work and of course raising the twins."

"Oh! You have twins! That's so cool! My brother's best friends were fraternal twins and they were so much fun to be around. What are their names and ages?"

"Their names are Bryce and Grace and they are eight years old."

"Really, my Ethan is eight years old, too. My daughter, Hope, is thirteen."

We nod and smile to one another in understanding as parents usually do when speaking about their kids. I can't seem to pull my eyes off this woman, but am beginning to weird myself out with my own behavior, so I turn around and notice Victoria as she waves me over back to her. I feel guilty because I shouldn't regret walking away in this moment but being the southern gentleman I am, my wife beckons so I must go.

"It was very nice to finally make your acquaintance, Lizzie Macintyre." Turning to Mark and seeing his obvious knowledge that I'm intrigued, he outwardly laughs at me, grabs me by the shoulder, and shakes his head. "Mark, I'll call you next week?"

With a reddened face and needing to hold in his laughter, he shakes his head at me. *Damn you, dickhead.* "Oh, I bet you will."

I take a final look over my shoulder at her amazing mile-long legs and practically trip a waiter passing by. He mutters "asswipe" under his breath. I deserved it, too.

When I reach Victoria, she introduces me to the new tennis pro at the Country Club. For some reason, I get the feeling she wants me jealous. It doesn't work because all I can think about is what is attached at the top of those mile long legs steadily walking away from me.

Chapter Twenty-two

Removing The Cogs From My Brain...

Jack

Tossing and turning all night long, I feel off and really irritable this morning. I assume it's because of the Trust Fund meeting scheduled for today. The one I was asked to keep from Victoria. Thinking I just really need some relief to get me centered again, I nuzzle Victoria around the neck and lightly touch her arm up and down. She's pretty deep in sleep, but my guilt isn't as hard as my dick, so fucking her wins out.

I lightly kiss her all over her face and neck until she begins to whimper. Moving her body from her side to her back, I begin to lick her over her chest around to each nipple, sucking them each until they are no longer flattened disks but hard pebbles. Victoria's nipples are always so responsive and I love that I can make her come with nipple play alone.

I work my way down to her core but continue touching her up and down her sides, causing her to have goose bumps everywhere. She begins to push her pelvis upward, trying to find her much-needed friction. *Nope, not that easy today, sweetheart, I have a much better plan.* I'm really in a particular mood today and I know I need something a little more…creative.

She fully wakes and moans. She undresses quickly when I ask her to remove her cami top and boy shorts. "Put your arms above your head. Hold on to the headboard and do not let go or I WILL stop." Knowing I mean business, she complies.

I move my mouth slowly across her stomach and lick across, hip to hip. I reach the bare mound of her sex and inhale deeply. "Fuck, baby, you smell so good." I take my time when my own body wants me to rush, I hold back, savoring her flavor and scent. Not too urgently, I very slowly lick around the bundle of nerves that begin to swell when I touch them more firmly. I press my hands to her hips, holding her down. I leave the sensitive nub and tease her viciously with just the tip of my tongue moving to locate the seam which separates her lips. I plunge my tongue deeper… looking, reaching, seeking what she and I most want me to find. My senses are overwhelmed: sight, smell, taste, feel, and most wickedly I hear her deep moans as I insert my mouth as deeply as I can reach. She's worked up, but not enough. Not for what I have planned, because I need her wetter than ever.

I insert first one, then two fingers inside her, moving them in and out. As I lick her clit, she builds toward her climax. Knowing her body so intimately, I'm never fooled. She's the fiddle and I'm the string bringing out the beauty of her music: her orgasm. I stroke along her g-spot, and just before she plays that song for me, I pull my fingers and mouth away. She yells her frustration. No, definitely not happy with me at the moment. *That's okay, baby, I have serious plans.*

I lean back on my knees and toss her onto her belly so quick she doesn't see it coming. She's so well connected to me she never releases the headboard, her arms just end up crisscrossed. *Good girl.*

Grabbing her hips, I pull her up on all fours and reach under the pillow for my secret stash of goodies. She jumps when she feels the liquid pouring in between the cheeks of her ass. "Ahh," she cries out in surprise. I always take my time getting her ready to receive me. This is the only way to do this and do it well. Too many women despise ass play and it's because their man doesn't know what the fuck he's doing. It's about preparation and you cannot rush it. Using my pinky, I insert it into her well-lubed ass very, very slowly. Encouraging her to relax and working my fingers slowly, I build up to three fingers until propped up before me is a fully lubricated, beautiful asshole ready for prime fucking.

I reach for my secret stash and grab the graduated size butt plug. Removing my fingers, I replace them with the plug about two inches inside and hold it there. Twisting around on my back, I lie in between her legs, reaching my head up to her clit to begin licking her bundled nerves slowly. I use my other hand to bury first one then two fingers in her pussy, stroking in and then out. She moans louder and louder, trying to thrust her hips, but I manage to hold her still. "Not yet, baby, just wait. You can't come 'til I'm ready and I've not even started."

"Shit, Jack! I want to come so badly. Please…let me come, please!

I focus on finding her g-spot as opposed to just thrusting my fingers in and out. When I find the spot, I'm looking for, I rub firmly while drawing her clit up into my mouth and sucking fiercely.

"Fuck, Jack! Jack, please I'm trying to wait but, please HURRY!" she desperately cries out.

I withdraw my fingers and mouth just at the point where I can feel her clit enlarge on my tongue, just about ready to explode. Mastering cunnilingus or oral sex, really is an art I've proudly become an expert in.

I quickly jump up on my knees and plunge my hardened cock very shallowly into her pussy. I'm careful to lean backward to avoid contact with the plug. I push her head to the mattress, leaning her far forward. I reach around, locating her clit, and begin to circle my fingers around it.

"Are you ready to come, sweetheart?"

"Yes, oh yes. Can I? Please?"

Driving her crazy with my shallow thrusts, I pant, "You know the deal, don't you, baby? Only when I give the signal."

She grunts and moans her frustration. I press harder on her clit and start increasing the speed of my thrusts. Then suddenly, as I slam my cock into her, I also slam the plug all the way in, in one fluid motion. Everything happens at once. I pinch her clit with my right hand and reach around and pinch her left tit with the other. "NOW!"

"Jack, oh god, Jack, Yes! Fuck me, Jack! Fuck me like you own my pussy…Shit!"

I continue thrusting hard and my cock is squeezed by the contractions from her orgasm tightening down on me. It's so tight it hurts, in a great fucking way. I hold back, just enjoying the way she falls apart under me. The only thing that would make this better would be mirrors on the headboard. Hmm? May have to install one. I thrust harder and harder and soon I feel her beginning to squeeze again. "I'm about to go again, baby. I'm almost there." I stroke her clit around in circles and still enjoy her tit in my other hand. Suddenly, her upper body flails upward and she's screaming loudly into her second orgasm. Fuck, I love a multi-orgasmic girl. There's nothing hotter.

Finally, the squeezing of my dick sends me over and I'm like a fast-moving piston enjoying the hell out of the warmest depths of my wife's cunt. "Well, fuck me that felt good. D-A-M-N!"

We both collapse on the bed, and when I have a moment of clarity, I remember it's time to take care of my woman. I stand up and carry her inside our beautiful walk-in shower. Our multi-jet shower spray massages and brings all of her limbs back to life. I carefully remove the plug and begin to lather her body up with her bath soap.

She's made me feel so good this morning, removing all the cogs from my mind that it's only fair I rejuvenate her body as well.

After play, avoided by so many for reasons I'll never understand, is in many ways the most important part of sex. This is when communication is at its best and true, loving connections are reaffirmed. This is when we can chat openly about the sex acts we just enjoyed and discuss limits, boundaries, and future ideas to try. It's about communication.

After a lengthy morning of hot sex in our bed, followed by a shower massage, Victoria surprises me with her own version of a shower massage and it involves her on her knees sucking me off. Yeah, orgasm number two feels mighty fucking fine. Bring it on; I'm ready to deal with asshat auditors now.

Chapter Twenty-three

My Life, In Little Tiny Pieces...

Jack

"Jack, I have the conference room all set up for your eleven a.m. working luncheon with your mom and the auditors," Patricia's voice rings aloud in my office.

"Thanks so much. Heading there now."

"Oh, and Jack?"

"Yes?"

"Mrs. Loving requested I not advise Victoria you are in an audit meeting in the event she should call in or drop by."

Now that I *didn't* expect from my mom. She asked me not to tell Victoria but now she's issuing directives to my assistant to make sure Victoria doesn't accidentally find out the auditors are here. That's unsettling. "Thanks for the info…and the discretion. Your loyalty is extremely valued, Patricia."

As I move toward the conference room, irritation flares within me. Telling me what I should say is bad enough but speaking to MY assistant is crossing the line. Mother and I will have a private chat.

When I approach the door, I notice the window glass has been changed to opaque, thereby denying passersby a glimpse of the room's occupants. Now, that is *very* significant. We rarely use the privacy glass. It's a cool feature, but unless you are hiding someone, it's truly not necessary. A warmth flows over me and I stop dead in my tracks. My uneasiness is back full force and I suddenly scan my brain for critical reasons to avoid walking through that door. The knob represents a scalding metal and I know in the pit of my stomach things are about to change. I can feel doom coming through that door. Through that glass. Suddenly, I hate that opaque glass and conjure images in my mind of contractors tearing this conference room to shreds.

Taking a deep breath, I open the door and notice everyone seems very serious. No smiling faces, just pure business. Other than Mother and her long-time financial advisor, there are two men and one woman whom I don't recognize. I greet the room with a head nod and a general "good morning, everyone" to the room at large.

I look to Mom and she makes general introductions. "Everyone, may I have the distinct pleasure of introducing my brilliantly talented son, Mr. Jack Loving, Jr." I can't help but give an eye roll to the "brilliantly talented" reference, but it's nice to know Mom thinks highly of me; I just don't like the lengths she's going to, to keep my so called 'brilliance' off track.

"Jack, this is our new auditing firm for the next, oh, four years and eleven months." She smiles to them and everyone shares a joke about hoping to live that long. A pain moves through my heart to think of my mom as deceased. It will absolutely paralyze me when it happens.

"Mr. Morton is the Managing Partner, Mr. Sears is the Assistant Partner, and Miss Collins is the lead Auditor for the Bowes Family Trust." I shake each hand directly and give a head nod to Mom's financial advisor. "Jack, Miss Collins is the niece to my dear, longtime friend from the Club, Mrs. Collins."

I smile pleasantly to everyone and offer to sit down and move along to business. I'm really anxious to know what's got Mom so worked up. Mr. Morton gives a lengthy speech about his appreciation on his firm being selected to the five-year contract as well as explaining his plans on conducting annual audits, etc., blah, blah, blah. Just really wanting to hear something I haven't heard before, it's hard not to become almost cross-eyed listening until he gets to the part of the presentation discussing irregularities. Now, this gets me interested!

Mr. Morton seems to focus his attention directly on me. "While familiarizing ourselves with the work of the previous auditors, Miss Collins was intrigued with a single line item expense buried in a general account. There was a footnote on the item and she noticed on the working papers it was crossed through repeatedly. Her piqued curiosity led her to three previous annual audits finding the same line item, but the amount has increased exponentially over time. Concerned that it had been misclassified, she wanted to essentially clear the slate and correct the error moving forward. When she contacted the previous auditor, she didn't like the non-answer she kept receiving."

Listening intently, I watch Mr. Morton and Miss Collins. I also watch Mom's grave expression and notice her pen tapping her paper, obviously upset. I stop him momentarily and ask specific questions to Miss Collins to which she supplies very proficient answers and I'm immediately impressed with her expertise.

"Miss Collins spent nearly forty hours investigating this issue and nothing was making sense. You certainly must know there is an accounting procedure for every transaction that must be followed. When something is askew, we comb the records looking for the cause. Most often, it's an unfortunate case of human error. In this case, the more we looked, the more suspicious the records turned out to be. Each time we followed a clue, we were stonewalled for answers from the previous audit firm, specifically the managing auditor. You must realize this is a major red flag to an auditor. Transparency is always your friend and stonewalling another audit firm when transferring clients is completely unprofessional," Mr. Morton explains.

As he is speaking, I grow concerned about his "you must know" and "must realize" comments. I am beginning to get the sense an impropriety has occurred and they believe I know something about it. The hair on the back of my neck stands on end, and my blood pressure increases with each passing second. Just as my thoughts come together and I'm about to ask what the fuck they are trying to infer, Mr. Morton directs Miss Collins to explain further details.

"A break finally came when a low-level auditor called me at home late one evening. She was extremely nervous and told me that money was withdrawn from the account in cash on multiple occasions over the past three years. Her previous boss, who just last week suddenly resigned, was assisting with covering everything up. Due to the sizable amounts of the withdrawals…"

I immediately sit forward in my chair, looking over at Mom with a murderous look on my face. I'm rushed with the realization that funds have been embezzled from the family Trust and I'm outraged! I know Miss Collins is speaking, but I cannot focus on her words while I attempt to comprehend what these people are trying to tell me. She closes her eyes and solemnly shakes her head in a look of defeat I've never seen cross my mother's beautiful face. A thousand questions run through my mind but most critical is, "HOW MUCH?" I yell across the table, causing Miss Collins to jump in reaction to my harsh words and no doubt volume.

Mr. Morton opens his leather binder and passes Mom and I each a single sheet of paper. I don't even want to look at it because deep down, I know my life is forever changed.

BOWES FAMILY TRUST	
Schedule of Unidentified/Fraudulent Withdrawals	
Prepared by: Miss C. Collins	
Fiscal Year Ending	**Amount**
2013	$880,000.00
2012	$525,000.00
2011	$225,000.00
2010	$100,000.00
2009	$0.00
Current 2014 (unaudited)	$1,370,000.00
Total unauthorized expense:	**$3,100,000.00**

Looking at the paper carefully, I review everything again. Surely, I missed something because this cannot be happening. Someone is embezzling money from my family Trust. I go through so many ranges of emotions and my heart is absolutely pounding through my chest. Continuously staring at the paper for answers, I'm frustrated that it's not showing me any. "Fuck!" I stand up, pacing the room, carrying this piece of paper like I will discover some truth and reason to void everything these people are telling me, but nothing materializes. The room is completely quiet and the chart is viciously mocking me with silence.

"Jack, there's more." I turn, looking in the direction of my mother's voice and I instantly get a feeling my world is about to implode. I suddenly feel very weak and barely make it into a nearby chair. "Miss Collins feels strongly that she knows the identity of the person making the withdrawals."

Swallowing and taking a deep breath, I know in my heart who she will say, so I save her the agony on saying her name, "Victoria?"

She shakes her head 'yes' and I feel like my breath has left my body and I just might faint. I look down the table to Miss Collins,

"Explain the exact details to me. Leave nothing out and you need to be thorough."

Over the next hour and a half, the facts of each and every transaction are laid out before me. There has to be a logical reason for all of this, but I keep silently asking, *why? Why? WHY?*

I have always trusted Victoria with all of my assets. Everything! She can buy whatever she wants or needs from my personal accounts. There is absolutely no reason to embezzle so much money from my family Trust. I made it a point when we were first married to include her in all financial decisions. I didn't want her to feel the sting of my money the way Erin did. Granted, I didn't know at the time Erin felt constricted by my money, but I knew it made her uncomfortable to be around wealth. Very few spouses in this country are married to people as wealthy as I am and I put zero limits on that money. I gave her full access. So stupid. I guess the joke is on me.

Mom and I want this money to stand for something good. Granddaddy Bowes scrimped, saved, and built a business all the while remembering what it meant to be poor and never forgetting his roots. His legacy, our family mission, is to do good works helping our community. Now that mission is tarnished by mixing our good money with something black, something potentially evil. As it is, I don't have a clue what it was used for. For all I know, our money was used for tainted ventures. Or blackmail! God, could someone be blackmailing her? FUCK!

I stand from my seat and address everyone. "First, I want to say I appreciate everyone's time here today. Miss Collins, my family, owes you a debt of gratitude of which I can never repay. I commend you on your professionalism and obvious good work ethic. To know this went on for years and we knew nothing…" I shake my head, still in disbelief this is happening to me right now. From my own wife no less! "Your attention to detail and obvious persistence brought the hidden cr-crime… crime, to light." This is so hard. Knowing I'm about to break, I need to get out of this room. Now.

"I am shocked to discover this occurred and I assure each of you that I intend to get to the bottom of it. In the meantime, I would ask that each of you keep these details strictly confidential. I have several calls I need to make and guidance to seek. So, if you will excuse me."

As I move to walk away, Mom says, "Jack, I need to inform you of changes I'm making to my side of the Trust." I shake my head because I knew she would do something. "My attorneys will remove Victoria as alternate beneficiary. I need to put protections in place to avoid this in the future. We need to discuss what those will be at a later time." I nod my head, just really wanting to leave this room.

Mom stands up, grabs by arms firmly, and looks me in the eye, performing the mandatory "Mom check" and hugs me tightly. "I love you, Jack" she whispers in my ear. I nod because I'm too emotional to say anything to the person I respect most in this world. The person who took a well-funded family Trust and turned it into a massive one whose assets could support many future generations of the Loving family. I can't ignore my feelings of failure that the money was lost while on my watch.

Leaving the office, I decide to hit the gym. There is no way I can go home feeling as jittery as I do right now. I have so many scenarios running through my mind. I still cannot believe Victoria would do this. And for five fucking years! I feel so stupid for being duped, yet according to the auditors, this was so thoroughly hidden it was a stroke of luck it was found in the first place.

I have many people I need to consult with, but first of those is my trusted friend Mark Chesney. He's a smart man when it comes to investments, and more importantly, I just need a buddy right now. After I beg him to drop everything he's doing because "I have an urgent and very serious personal matter I need help with", he meets me at the Club for racquetball. Just what I need to work out aggression.

After I relay the entire story to him, he stops playing and turns to me, looking as though he may faint and it has nothing to do with the game. "I don't know what the fuck to say, I'm flabbergasted!"

"Trust me, I know. My life just imploded!"

"When are you going to question her?"

Picking up the ball, shaking my head, and looking to the floor, I say, "Soon, but I don't know what to say. This is a crime, Mark. A fucking CRIME! My WIFE… my *wife*, Mark… she stole from my family. I can *never* forgive that. I *won't* forgive it. My family Trust has controlled my entire life—for the good and the bad, it has. It caused my first love to walk away from me and now it's caused my wife…it's caused my wife to…*steal* from me."

I swing with every bit of strength I can muster. Mark seems to know I need a few minutes and doesn't press me. "I need to consider the kids but my marriage is in free fall. I already know that. For her indiscretions in the past, it was fun to punish her reddened ass for being bad but this isn't about a good spanking, this is about how she fucked my family financially. I just want to wring her damn neck!"

Even working through the punishing game, we continue our discussion, Mark seeming to know I need to release my pent up aggression. "Well, if you're just looking for some discreet fun, I can hook you up."

"Naw, man! You're not pretty enough for me!" I manage a laugh for the first time this afternoon.

"Fuck you! Seriously, I know a lady who runs an escort business. Just fun times; no complications, no gold diggers!"

I stop playing and stand there, bent over and exhausted because I have played too fucking hard. Processing what he's telling me, I look at him questioningly, "So have *you* ever used this escort business?"

"Absolutely." He quickly responds, not looking a damn bit sorry about it.

"Really?" I stare at him like a deer caught in the headlights. "You? You can find dates anywhere. Why do you need that?"

"Like I said, it's easy—no relationships, no expectations, no gold diggers. There are some that just escort you to events and that's it. Others are known to enjoy some between-the-sheets action. It depends on what you're looking for and what your tastes are." He smirks at me knowingly. He and I have enjoyed conversations in the past about our affinity for all things BDSM. "Besides, you'd be shocked if you knew the people that used escorts routinely. It's a dirty little secret around here."

Still not believing that something like this exists in little 'ole RVA, I just shake my head incredulously. "I think I have enough problems right now, I don't need any more."

Mark leans over and pats me on the back, "Well, bud, let me know if you change your mind."

"Actually, I'd like you to consider joining our team of financial advisors. I trust you and I'd like your input in all of this mess. Mom plans to make some changes to prevent this kind of thing in the future. She has her longtime financial advisor for her part of the Trust. I'd like someone who I know has my back looking out for me as well."

"Sounds reasonable and I'd be proud to have your business."

He asks me some general questions and we decide to meet tomorrow to go over more specific details. Mark is an extremely busy guy, so the fact he's dropping everything to help me, even though I would assuredly be his largest client, well, it's a testament to the kind of friend he really is.

Leaving the Club, I phone my attorney and give him the shocking news. It's times like this that having his personal cell is most beneficial. We make plans to meet first thing tomorrow morning.

"You cannot let on that you suspect anything, Jack. I know your life has been blown to shit, but say nothing. This is a legal matter now and anything you say from here on out can be used against you."

Great. Now I have to act like the doting, happy husband. Time to close ranks, I guess.

Chapter Twenty-four

Fully Exposed...

Victoria

*J*ack is back to being his occupied self all of a sudden. Last night he didn't come to bed. This morning he left before I awoke, and when I called his office, Patricia said he was unavailable to speak with me. Odd, really, because she normally comments where he is or what he's doing but not today. Come to think of it, she was tight-lipped and rather curt on the phone. I'll need to have Jack put her in her place about proper communication when speaking with HIS wife.

I've left several phone messages and texts on his phone, with no answer. What the hell is going on? He didn't come home for dinner, and considering it's almost nine p.m., I'm getting rather worried. Maybe he'll answer a text if I get shitty or use the ultimate weapon, our children.

9:00 WTH??? Where RU? The kids and I deserve to know when you'll be home.

9:05 Working on a big problem. Tell kids I love them. Don't wait up.

9:06 What's going on, Jack? Call me!

It's one a.m. and he's not home. This REALLY pisses me off! I deserve a phone call at least.

Waking up the next morning at six a.m., I run through the house, no Jack. He hasn't been home because the shower wasn't used this morning. I check the other bedrooms, his office, and nothing. Dammit! I decide he isn't going to avoid me any longer. He'll face me directly, in his office, whether he likes it or not.

I dress in one of my best power suits. Red. It represents strength yet it's sexy with an above the knee skirt and black frilly blouse. It's this season's Marc Jacobs and I love it. I decide to make a statement to my dear husband, especially with the surprise undergarments. He's avoided me long enough, and mama needs a little excitement, so I plan to remind him of the "power of the pussy."

Strutting past the receptionist—she knows who I am—I enter the elevator and press the number fifteen. The view from the fifteenth floor is incredible. You can see all of Richmond from there. Of course, Jack's offices are on the top floor as well as his father's. Associates share the tenth through fourteenth floors. The practice has grown over the years. Jack Sr. along with the Bowes Family Trust purchased the building about twenty years ago. The bottom floors are used for rental property and allow the firm room for future expansion. Quite clever. I believe it was Sarah's suggestion and all hail the mighty Sarah Loving.

When I arrive on the floor, all eyes suddenly come to me. Normally, I feel them watch me in a jealous sort of way, but today it's rather odd. The eyes seem to follow me in an inquisitive, almost abrupt way. *What in the world is happening?* Immediately, I'm concerned that Jack is in some sort of trouble. I can feel my heart begin to flutter and my hand moves to my throat. My legs suddenly feel very weak and I'm lightheaded. *Oh, Jack, what in the world is going on?*

As I approach Patricia's desk, she rises with a nod and brief greeting, "Mrs. Loving."

"Good morning, Patricia. I need to see my husband right away." She looks rather startled and asks me to take a seat. Apparently, he has stepped away for a moment and she needs to find him.

I see her enter a room and she exits quite a while later. I don't enjoy being left and forgotten about. This girl doesn't seem to worry about my perceptions which will not serve her well when I ask Jack to discipline her.

Returning from the long hallway, Patricia walks around her desk, motioning for me to follow her. "If you will please follow me, Mrs. Loving? Mr. Loving requested that I direct you to the large conference room."

"Well, it's about time. I was beginning to think you had forgotten me." She makes a smirking sound and I turn to face her and she gives me the coldest look. Honestly, the gall of this girl to treat me so rudely; I'm really shocked.

Trying to recover from her bad attitude, my attention is drawn to loud voices coming from the conference room. I can't make them out, but someone is not pleased. That's odd...my heart is racing. On the other side of this door is my husband, but I feel fear for some reason. There's bad news in that room. It's permeating through the walls. I stand before the dark wooden door, staring at the polished wood grain. Interesting, I've never noticed the excellent quality of the construction materials before. Something is telling me to run—RUN!

I immediately try to disregard my irrational thoughts and reach down to the knob. It almost feels warm. Is this a sign? Opening the door, I walk in and find a room full of people and they are all quietly staring at me. No one is speaking and they don't look amused. Some I recognize immediately: Jack's parents, Ed, their longtime financial advisor, Mark Chesney whom I know is a financial guru and philanthropist, another attorney whom I have seen at many parties but don't know his name, and five others I don't recognize. After scanning the room, my eyes return to Jack in silent query asking, "What the fuck is going on?"

Obviously reading my thoughts, he responds, "Victoria, we've been waiting for you. Good of you to join us."

Jack

Victoria stands there in her sharp, beautiful red suit, outwardly looking every bit the polished society wife. Yet, I recognize the inwardly scared little rabbit out of her mind with fear and instantly my heart feels for her. She is, after all, my wife whom I love, mother of my children, and until recently, the most trusted person in my life. I can't believe this is happening. Part of me wants to clear the room and handle this privately because there has to be a logical reason. However, the analytical side of me agrees with my outside law counsel that this must be conducted very carefully and formally.

No matter how my heart may break, this is embezzlement. It's a crime and bigger matters are at hand. Fuck, I can't believe this is happening. My biggest personal concern is my beautiful children. Their mother is in big trouble. Their financial future has been jeopardized if she stole from them. As the youngest heirs to the Trust, this will be their responsibility one day. Will she go to jail? If not, who will they live with? I'm so scared for their broken hearts and I will do whatever I can to soften their blows. God, I can't believe this is happening! I keep saying that over and over but it's true… I CAN'T believe this is happening!

My lawyer and Mark both agree I must tread very carefully. Everyone has been crunching through my assets and attempting to minimize my exposure. They've looked at my estate and valued it at close to half a billion dollars. I was shocked to learn it's so high. It's never been important to me to ascertain the real value, so I honestly didn't know it. Mark, whom I already knew to be a smart man, has been a tremendous asset over the past twenty-four hours. I don't think he even went to sleep last night. If I'm not careful, Victoria could get half of my net worth in a divorce settlement. The pain of that is so sickening that I can barely breathe. Divorce? I never thought for one fucking minute this would be what I was thinking when I felt antsy yesterday morning. Shit, I can't believe this is happening! Half of my estate in a divorce settlement…that would mean that I'm literally unable to help fifty percent of the charitable causes I would have otherwise helped. That's a powerful blow I could never come back from. That's a blow that the Richmond community would never come back from because I have always known Victoria doesn't exactly share my philanthropic vision. The many years and effort of family members before me who built this money could be lost in a fucking divorce! FUCK, I CAN'T BELIEVE THIS IS HAPPENING!

Momentarily lost in my thoughts, I refocus on Victoria standing before me, totally unaware of the bomb I'm about to ignite. Suddenly, my mouth is dry and I feel really nauseous. I raise my hands to my forehead and stare at the prepared reports in front of me. Taking a deep breath to find the courage, I'm about to speak when Mother reaches over and lays her hand on my forearm, gently rubbing and patting my arm twice. No words are spoken, but the message is loud and clear… Mother is in charge and it will be okay.

She begins, "Victoria, please sit down," as she points to the chair at the head of the long rectangular table. I can only imagine what it might feel like to sit in the "hot seat" staring down all of these people. Her only advantage is she knows the truth and let's not forget a full night's rest. The rest of us have barely slept or left these offices since my world blew apart. Even Mother and Father have dug into the details, calling in favors to see bank video feeds as well as combing over every possible scenario to get me out of this mess. It's times like these that I am truly in awe of the strength and intelligence of my parents. Patricia has stayed all night, making phone calls, organizing meetings, providing food, and preparing reports. She has proven her dedication and commitment to my family and I mentally remind myself to give her a raise and guarantee her a job for as long as she wants it. The auditing firm and the financial advisors, they have all worked tirelessly to prepare us for this moment. The truth… revealed.

"Jack, what's going on?" she speaks directly to me at a frantic, quivering clip.

Mother breaks in, "Victoria, I need you to answer some questions for all of us. It's very important that you be honest so we can get to the bottom of a situation that has come to light." Mom introduces everyone at the table with the exception of one man sitting off to the side near the door. "Every five years, the Bowes Family Trust mandatorily changes its auditing firm. This is done for many reasons, including our need to ensure that we are abiding by the terms of the Trust as outlined by the original benefactor.

"As you know, I was the sole heir until Jack turned eighteen years old. I shifted fifty percent of my assets to his Trust account. As it currently stands, Jack and I are the only authorized legal owners of these accounts. Therefore, we are the only authorized individuals who may make withdrawals. We are here today to try and ascertain why, over the last five years, $3,100,000 was withdrawn without authorization."

The look on Victoria's face as Mother speaks goes from shock to almost dry heaves. I know from looking at her that she is absolutely guilty. Of course, I watched the bank videos, but until this moment, looking at her, I still didn't want to believe it. I can't believe this is happening.

"Victoria, did you make any unauthorized withdrawals?"

Her face turns completely white. She opens her mouth to speak then promptly closes it.

"Jack made it very clear early on that he did not want to hide anything from you and therefore invited you to attend open meetings over the course of your marriage. You obviously had knowledge of these accounts and offered input on charity disbursements from Jack's Trust account. The question is, did you withdraw this money yourself or with the help from others for reasons other than legitimate charitable causes?" Victoria just stares at Mother, obviously lost for words. Her eyes glide to mine, begging for my help. I can't stand it. The pain I see there is killing me. Her breathing is almost shallow and her torso begins to slightly sway side-to-side.

"Vickie, talk to me," I implore her. "I need to know if this is true." She just stares at me, lips apart, and her eyes begin to well up with tears. I'm so conflicted because she is my wife of ten years, my responsibility, but she has most likely committed a crime. I stand up suddenly and quickly walk to her, gently grabbing her elbow, "Come with me."

Suddenly, Detective Wallace moves from the corner and blocks the doorway. "Mr. Loving, I'm sorry that can't happen."

"I'm just taking her to my office to speak privately."

"That would most definitely not be in anyone's best interest, Jack," my personal lawyer chimes in. I look between the two men and realize this is out of my control. I'm powerless at this point, but I can do the right thing for my wife whether she deserves my support or not. She is the mother of my children, and right or wrong, they would expect it.

I look around the room slowly and my eyes fall upon my beloved Mother. I know she will not be pleased, but all I'm thinking about is my kids. I turn to Victoria, squeezing her elbow, "You probably need to leave with Detective Wallace now. I will retain independent Counsel for you. It's probably best you not say anything."

I remove my hand and she throws herself into my arms and begins sobbing, her face buried in my neck, calling my name over and over in desperation. Her piercing, wailing cries startle me and are the first sounds she has made since walking into the room, and the vibrations ripping through her body are more than I can bear. Her legs begin to falter and I reach out for her before she hits the floor. Her tear-stained face and near-hyperventilating distress cause such confliction in me. I've never seen her like this. Actually, I've never seen anyone like this and it's so unlike the strong character I know she always maintains. There's more to this story. I feel it deep in my bones, but now is not the time, especially in front of a room full of witnesses. Now, this moment is about basic human compassion and dignity. As lost as we both are right now, she's still my wife. Ultimately, my responsibility.

Turning to the room while holding Victoria in my arms, I find my voice, speaking with as much determination and strength as I can bear, "I want everyone to leave with the exception of my parents, Detective Wallace, and my lawyer." They all look at me with stunned faces and it suddenly occurs to me that they are as affected by Victoria as I am, yet they don't move. "Now!" I bark. Everyone quickly gathers their belongings and heads out.

Agent Wallace watches the door closely and begins addressing Victoria in a very professional tone, "Mrs. Loving, my name is Detective Wallace and I was asked here to review the evidence of missing funds which were allegedly removed from your husband's Trust account. Would you like to tell me what happened—"

"No—be quiet, Victoria. Don't say anything," I interrupt him.

"Mr. Loving, I realize you invited me here today, but this is a very serious alleged crime and we are in a formal stage now. You cannot, and WILL NOT, interfere with my questions to her even if she is your wife. Are we clear?"

"She is entitled to legal representation, Detective!" I throw back at him with a raised voice.

"Jack, settle down son." My dad moves to stand near me with raised hands in a 'calm down' motion. Turning to the Detective, Dad asks, "Are you formally charging her at this point?"

"My plan is to take Mrs. Loving to the station where she will be questioned. I'm not arresting her."

"Okay, we understand. In that case, let's walk together to your car." Turning to Victoria, Dad says gently, "We will call someone to meet you there. You have my word." Victoria sobs harder and begins climbing my body like a vine, begging me to stop them from taking her. I can't do anything at this point and I don't really know what I should do. Fuck! I can't believe I'm dealing with this fucked up disaster. I pull her hands from around my neck and she claws my skin as I pull away, leaving a searing, burning pain in the path of her nails. Her desperate need to hold on to me is killing me in the worst way.

I manage to get her standing on her own power and wipe her face of tears. "You need to walk out of here, head held high. I don't know when I will speak to you—"

"Jack, it will be impossible considering the circumstances. You need to say goodbye now." My lawyer is just looking out for me and I know it. This is a major, major situation and if I was the attorney, I wouldn't let my client near her with a ten foot pole.

"Take care, Vickie." I softly kiss her lips and she tries to deepen it but I deny her and pull away. I barely have the strength to turn around, knowing I can't handle watching her walk out the door with Detective Wallace.

Moving to the large picture window overlooking the city, I think I might die. If these windows opened, I'd throw myself onto the city sidewalk. I hear the click of a closing door and my knees are jolted with pain and I suddenly feel the rough fibers of carpet against my palms. A small, warm hand touches my shoulder and squeezes. I don't even need to hear her voice or see her face to know it's my mother, and she's here for me. No matter what, she loves me unconditionally.

Chapter Twenty-five

Wake Me Up Any Time...

Lizzie

Janice called me the other day to get my take on voyeurism. She started out by asking what I thought about it. Did I think it was morally wrong to do that to a stranger? General questions on the subject. Normally, when my friends call me with questions, I answer what they ask and don't delve too much, figuring they will ask me for specifics if they really want my take on a subject. I didn't anticipate that phone call would be a precursor to what I would learn on girls' night!

Five hours earlier...

So my friends and I dared to change the scenery up a little bit and we ventured all the way next door to Conch Republic, from our usual hangout of The Boathouse. Considering my condo is within walking distance, for me it's no great ordeal and very convenient. I enjoy both places quite a bit, especially not worrying about a DUI. Besides, what's not to enjoy about a waterfront restaurant overlooking the James River?

Tonight, Janice is in rare form. Normally, she is the most subdued of our group if there were such a designation that must be made. Not tonight, because she made it clear when she first walked in, "I'm getting blitzed!"

We all chat through the first few rounds making typical conversation, alcohol flowing freely, everyone complaining about their spouses or boyfriends. Then Janice, out of the blue, pipes up saying, "So what's everyone's opinion about voyeurism?" Our group stares at her, then we look at one another and burst out laughing. "I'm serious!"

"Well, I don't have a problem with it, per se. Why?" Jenny asks.

"Robbie came to me with an idea he wanted to try." We all look at her, eyes wide, waiting expectantly. "He wanted us to go shopping and specifically asked that I wear a mini skirt and no panties."

"So, did you do it?" Marianne asks. Janice grins like a Cheshire cat. "Janice! You've been holding out on us, you little minx, you!" Janice bursts out laughing.

"We went to one of the department stores in the mall. He wanted me to buy the tallest pair of black 'fuck-me' pumps I could find. He had this shopping trip planned out in total detail. The store, the time, the chair he wanted me sitting in, everything exact. So I find a shoe I wish to try on and give it to the male sales clerk, who, by the way, was very easy on my eyes. I sit in the chair and Robbie sits two rows over, directly across from me. We were the only ones in the section because who shops for shoes at eight forty-five on a Thursday night, anyway? The clerk brings my shoes, and as you know, the clerks still fit you in those types of stores…" Jenny shrieks and laughs hysterically, anticipating the story. "Anyway, Robbie is sitting behind the clerk who is on his knees bent over, preparing to assist me when

Robbie holds his hand up, making a letter "V" very slowly directly in front of his face…" Janice proceeds to demonstrate the exact way Robbie did, "Implying I should spread my legs, ladies…and I DID!" The entire table howls with laughter and disbelief. "Then Robbie sticks his tongue out at the bottom of the "V" in a licking motion, indicating that I should gyrate my hips for the sales clerk." Jenny and Marianne are falling over, dying with laughter, drawing attention, yet again, from other patrons.

"Janice, first off…I have to know, what was the clerk doing?" I ask.

"Well, it was interesting because I don't think he was initially paying attention to the fact I had a mini skirt on with no panties. It was only after I moved my hips forward in the seat that he began to notice something was up. Boy, did he notice! He glanced, then looked away real quick, then tried to be sneaky and take a quick peek but his jaw just dropped down and he sat frozen. It was weird because I started feeling more comfortable and taunted him a little. I felt so dirty and definitely minx-like, Marianne!"

"Damn, girl! I can't believe you did that. That takes a lot of guts," Jenny says.

"What was Robbie's reaction while this was going on?" I ask.

"I know exactly his reaction because I've seen the video and heard his heavy breathing. He videotaped it with his cell phone. He was really into it."

"Oh my gawd, that's so kinky!!!" Marianne cries out.

"Okay, finish telling what happened!" I demand and everyone agrees.

"My legs, which were already spread, opened a little more when I knew I had his eye contact. At this point, he was literally four feet in front of me. He was like a deer caught in the headlights! My ass cheeks were at the edge of the seat and my pussy was on full display. Anyone walking by would have gotten a free peep show. He just sat back on his heels, jaw slack and then swallowed very loudly. I could tell he was struggling and I wanted to laugh, but I held it in. Then, Robbie stood up behind him, closed his fingers together, and put his hand in his pocket, meaning I needed to close my legs. Which I promptly did, causing my shoe boy to groan, loudly, and shake his head as if he was clearing his thoughts. I simply told him, 'I'd like to try the heels now, pretty please,' and he let out another longer moan and slipped them on for me. I'll be honest, it was one of the most erotic experiences of my life and also one of the dirtiest."

"Then what happened?" Jenny asks.

"After I made sure the shoes fit, Robbie paid for them and he took me home and fucked me harder than ever before. *Of course, the shoes just had to stay on!*"

I feel the warmth as it travels up my outside thigh. Gentle touches that are feather light, then firmer, then barely a whispered touch. My sleep filled haze is slowly clearing as the warmth travels to my other leg, beginning at the top of my foot and moving slowly up the back of my calf. My leg trembles from reflex when my large toe is covered in wet warmth with a noticeable intense silkiness on the underside. As my toe is sucked, I can feel hard nibbles on the outside edges while the firmness on my calves increases. A slight moan escapes my throat as I fight to control the feelings somewhere between a tickle and pure, erotic bliss.

Large hands move to the inside of my knees, pushing them open and trailing up the inside of my thighs. Opening my eyes fully, all I can see is the yellow tinged light from the outdoor street lamp peeking through the slats of the mini-blinds and the blue hue shining from the digital alarm clock. The obvious darkness enveloping the room shares no hint of the source causing my pleasure. Suddenly feeling uncomfortable and confused, I quickly shut my legs, closing off my most intimate assets.

Feeling rather confident of the source, I take a deep breath and began mulling over my next move: acceptance or rejection. While willing my brain to think quickly and act, my knees are forced open and the sensation of an inhaled breath on the outside of my panties knocks me totally off kilter. The ensuing abrupt contact is delicious when his face moves hard against my panties and moves up and down once, twice, three times. My hips uncontrollably lift upward but are quickly pressed firmly into the mattress and the assault continues. My voice quivers uncontrollably as the heat travels all over my body, taking over all my thoughts and ability to reason.

"You smell so good. I feel like it's been forever since I tasted you on my tongue." The grinding of his face in my now-raging core and the sounds he makes inhaling my essence, turns me on and my body responds automatically. It's been so long since I had any real contact with him and I need it so desperately. Feeling my panties pulled to the side, I anticipate the next few seconds like never before. I know what is coming—the warmth that will feel so good and will cause my blood vessels to constrict. Then, I *feel it,* the moist tip of his tongue inserted on the edges of my entrance, slowly traveling around and around, teasing me. I try to point my hips downward, wanting the contact on my clit, but he denies me. He knows my body is quivering with need and yet he draws me out, begging for me to climb higher and higher. After all this time, he can still play my body like a string orchestra. "Be still or I'll stop."

My body knows his commands and instantly ceases all movement. I suddenly want this so badly and I'll do anything at this moment. Anything. He holds my hips on either side, and with a stiffened tongue, plunges it in my pussy as far as it will reach. The edges of his teeth just barely scraping over my clit. His breath over my bundle of nerves causes a sensation so fantastic I could literally melt.

He rewards my stillness with moving his tongue up near my swollen, sweet bud. Slowly, oh so slowly, he moves his tongue around the outer edges of my clit, not exactly touching it, but enough to set me on fire. I moan loudly, begging him to please take me and finally he does. His tongue flicks over and around my clit furiously and I begin to build. I am overwhelmed with how quickly he is taking me higher and higher. Surely the long absence has left me edgy and needy. Suddenly, I feel fingers entering me, rubbing deliciously in search of my g-spot, and just before I start to see white stars behind my eyelids, he sucks my clit into his mouth and fucks me hard with his fingers.

"Ahhh! Oh, damn! Oh shit, Jeremy that feels so fucking good. Please don't stop!" My pussy takes advantage of his fingers and rides them hard, enjoying the delirious wave of euphoria as it leaves me in a weakened state. I don't use drugs, but if this is anything close to a great high, I understand the addiction.

Helping bring me through the most intense orgasm I've had in quite some time, Jeremy moves up my body and begins kissing along my neck to my earlobe. Whispering in my ear, "You are so fucking hot when you come, baby. You're beautiful, so fucking beautiful."

I allow his words to sink in like a soothing balm that caresses my heart and soul. It's been so long since my husband spoke this way and was present enough to initiate our lovemaking. I didn't realize how much I missed being touched until this exact moment. He leans down and kisses me chastely then deeply and the kiss quickly heats up to where we are both breathing hard, almost gasping for breath.

He lowers his pelvis and I can feel his erect penis gliding up and down through my lips and over my clit. The feeling it brings over my already sensitive nub feels amazing as my drenched wetness coats the shaft of his cock. He thrusts his hips like a piston soon, causing his head to roll back and around. "Your pussy is like silky heaven, Liz. God, I've missed you." Then he leans down, kissing me roughly, and without warning switches the thrusting angle and buries his cock deep within my walls.

"Oh, damn, Jeremy…that feels so good, so big!" The feeling catches me off guard and it takes a moment for my body to adjust to his length and girth. Jeremy is amazingly endowed and I have always felt so full when he's inside of me. I scream out loudly due to the impact and soon find my hips reaching upward and moving in tandem with his gyrations.

"Rub your clit, baby, rub it hard. I need you to get there. I want us to come together." Not hesitating a second, I use two fingers to press circles firmly over my clit. Within minutes, my heightened state brings me just to the edge. "Fuck! Baby, you're squeezing my dick and it feels so good. I can actually feel the movement against my cock when you're rubbing your clit. Please tell me you're close."

The moans escaping my mouth quickly answer his question and I concentrate hard to squeeze my vaginal muscles as hard as I can, sending me over the edge. He holds my hips and slams hard into me several more times before I feel him enlarge within my walls, spilling his seed deep within me.

We lay there holding one another, could have been minutes or hours, I don't know. I'm sexually sated and it feels great. Realization dawns on me that Jeremy seemed present during our love making. He wasn't drunk and the fact that he could get hard was a major miracle. I know I should probably keep my mouth shut and just enjoy the moment, but I'm curious to know what has brought on the change.

"Jeremy, thank you for what we just did together. I have been so lonely recently."

He sighs deeply and doesn't answer right away. "I know I haven't been the best husband to you or the best father to the kids lately. I'm very sorry. I recognize my drinking has gotten way out of hand. I really love you, Liz."

Tears begin to fill my eyes as I listen to his words and think about what I should say next. We've been here before. Unfortunately, many times he would make promises to stop drinking and would eventually falter. I've gotten to a point in life where I can't rely on him. I know promises are just words. Action is what really counts. "I just want you healthy. The kids deserve an active father in their lives. It's not about our relationship anymore, Jeremy. It has to only be about the kids."

He shakes his head solemnly in agreement. "I know. You need a husband, too, though. I'm scared to lose my family. I have to fix what's wrong with me. I didn't drink last night, and when the fog began to clear, I saw you lying there and my dick got so hard. Seeing you dressed in that nightie of yours, fuck, I wanted you so bad. The way your legs were open...I saw the impression of your lips through your panties and I needed a taste. I felt like a starved man before a buffet feast. Your body is amazing, baby, and I selfishly must admit my balls have been twenty different shades of blue."

We both laugh at his self-description. It feels like forever since we actually had normal sex. "Trust me, I've been pretty horny myself. The batteries in BOB have been changed several times. Actually, I'll admit I have a collection of BOBs these days. They include different sizes, textures, colors..." I'll be honest, it feels really good to laugh with him. Lost intimacy has got to be the thing that hurts the most. Basic human companionship is taken for granted every day until one day you wake up and it's not there anymore. It can take you on a road to depression.

He strokes up and down my back with his fingertips. The sensation and ensuing chill bumps are evidence that my body always responds to his touch. "All I ask is that you give me a chance. I've fucked up so badly. The things I did to feed my addiction are appalling. I'm mortified and embarrassed, Lizzie."

I look deeply in his eyes, looking for signs of deception, and today, I don't see any. As anyone knows, when a family member has a problem, each day is a new day. He has to truly want to get better on his own. "We can't guarantee anything, but if you set a pattern of improvement that's hard to ignore, anything is possible. It's a day-to-day assessment, Jeremy. My focus today is the same as it has always been and that's my children."

He grabs me forcefully and squeezes me to the point of almost hurting me. Whispering close to my ear, "Oh, baby, you have no idea how happy that makes me. I just want to put my family back together. I promise things will get better. You'll see!" With that, he sucks gently on my earlobe and soon reignites the fire within me. After two hours, we finally reemerge and I can barely walk. So far so good, but every family living with an alcoholic knows that each day brings new challenges. Unfortunately, that often leads to *many* broken promises.

Chapter Twenty-six

The Children's Hospital Christmas Gala...

Jack —December 14: two months later

Everyone around me is seemingly buzzing along with their lives. The holidays will be here before anyone is ready. The happy smiles plastered on strangers' faces sicken me. The Christmas music that practically follows me everywhere I go pisses me off. I'm definitely not happy, not by a long shot. My wife is most likely an embezzler who stole from me, or more specifically, stole from her children's inheritance. Obtaining any real answers from her attorney as to why she did it in the first place, is not happening. It makes no sense to me at all. Her closet is exploding with every brand name sold on 5th Avenue and she has seemingly the easiest life of any woman I know. She's been provided with everything her little heart has desired. I'm sick with disgust that I didn't figure this out long ago. Where the fuck did the money go in the first place because I'm totally baffled? I've tasked my friend Mark with trying to at least solve that mystery for me. He has a friend who is a forensic accountant and they are combing through records as we speak.

My lawyer wants me as far away from Victoria as I can get. If he could force me to Antarctica, he would send me. Everyone is very concerned about my lack of a pre-nuptial agreement. They are all assuming we will get divorced and seem to be proceeding as if it's been decided already. Funny thing is, no one has asked me what I want.

My kids are totally devastated. They have a million questions and I can't answer any of them because I lack answers, too. At this point, Victoria has only been questioned by the police. No charges have been filed. Detective Wallace says that they will charge her when they are sure there are no holes in their case. Until then, she's a free woman. My father arranged for her to have a suite at The Jefferson Hotel. The nanny takes the children back and forth so they may spend time with her. I try not to ask a lot of questions about their visits. It's obvious everyone is making the best out of a bad situation. I haven't spoken to Victoria since the day in my conference room two months ago. Today, I'm just a bitter bastard. So a Christmas Gala, even though it supports one of my favorite causes, Children's Hospital, is not enough to put a smile on my face.

I've tried to limit public appearances for obvious reasons. We've done our best to keep the situation under cover, but I know it will come out soon. If I hadn't already agreed to MC this event, I would not. In fact, sticking a fire poker in my eye seems like more fun. I'm just not in the mood for happy celebrations or undoubtedly plastering a fake smile on my face as I beg people to hand over their cash. *Fuck! I'm so screwed.*

Dressed in my favorite tuxedo, I arrive at The Jefferson early and head to the ballroom. Mom has a meeting planned amongst the organizers to make sure things run smoothly. I'm given a rundown of the timeline and can't help but focus on the final bachelor auction indicating the end of the festivities. I silently will the night to hurry so I may take the monkey suit off and get the hell home.

As the first guests begin trickling in, I remind myself to stay present and greet all the guests amicably. The room gradually fills within an hour, and soon I've shaken hands with many of the state Representatives from the Commonwealth of Virginia, partners from most all of the prestigious law firms from Richmond, and many doctors from various specialties around the state. The room is a verifiable Who's Who of well-known individuals.

Knowing we have a strict schedule to maintain, I habitually check my wristwatch for announcing dinner in just under fifteen minutes. I look up to notice Mark sashaying toward me with the familiar woman on his arm. He smirks with every step because he notices I can't seem to stop looking at her. There's something about her that is so intriguing. Her red dress, which hits just above the knee, showcases her black stockings which seem to have silver rhinestones sparkling throughout. Her stiletto heels show off her firm calves which undoubtedly connect to something just as scrumptious hidden under all that fabric. Scanning up her body, I can't help but notice her exposed cleavage pouring from the top—the soft swells of her breasts as they are pushed together and shimmer with some type of glittery spray. Willing my eyes up to her face, I quickly realize my intense evaluations of her have been noticed. She is staring back at me with a questioning eye, but what really gets my blood rushing is her bottom lip trapped to the side by her top teeth. Immediately, images pour through my mind of tasting that mouth and biting that lip. Wondering what she tastes like and…feels like. FUCK! I can't think this way. No matter what's happening, I'm a married man. Period.

Thankfully getting my mind out of the gutter, Mark interrupts my wondering thoughts. "Ah, Jack? You remember my friend Lizzie Macintyre, right?"

"Oh, I certainly do remember Lizzie." Almost stumbling with my words, I make a quick save and remember my engrained manners.

"You look quite beautiful. Thank you for attending our fundraiser this evening."

Her cheeks redden and she looks downward momentarily before replying, "I've been looking forward to this night for quite some time. It's most definitely a worthy cause." She turns to Mark, who is clenching her hand in his elbow like she might bolt. "Mark was kind to invite me."

I stare at her, memorizing her face in its entirety. The eloquent lines of her lips painted with red. The length of her neck as it blends into her flowing hair. This woman is mesmerizing to me. Why? I do not know. It suddenly occurs to me that I'm not breathing when a cough rises up into my throat. I'm embarrassed. Mark chuckles and hits me on the back. "You okay there, Jack?" I barely manage a nod of the head and can't fathom looking up because I know I've just made an ass out of myself. Finally recovering from a coughing fit, but not my most assuredly red face, I am about to make my departure when Mark speaks, "Oh, Jack? That person who is looking into that business we discussed has made some headway. He believes he may know the destination."

Suddenly, I'm on high alert, watching him with bated breath. "What did he learn?"

Mark cuts his eyes at the beauty on his arm and gives me his questioning eyes. She apparently notices and excuses herself to the ladies' room. Thank fuck because this is huge to me. "Well first, you have to know that it didn't settle right with me that Victoria would embezzle that amount of money without evidence lying around to show how she spent it. So, I had a hunch and asked someone to look into a few things and I think it paid off."

I feel my blood pressure begin rising and want to jump out of my skin. "Mark, this has tormented me day and night. The idea that millions would be stolen, by Victoria no less, is unfathomable to me. She already had access to our personal accounts and could purchase anything her heart desired, so it didn't make any sense. So, if you have answers, I *need* to know them." He shakes his head in agreement, his eyes revealing sympathy. "Well?" I question rather loudly then look around and notice others have turned our direction.

He looks around as well, and with a head nod, guides me to a private alcove. "I asked about her family. Seems her father was in quite a bit of debt to the wrong people."

Suddenly, I feel a warm rush race through my body. I begin feeling slightly faint and reach out toward the wall to support myself. My mind is spinning with thoughts. *Her father? Whoa, wait...Ingrid...she said there were raised voices during a visit. That shithead!* I *never* liked him. He was always so condescending to Victoria and her mother wasn't much different. I always thought she had a shit upbringing, but Victoria always downplayed her past like it didn't matter. She never wanted to delve too deeply into her family life, but I could always see pain in her eyes. What I don't understand is why she didn't confide in me.

"You're fucking kidding me."

"Nope. Apparently, he has a gambling fetish, but interestingly enough he doesn't have any outstanding local markers because we asked around. There's no doubt, though, that he's well known in the arena." Mark looks at me with pity in his eyes because he knows Victoria did this to help her dad, but we'll never prove it. If he's well-known locally for having a gambling problem, but doesn't have any current debts, does that mean she paid them off?

I look down, shaking my head, not knowing what to say. In all probability, money that was always well intended for the good of Richmond was used in a dark way to pay off sleazebag gambling debts. I suddenly feel very sick. The bile begins to rise up into my throat when Mark's hand taps my shoulder in comfort. Regardless of my weak stomach, all I want is a drink. A very strong one.

"Jack!" A shrieking voice sounds from behind me. I turn to find my mother approaching me with desperation in her eyes. *Oh dear, please tell me she doesn't know about these gambling debts.* I truly don't believe I could handle the disappointment in her eyes.

I try and plaster a fake smile on my face, "Yes, Mother?"

"The schedule! Aren't you watching the time? Come on, Jack. I'm relying on you." Her pleading eyes tell me I need to move through the current destruction which is my life and focus on what's important.

"Sorry, Mother. I apologize." I leave Mark with a knowing head nod, and as I'm walking away, she grabs my elbow to halt me. She reaches up and gives me a loving hug. No words are spoken, but she always knows when I'm emotionally struggling.

"Not necessary, but I do need to tell you about a vocal act we arranged at the last minute. I didn't know how you'd feel about it so I didn't want to tell you until I had to." With narrowed eyes, I wait for her to respond but she just looks at me with an upturned eyebrow and a 'you ought to know' look on her face.

Suddenly, recognition crosses my eyes and I inhale sharply. "Erin?"

She nods solemnly and waits for me to respond, but I just don't know what to say. Finally, she explains, "A member of the committee recommended her because she is back in town. She volunteered her services, Jack, and the committee voted yes." She hesitantly reaches her palm to my face, "Are you okay?"

I nod my head firmly. Knowing I only want the best for Erin, I reply, "That's fine. She will do a great job, I'm sure of it." Mom's chest releases a large breath like she's been scared to hear my response. "Let's get this show started." With that, I escort my mom inside.

Everyone is standing around, drinks in hand, chatting up the well-to-do when I approach the microphone. "Good evening, everyone." Only gathering about half the room's attention, I speak louder. "Good evening, everyone!" Waiting to have most eyes on me,

I begin, "Welcome to the Children's Hospital Christmas Gala." Everyone claps. "Ahh, I'm glad everyone is clapping already and having a good time. For those of you whom I haven't met, please allow me to introduce myself. My name is Jack Loving. More specifically, I should say, Jack Loving, Jr. because the dashing man seated with the most beautiful woman in the room at the head table, which, of course, is my mother, Sarah Bowes Loving, is the original Jack Loving, Sr." I hear a round of chuckles and an actual catcall from the back of the room. "In any event, I shall do my best to keep the evening moving along in hopes I won't bore you too terribly much. We have a musical guest this evening." I look around the room carefully, but she's nowhere in sight. "The lovely Erin Hughes has recently decided that she prefers southern hospitality to west coast life and has moved back home. Tonight, we are all in for a great treat since she will gift all of us with her beautiful voice." Knowing looks and head shakes with smiling faces appear around the room and I'm very pleased for Erin. "In any event, let's begin. If you will move to your assigned tables, we shall begin the dinner service."

Still standing at the podium, my eyes move across the room. My elevated level allows me to see the room better and she comes into view—the beautiful brunette with nearly waist-length wavy hair. She moves with such grace and dignity yet her sex appeal is undeniable. Sensing my eyes on her, she looks straight at me and blushes. Looking downward to avoid my eyes doesn't hide what's written all over her face. I affect her just as much as she affects me. Forcing my eyes away, I land on a smirking Mark. He knows. The fucker always knows. I don't know what their relationship is, but in any event, just being in her presence makes him a very lucky man.

Chapter Twenty-seven

The Children's Hospital Christmas Gala...

Lizzie —December 14: two months later

Jack's eyes have been watching me. Ordinarily it would be very unsettling to be watched by someone I don't really know but there's something about him. He has this calming sexiness to him. Not only is his body every woman's erotic dream, but he has this presence that just lets you know he's a really nice guy.

Making my way over to our table, I feel eyes boring into me from the opposite side of the room. When I look in that direction, I find a death glare being shot my way. Cindy Hall apparently has a major problem with me. Her obvious sneer is practically so big that her nostrils seem ready to begin flaring fire. This woman cannot stand me. I haven't done anything to her personally, but she seems to think I'm some sort of competition. With an upturned chin, she strides away with a wicked smirk on her face. Dammit, she's up to something.

"Oh, Lizzie?" I hear from beside me. "Can I have a quick word?"

I look around to make sure no one is in our immediate space, "Absolutely, Ms. Martin." Immediately, I sense her strong happiness with an extra kick in her step and twinkle in her eyes. Never before have I seen her so glowing before.

"I have news, dear Lizzie. Very good news, in fact. My sweet Henry has convinced me that we both deserve a life of sheer bliss. He has asked me to travel to France with him next week to celebrate the holidays."

Feeling warmth for this lady whom I have grown closer to these last few months, it thrills me that she will be spending Christmas with Henry. "I'm so pleased for you. Henry is a lucky man, for sure."

"You best believe he knows it, too!"

"So why did you change your mind? I thought you needed something more permanent before visiting overseas?"

Looking at me with strong, determined eyes, I immediately sense there is more going on. Little do I know, she is about to change my life. "He wants me to go with the intentions of considering a permanent move. I haven't told you, but Henry is serious about marrying me."

With assessing eyes, she waits for my response but I'm still processing her words. "Ms. Martin, I'm confused. How can you marry Henry if he's already married?"

She looks down at her clenched hands, "He and his wife have been separated for around three months now. He confessed to her that he'd fallen in love with an American and wouldn't you know, she was finished with him just like that! Apparently, she doesn't care for us very much."

My expression must have been quite comical because she burst out laughing. "Well, as long as you are both happy that's all that really matters I guess. He seems to care deeply about you."

"He always has Lizzie. Sometimes, you have to hold out long enough because you won't get anything long lasting when you give away the milk for free! Plus, he's promised me an endless supply of my favorite roses."

I might just die in a fit of laughter. She always has a way with words. "You're probably right, Ms. Martin. Besides, who can turn down a lifetime of roses?"

"Apparently, not me!" she smarted. She begins looking at me closely, reading me in that way she always does. "Lizzie, how are things with your husband?"

Wow, with just a few words I go from happy to depressed. "Not very well, Ms. Martin. He claims he will stop drinking and he does, for a few days. Then, he just goes right back to getting drunk. He's still living with me, but I think I may need to do something about that as well. I initially thought I was doing what was best for the kids, by letting him stay there, but I fear I was wrong."

"Oh, honey, you know what you must do. Just do it. That man is dead weight on you, bringing you down. I have faith in you, my dear; you're made from strong stock." Looking very serious, she looks around us, making sure we're totally out of earshot. "I'll be very blunt. I'm considering giving you the business to run, Lizzie. I don't have any family to speak of and I can't run the business from France. You are a very bright girl, have a great mind, and my dear, I think you understand more than most that I provide an essential service in Richmond. While most may not understand what we do, we truly don't hurt anyone. We aren't the typical cheating escorts that some may envision. Our clientele have specific confidential needs and we do it with class. I think you're just the person to take this business to the next level. We could be equal partners or we could discuss something different if you have another idea." I'm totally shocked and blown away, so much so that I'm completely mute. "What are you thinking at this moment, Lizzie since I currently don't seem to have a clue? Do you have a problem with the equal percentages or something?"

My mouth opens, closes and reopens. I'm so blown away considering all the possibilities this would bring. Fear is the overwhelming feeling I have at this split second: failure, public scrutiny if I were revealed, Jeremy's opinion, and knowing this is probably illegal—jail doesn't suit me. "Truly, I don't know what to say. I'm flattered you would want to choose me to run the business. But why exactly would you choose me?"

She laughs while shaking her head. "I knew there was something about you when we first met. In a way, you remind me of my younger self. We're survivors! You've struggled, but you created a solution for you and your children. I admire you. I have faith in you. Plus, Mark thinks you will kick ass. I trust him implicitly."

Inhaling quickly, I could almost fall over with her words. Especially about Mark. I wish he had forewarned me. "Mark knows about your plans?"

Nodding solemnly and with a knowing twinkle in her eyes, she replies, "He does. We're very close and we've discussed it plenty. I trust you, Lizzie."

Shaking my head, feeling like I'm in a dream, I say, "I don't know what to say."

She smiles brightly and exclaims, "You say yes!"

Suddenly filled with greater worry, I lean in and whisper, "Ms. Martin, I don't know anything about the ah…you know, sex part of the operation."

She lets out a bold laugh, "Well, dear, I didn't either at first. At least with me being a phone call away, you'll have a consultant on speed dial. Seriously, though, if this takes place, you and I will have a much more serious conversation. I don't keep written records." Pointing to her temple, she continues, "The vault will have to be transferred to a younger version of myself." She smiles, leans in, and kisses my cheek. Before walking away, she adds, "It's a lot to consider. Think it over and come see me on Monday. I'll have lunch catered at noon." Not waiting for my answer, and with those parting words, she walks away. Somehow, I just know my life has been irrevocably changed. Again.

Chapter Twenty-eight

The Children's Hospital Christmas Gala...

Victoria —December 14: two months later

itting in my hotel suite, I begin pacing back and forth across the floor. Panic has nearly overtaken me. Chewing on my nails, I consider my options. I know he's in the building. Not having any direct contact with him for months, I don't know how he would feel about seeing me or having me show up at the Gala. I keep glancing at the beautiful, custom-designed gown I ordered long ago for tonight's festivities. It's so beautiful and so me. Being the special occasion I knew tonight would be, I planned ahead to make a grand statement with my dress. The one shouldered, winter-white adorned with crystals and sequins, is designed to fit me like a glove. The low V-cut crisscrosses over my bountiful breasts and the line of crystals travels down and around my side to accentuate my husband's self-proclaimed favorite asset—my ass. Thinking of how his eyes would enlarge seeing me fully dressed for the evening sends a shock of grief through my heart. Knowing I have missed out on his heated stares and warm touch as he ravishes my body crushes me into a million pieces.

I move to the full-length mirror located in the bedroom suite, carrying my gown in front of me. My eyes peruse the reflection, and even though I see beauty contained within the thousands of handmade stitches lovingly created by superior craftsmen, it's overshadowed by the ugliness of my tear streaked face. My swollen eyes don't hide the darkness contained therein of a little girl so unsure of herself, filled with a constant desperation for love. Staring at those lost eyes with a trembling lip, I speak, "Oh, Jack, how I have missed you so much. I've made a huge mess of things. Your trust, broken in so many ways, as I squandered away a beautiful life. I haven't told you about so many things and now my lawyers want me to speak to no one when all I want to do is tell you everything. So much shame for the control, my parents have over me. Total embarrassment that I stole from the very people who have shown me nothing but kindness. I'm scared I may be sent to prison for everything, and truth be told, I deserve it. My great desire is to tell you, I love you, Jack Loving, so much. Facing the world without you in it is incomprehensible."

My eyes travel back to the beauty before me and I think about my beautiful children. They will grow up with the stigma attached to my wrongdoings. Knowing I stole from their family Trust, they will never have faith in me again. All of my charity work, which I despised more often than not, I would take back in a heartbeat. When you're an outcast, you tend to appreciate everything you used to have and I had it all. I had the unique opportunity to bring about real change by helping others and I never appreciated it. I'm such a fool.

My phone rings again, and looking at the display, it's the person I truly fear. Mother. "Hello, Mom?"

She breathes heavily into the phone, "Well, I don't hear any music in the background so that must mean you're still in your suite in the ivory tower."

My hand begins to tremble and I return the dress to the closet. "Yes, I am still in my suite at the Jefferson—"

"Well, why haven't you left for the Gala?" she interrupts by yelling into the phone. "We're on a deadline, ya know. Get your ass downstairs and round up some cash for your father!" My mouth is desperately dry and I reach over to the bed to settle myself because I'm suddenly weak and dizzy. "I can't go to Jack with this, Mom. Don't you understand this is why I'm in so much trouble as it is? He's not going to give me any more money. I haven't even told him why I took it in the first place."

"I don't care, Victoria! Your dad has until midnight tonight." Suddenly, her tone becomes more solemn and she speaks just above a whisper when I hear, "He was taken yesterday afternoon by some goons from Atlantic City. They kidnaped him, Victoria. I need him back." She begins to break down, sobbing. My mother is a very strong woman and I've only ever heard her cry once when my grandmother died. She's never been one to show emotion so I know this is serious.

"I didn't know they took him. Why didn't you say that when you called last night?" My words are met with silence. My dizziness strengthens and I suddenly feel very nauseous. "Mom! We must call the police!"

"NO! You will *not* call the police. These are dangerous people, Victoria, and they are nothing like your high society snobs you party with at fucking Galas. They will murder him and then they will come after me, then you, then your children. Is that what you want? Do you want their deaths on your conscience?"

Hearing her words and thinking of my innocent children kidnaped forces the bile up in my throat and I race to the toilet just in time. I set my phone on the sink and I can still hear my mother's rants through the earpiece. Once I have purged everything, I rinse my mouth and return to the phone. She's so full of herself that she failed to notice I was away from the phone, much less getting sick. "Okay, Mom, I will go to Jack," I whisper reluctantly.

She brightens up instantly, "Yes, yes that's what you must do. Go now! Get the money and bring it to me straightaway. I'll take care of everything."

Feeling totally numb yet full of crushing fear, I begin to get dressed. Noticing immediately that my skin tight dress is now loose, I begin installing my public mask. No matter what, I'm still Jack's wife and he has an image to uphold. More importantly, though, I have children to protect and so help me this is the last bloody time I'm helping my father.

As I walk toward the main ballroom, I begin to hear music. A female's enchanting voice is entertaining the crowd. Approaching the door, I notice the dinner service is finishing up and I carefully peek in, trying not to draw attention. Knowing Jack is the MC for the event tells me he will be sitting at the head table. My stomach is full of butterflies as I strain to catch a glimpse of him and his beautiful body. The Armani black tuxedo—his favorite—fits his physique perfectly. I'm instantly reminded of many nights dancing in his arms, feeling so happy and complete. *Oh, how I didn't treasure those moments as I should have.* My heart aches at seeing the smile on his face as he chats with passersby. He shakes hands and all I can do is stare at his fingers and reminisce about the thousands of times he used those fingers inside my pussy, drawing out the strongest orgasms he could from me. Oh god, those masterful hands. I begin to sway and suddenly feel warmth between my legs. It's a feeling I haven't felt in months since I've begun my self- imposed orgasmic exile. I don't deserve any satisfaction right now let alone at my own hand.

As I recover from my moment of remembered bliss, I fail to notice the new male voice singing but am shocked into reality as Jack suddenly stands and pulls out the chair next to him for a beautiful woman. He grants her a large smile and his face lights up. They appear to have a loving embrace and my legs feel weak as I reach for the wall. I close my eyes to muffle the sights and sounds of laughter and holiday celebration, drowning out the breaking of my soul into a million pieces. When I reopen them, I barely notice the tears pouring down my face when she turns to sit and I see the face of Jack's first love. *It's finally happened, Erin's back.* I've been replaced.

Chapter Twenty-nine

The Children's Hospital Christmas Gala...

Jeremy —December 14: two months later

Spending the day with my new counselors and support coaches while creating a manageable plan for my sobriety has been mentally exhausting. I can hardly believe I have lost so much time away from my family. Alcohol has taken over my life, and never in a million years did I think I would be in this situation. I know it's tenuous at best and I'm in a fragile state right now. Knowing my counselors understand my struggle and seeing the progress my support coaches have made gives me great hope. But it's an hour-by-hour struggle. Hopefully, one day it will turn into a day-to-day struggle. I can't fathom anything any greater right now.

I have so many amends to make with Lizzie and my kids. Now that the fog is beginning to clear, I have many questions. First, where is she working? It's obvious she's bringing money in because we're not on the streets. Losing our dream home still feels like a knife to my gut. So many years working and saving and providing, all lost. Becoming one of the nation's mass of unemployed and failing to provide for my family took all of my confidence away as a provider and man, but alcohol took my dignity.

Finally, I'm trying to take control of my environment. So, I decide to take an inventory and catch up, so to speak. My eyes scan the kitchen cabinets and I find full selections of various types of food. I even find fresh steaks in the refrigerator. I notice new tchotchkes lying around I've never seen before; the place looks well-decorated overall. From first glance, this doesn't look like the home of a family who is struggling financially. That thought causes an ache deep in my gut and I'm so afraid to even ask about it.

Walking to the children's rooms, I notice new clothes hanging in their closets with price tags. I also see normal stuff you might find in a kid's room. I smile when I see a framed picture in Hope's bedroom from Ethan's second birthday party. We had a big outdoor birthday party at our home and the three of us were making silly faces when Lizzie snapped a photo. Hope always loved that photo and it has been in her bedroom ever since.

Long ago, Lizzie announced we needed separate bedrooms. It made no difference to me because when I passed out, I just chose a bed. I didn't care whether it was mine, hers or one of the kids'. I just didn't care. Moving to her bedroom, I hesitate before going inside but she is my wife and one thing I want to immediately remedy is sharing one bedroom. So, realizing I'm taking a risk by going in uninvited, I go anyway. I pull open the door to the walk-in closet and notice the same, full racks with tags. In the back of the closet, I see about a dozen full-length fancy dresses. I look at the closest tag and $430 is clearly labeled. WHAT THE HELL? I realize I have been out of it for quite a while, but since when can she afford shit like this? I'm left shaking my head with so many scenarios running through my mind with no answers.

I'm racked with guilt for being out of the loop, for not already knowing these answers, for essentially abandoning my family. And now, for thinking the worst about my wife's new profession. As curious as I am, I'm depressed to know that I probably don't deserve the answers and deep down maybe don't want them because it's my fault. Everything is my fault.

For so long, I have been without my beautiful wife's touch. Her flawless skin and exotic scent that always causes my dick to harden whenever I'm near her. I hate that I was stupid enough to not realize I was missing it while in my alcohol haze. The smell of her hair, the taste of her lips, the sweet tanginess of her pussy. I'm such an idiot. I swear to god I will never allow anything to control me ever again. I have to get my wife's trust back. Without her love, I am nothing and will surely die. When I think back to the allure of the bottle, yeah it gives me a great high, but it came at a tremendous personal cost because I couldn't maintain an erection. Here I have this drop dead gorgeous wife and can't get my dick hard even with her lips wrapped around it? I'm mortified that I ever thought the high from alcohol was enough to replace the high of an orgasm and personal fulfillment with Lizzie.

Lizzie left me a note that the children were at the sitter's house. I stare at the note, rereading it, and it occurs to me that I don't even know who the sitter is. How pathetic of me! She said she was working. Where? I don't have any idea, but I would surely enjoy some time with my kids right about now.

I decide to stay busy because silence is not my friend. She has always taken care of the housekeeping, but that's a chauvinist role I've imposed on her. Thinking I have so many bad days that I need to make up for, I decide to help out around the apartment. Keeping busy equals progress for me. I pull out the vacuum, and after figuring out how it works, I vacuum our entire place. Next, I begin work on the bathroom. I honestly don't know how anyone has the stomach to clean a toilet, but it's not beneath me and Lizzie does it all the time, so it's my turn. Armed with rubber gloves, I begin the disgusting job and just then I hear the doorbell. *Saved by the bell!*

Answering the door, there is a lady standing before me in a fancy ball gown. Her hair is styled in a fancy way, twisted on top of her head and she has this weirdly intense smirk on her face. There is something about her that is oddly familiar; however, I can't seem to place where I know her from.

"Hello. Can I help you with something, ma'am?" She smiles boldly at me then her lips flatten. Her eyes travel my body up and down, landing on my pink rubber gloves. With an inquisitive look, her eyebrows raise with the lingering question. I suddenly become very nervous and laugh quietly before finding my voice, "Oh, I ah, well, I was, ah… cleaning. Any-wayyy…"

She finally speaks, "Mr. Macintyre, you must not remember me. I had hoped you might." She turns, slightly peering toward the parking lot, almost as if she were nervous. "I was hoping to speak with you if I could. My name is Cindy Hall. We met once before at the Country Club." She looks at me very intensely, willing me to remember.

"Oh, yes! Now I remember. Please, won't you come in?" I step aside, directing her to sit. "Lizzie isn't home right now. Can I offer you something to drink? You look awfully dressed up; I wouldn't want to spill anything on your beautiful dress."

Moving toward the couch she sits, shoulders back, legs crossed at the ankle, and she exudes an air of refinement and behavior fitting of a proper lady. I'm suddenly very intimidated by her presence. "I appreciate the kind offer, but no thank you, Mr. Macintyre." She pauses and looks down at her clenched hands. It's obvious she is struggling for some reason.

"Ms. Hall, as I said, my wife isn't home right now. I'm actually not sure when she'll be home. I'm sorry you made the trip. Can I have her call you later, once she returns?"

"Actually, *you're* the person I need to speak with." She swallows hard and takes a deep breath. "I must tell you something rather disturbing and I fear you're going to be rather upset."

I stare at her, totally clueless, silently begging her to get to it. Then it occurs to me, I don't know where Lizzie is. *What if she has been hurt!* "Ms. Hall, are you here to tell me Lizzie is sick? Is something wrong with my wife? Please tell me!"

She raises her hands to me in a 'calm down' motion and shakes her head swiftly. "No, no, no, she's safe! Nothing like that." I immediately calm down, but become agitated; I'm quickly losing patience with this woman. "Lizzie is a prostitute."

Oh my god. I did not just hear that. She did not just call my wife a hooker. I'm suddenly filled with rage and contempt for this imbecile. "WHAT THE FUCK DID YOU JUST SAY ABOUT MY WIFE?" I roar at her. I probably haven't ever screamed that loud. She immediately reaches back, attempting to disappear into the couch knowing she has totally pissed me off!

She jumps off the couch, moving toward the door, and just when she tries to reach for the doorknob, I block her path by jumping in front of her. I point my finger at her and become more enraged when I see my pink covered rubber finger. Ripping off the gloves, I implore her to speak. She holds up her hands in a silent gesture for me to back off and I try to speak but no words will come out. My throat is dry and I fall into the door because I feel like I might fall out before her. "I-I, ah, you're scaring me!"

"You think? You're scaring me, lady. Speak, now!"

She looks at me with eyes so huge in her face, larger than I've ever seen on another person. She must realize there is a consequence to dropping a bomb on someone's life and if you're too close you might have collateral damage. "Okay. This is very troubling news. I couldn't imagine you knew, so as Lizzie's friend, I decided you needed to know in order to help her. I figured she must have a shopping addiction or something because I'm always noticing her wearing very expensive clothes, and pardon me, but I know you've fallen on hard times, Jeremy."

"My hard times are NOT your concern! Get to the damn point. Why are you accusing Lizzie of whoring around?"

She becomes excessively nervous, glancing out the window and trifling through her purse. I sense she's ready to bolt and I can't let her leave before getting answers. Suddenly, everything about this woman is seriously irking me. Her hair, her stinky smelling perfume, the over zealousness of her impeccable manners, she doesn't seem like someone Lizzie would befriend, but I've been out of the loop for so long now.

She turns back to the sofa and carefully sits, waiting for me to get under control. "I will tell you what I know. For months now, she has been working on a charity alongside me for the Children's Museum. Our friendship has progressed and I am privy to a relationship between her and Mark Chesney. Do you know him?"

Suddenly, I recall who he is. We played racquetball together several times. We weren't friends, just occasional gym mates. I think he is rather wealthy, having a job in the financial arena. "I-I think I know who you're talking about."

"Yes, okay. Well, this all started when he appointed Lizzie to handle the disbursements for his personal contributions to Richmond's Children's Museum. Anyway, I started noticing they were rather touchy-feely with one another. Then, while at an event one evening at The Jefferson Hotel, I accidently came upon them in a hidden alcove while I was walking to the restroom. They were not discreet in any way. They were groping one another in plain sight. His tongue was all over her chest, Jeremy! It was so disappointing to see Lizzie in that environment. I never would have thought she would behave in a manner unbecoming of a lady. Even if she has fallen from economic stability. She...."

My body shaking uncontrollably, all I can really think about is getting to the liquor store but I NEED answers from this dimwit. "Look here! I'm desperately hanging by a thread. You don't get what I'm referring to, but you gotta move this along, lady. Answers, please."

"I understand. Just bear with me. I thought this was a simple affair. Then, I came upon some information that convinced me this is actually more of a crime. I decided it's best to come to you rather than the police. You see, I'm really doing Lizzie a favor. She needs to stay away from Mr. Chesney and I think you are the best solution for saving her."

I stare at her, mouth open, hardly able to keep up with the venom pouring from this woman. "Um, did you say that you and Lizzie are good friends?"

She answers quickly, almost too excitedly, "Absolutely, we've become great friends. That's why I'm devastated." She reaches into her suitcase-sized purse and pulls out several photographs. "Look at these closely, and then we'll talk about them." I carefully examine them and begin to feel nauseous. Lizzie is dressed up and he's holding her closely, too closely, speaking into her ear. She has the sweetest smile on her face. The second picture, they are walking together, with his hand on her lower back, just over her ass. She's mine and that's *my* ass he's caressing! I swallow deeply and close my eyes, not really wanting to look any further but knowing I must. The third picture is when my blood really begins to boil. Mark is holding Lizzie against his body. It appears as though they are dancing. He's holding her tightly in frame. Too–tight—too close. The fourth picture is a blown up version of the third. It shows… oh fuck, NO! His fucking tongue is licking her neck and her head is tilted with her eyes closed. She looks happy—very, very happy.

I should stop looking at the pictures, but I just can't. This is entirely my fault. I've driven her away from me with my alcohol and totally bad behavior. I lost my job, and then felt sorry for myself, falling into a deep depression. Not able to find a new job, I turned to alcohol instead of my wife. My behavior caused us to be evicted by the Sheriff and lose our family home I had personally designed and built. I drank so much I couldn't even get hard and fuck my wife properly. *How pathetic.* The daily focus was stealing every cent we had for booze, even pawning all of our valuables. When I even pawned her grandmother's jewelry, I was lower than low, but when I pawned my daughter's gold baby bracelet and both silver baby cups, I lost the right to exist in their lives. My Lizzie, MY Lizzie. Tears fill my eyes and I couldn't care less that I'm with this woman and she's witnessing my emotions. Looking at these pictures is complete torture. *What have I done?*

"You should really keep looking. I know it's hard, but you need the truth. Lizzie needs our help." Somehow I don't trust the gleam in her eyes. Something isn't right about her. She almost seems like she's enjoying this a little too much.

I resume looking at the pictures, turning to the next one. I immediately notice a different outfit which means another date. He is almost holding her up as if she has fallen into him. She has a sad look on her face but has longing in her eyes, for him. The next picture was taken at the same time, oh wait...that looks like...no fucking way! They're at the botanical gardens? Why? Lizzie loves it there. I guess that's why. This particular picture shows him, yet again, with his mouth at her neck. These are intimate pictures. They are not merely friends; these are individuals who are comfortable around one another. Too fucking comfortable.

Flipping to the next one, I'm struck with how amazingly gorgeous my wife is. She's so hot! There are even men looking at her provocatively in the background. She's wearing a beautiful black dress, oh wait, I remember seeing it in the closet just today. In this picture, he is standing behind her. She is touching a red heart necklace with diamonds that I haven't seen before and he is holding her closely, with his mouth on her ear.

The next one makes me nearly rip it in two and I probably would have had Ms. Hall not placed her hand on top of mine to deflect me. Mark's leg is between her thighs, fitted closely between her legs. Lizzie has a look of total exhilaration even with her closed eyes. To add salt to the wound, he is obviously pinching her nipple, regardless of the fact that it was through the fabric of her dress. I know my wife. That look on her face is the look of sexual satisfaction…I know that look! She was caught on film mid-orgasm. I've seen this exact face hundreds of times. There's no disputing it. "I know you're upset, but I must tell you what I actually heard Lizzie say to Mark after I took this picture. Prepare yourself because her words are the reason why she desperately needs some help and support from her loved ones." She offers a dramatic pause, supposedly to allow me to take a breath, but really because I know that she knows I'm hanging on her every syllable. Bitch. "She said, 'did you get your money's worth?'"

I look up at Ms. Hall with a murderous look and she rightfully flinches. She's enjoying her show-and-tell and her game is over. "You're not her friend, you lying bitch. I admit these photos are bad, but I must also admit that I've been a terrible husband and father. You have yet to explain the prostitution comment."

"There are more pictures I haven't shown you, yet." She pulls out two more. Lizzie is standing at a bank teller window with a large stack of cash. No freaking way she earned that much money working a regular job. The next picture, she is walking into the bank vault, cash in hand, presumably toward safe deposit boxes. We don't own one of those, never have. She's hiding money and she's selling her body.

I look around the apartment at the new tchotchkes I discovered earlier. My eyes land on an oil painting we didn't bring from our dream home. Moving in its direction, I notice it's signed by the artist and looks rather expensive but I can't say for sure because I know nothing about art. "That's from an art auction I attended recently. I recall it was quite pricey." My shoulders slump and I close my eyes, begging this woman to shut up. Thinking back to the children's closets, as well as Lizzie's, there were so many clothes. My mind's eye is connecting the dots and I'm sickened.

Suddenly, the bile in my throat is filling my mouth, and as I race to the toilet, I point to the door with an angered face, demanding her to leave the apartment. Barely making it in time, I hear the door slam. The reality of this situation is overtaking my senses and my body quivers and shakes hard. My eyes fill with tears as I fall back onto the floor, nearly missing the corner of the counter. Violent sobs overtake my body as images roll through by mind like a movie on the big screen. Recalling the pictures, her beautiful body being touched by the prick I only somewhat know. His mouth near her ear, on her lips. His hands touching her face, her stomach, her ass. That body belongs to me… *it is mine.*

Guilt overtakes me due to the wretched way I have treated her. I ignored her needs, her body, and mind. My stupid-ass self was so consumed with my necessity to be sloshed to avoid the painful reality of my failures as a man. Her body *is mine*, yet while I wasn't looking, she left me. And here I sit on the bathroom floor, a shell of my better, stronger self, bawling my eyes out because my wife apparently moved on. She gave what was mine away; she gave my pussy to another man!

What I don't understand is why she just agreed to work on our marriage if she is dating Mark? He obviously enjoys her company; that's completely obvious judging by the pictures. She seemed genuine when we made love. I don't get it. Why didn't she tell me she was doing this out of desperation? I'm sure I am responsible for this, so why not tell me and give us a chance to work through it? Why? As it stands now, it's like she intends to have a husband and a boyfriend on the side. I don't get it!

What about the money? That huge stack of cash, I saw her handing the bank teller. We've never handled large sums of cash. I rack my brain, desperately seeking logical answers and I can't find any. After brushing my teeth, I walk to the bedroom and lie down, staring at the ceiling. Trying my best to remember my lost, alcohol-filled days is completely frustrating. I roll over and face her packed closet when everything suddenly makes sense. Cindy's shrill voice in my head, "Did you get your money's worth?" I bolt upright in the bed, "Dear god, NO!" Suddenly, the bile rises in my throat once more. I dry heave over and over, having no control over my body. It occurs to me that just as I have no control over my heaving, I fear Lizzie lost control over her body, too. The pictures appear happy, but in a very morbid way I hope she was because the idea of having sex for money or being raped because I failed my family will cause me to lose my battle with addiction. There is no doubt about that.

This is entirely my fault. My beautiful, kind, gentle, loving wife and amazing mother is selling her body, not because she wants to, but because she had to. "THIS IS ALL MY FAULT!" I scream to an empty room, no one around to hear my desperate cries. I fall to my knees, begging the universe for forgiveness and compassion from the depths of depravity my wife has fallen to in order to survive. Lizzie has never been a materialistic sort of person, so seeing a stuffed closet is out of character, unless she is *playing* a character. Streams of tears fall down my face for the angel I love so much.

Not knowing how long I sit there, or how much time has passed, I stand up on weakened legs and wander into the living room. Lying on the coffee table like an unwelcomed gift, are the pictures. A parting shot, I assume, from Cindy. I don't even know the woman and can ascertain she has ulterior motives. I shift my eyes, trying diligently to avoid the unwelcome reminder when I notice a note:

If you want answers, come now to
The Jefferson Hotel Grand Ballroom

I stare at the note for long moments, considering my options. I know for absolute certain that I love Lizzie Macintyre with every breath in my body. The second thing I definitely know is that Mark Chesney needs to keep his fucking hands off what is *mine*. Forever. She and I have a lot to work through and so much we need to discuss, but I have faith in our love. Problem is, I also love alcohol, and right now, I need a fucking drink.

Chapter Thirty

Lucky Numbers...

Jack

The Gala is in full swing with everyone dancing, networking, and the occasional tipsy moment but overall it's a success so far. Mother organized an art auction, and thankfully, we were able to sell every piece and raise quite a bit of money. As much as I complained about having to MC the event, I have enjoyed it.

"Jack, dear, it's almost time for the bachelor auction."

"Yes, Mother. I'm on schedule, but there is one lot number I don't quite understand. It's called a raffle lot?" She looks rather nervous and peers around her almost as if she wants to bail on me. That's a sure sign something is up with my mother, and generally it will be at my expense. "Oh, no, no, no you don't. I know that look! What's going on?"

She sheepishly grins at me with the full knowledge that I adore her even though she drives me crazy sometimes. "Well, the committee members decided it would be fun to have a raffle as part of the bachelor auction and the winner would actually win dinner with you. Isn't that a great idea, Jack?"

I stare at her open-mouthed, clearly misunderstanding her last statement. With narrowed eyes, I ask, "Please, explain that to me again."

She leans in toward my ear and whispers, "Well, since technically you're separated you meet the criteria for being a bachelor, so it's fine." Pulling away from my ear, I look at her, dumbfounded because I can't believe she has arranged this.

"I'm not doing it, Mother. I don't need the attention right now. You *know* that."

"That's ridiculous and besides, it's for a good cause." She gives me that pointed motherly look that says, 'do as I say.' "At last count, the raffle has earned sixty thousand dollars, and that's a thousand dollars per ticket, so you must follow through."

My eyes must appear bulging from my eye sockets because I cannot believe so much money was raised just to have dinner with me! "Good gosh, who bought so many tickets?"

"That, my sweet son, I cannot reveal. I will tell you there were blocks of tickets purchased and quite a few single tickets. You're an interesting man, Jack, so why the self-doubt? People find you fascinating."

I exhale loudly, shaking my head in confusion. This is not going to go well, I just know it! "You owe me, Mother, and you know what they say about payback?"

"Sweetheart, I believe in fate and you are due for some fun and happiness, so if an old bitty shakes you up a bit with a little journey down the wild side, have at it I say!"

"*That's a visual I did not need, MOTHER!*" I hiss loudly before I walk away sulking, having serious doubts, knowing the guys are going to never let me live this down.

Returning to my MC post, we break the band momentarily in favor of the highlighted bachelor auction. I'm met with roars of laughter and cheers, quite a looser reception since the alcohol began flowing. I had forgotten how boisterous women can become when good-looking male specimens are pranced across the stage. We had a lot of ten bachelor's and they all "sold" for at least five thousand dollars each. Yes, a win-win for our charity all in good fun.

Finally, we arrive at the eleventh lot and just as I am about to speak, Mother walks up, taking the microphone. "Finally, the real moment you ladies have waited for!" Screams and whoops call around the room and suddenly I feel like I'm back at a college party. "The eleventh lot is our raffle lot. My handsome son here has offered himself for an evening of dinner to one lucky person. I can't even say 'woman' because men bought tickets, too!" I look at her horrified while the room snickers with laughter. "This lot was especially beneficial to our cause because we sold eighty-eight thousand dollars in raffle tickets!" Everyone cheers and I do as well while shaking my head, still baffled, because it's great for our grand totals this evening so I need to buck up and be happy. Ugh! "Okay, here we go. The winning ticket number is…can we get a drum roll, maestro?" The beating staccato of drums leads to….

#321214

I hear the number and scan the audience, waiting for the inevitable hand to raise signifying my dinner companion. Waiting, waiting, waiting…

Mother repeats the number and finally a hand timidly raises in my periphery. I turn to face the lucky winner and I cannot believe my eyes. The beautiful, long-haired brunette stares at me almost like a scared rabbit. Her response is definitely not what I would have expected. She looks absolutely terrified. Confusion marks my face as I look to her dinner companion and find Mark with his trademark smirk directed my way. *Fucker.*

"So we *do* have a winner! How exciting! Come up, dear, and meet my handsome son." She stares back with an expression of 'oh hell no.' "Sweetheart, it is okay. Jack won't bite." I hear a voice in my mind answer her back, "Oh yes he will but you'll enjoy the hell out of it." I glance at Mark and he carries a wolfish, knowing smile because he somehow caught that reference as well. The crowd chuckles, and as she moves toward us, I immediately have images floating through my mind of everywhere I would really like to bite her. Dammit, why does this woman seem to stir me up so much? "Oh, I recognize you! It's wonderful that you've won a date with my son, Jack. Tell everyone your name?"

With the microphone in her face, she looks at Mom, scared to death, then cuts her eyes to me for a split second before immediately turning her eyes downward. *Interesting. Hmm, that's not helping my growing semi-erection whenever this woman seems to be around.* She leans her body into the microphone. "Lizzie. My name is Lizzie Macintyre."

Chapter Thirty-one

Newly Defined Relationships...

Lizzie

"Well, bless your heart, you're one lucky girl!" is shouted from somewhere in the room. "I'll buy that ticket. I'll even pay double!" is yelled by another. I just smile at the hecklers and turn away from Jack, suddenly feeling very shy and not wanting the attention for some reason.

"Thank you, Lizzie, and congratulations for being our lucky winner!" Mrs. Loving smiles warmly at me and reaches in to hug me. She seems to be such a nice lady. "That concludes this year's bachelor auction and I will now return you to our wonderful MC."

Finally reaching our table, I shoot Mark a glare and he just beams with the biggest smile highlighting those high cheek bones and pearly white teeth. He bought that ticket for me and shoved it in my hand while the number was being called. I'm so embarrassed because now everyone thinks I actually paid a thousand dollars for a date with Jack Loving. Not that he's not gorgeous or anything, but I lose my flipping mind when I'm near him. He turns me into a mute schoolgirl who forgets she's a rather intelligent person.

Once seated, I lean into Mark, hissing so only he can hear, "You were a very bad boy, Mr. Chesney, and I may just punish you for embarrassing me like that."

No one can miss his loud inhalation as he looks at me with heated eyes that travel from my red lips to my nearly bare breasts. He reaches over and grabs my hand in his, caressing his thumb over the top of my hand. He leans his head toward me, sending tingles down my spine from the breath he warms my neck with. "Baby, if I could be sure you'd truly do it, I'd throw you over my shoulder and carry you to a suite and let you spank my ass 'til morning." I'm taken aback with the seriousness of his sexy words. Mark is a beautifully hot man and he knows just what to say to light my body up.

"I-I was just teasing you for making me walk the stage." Shaking my head at him and laughing together, we always seem to have a flirtation going on, yet at our core, we have developed a true friendship and I respect him. "Somehow, though, I will pay you back for the embarrassment."

"Look, it was ten grand well spent just to see the body language between you and Jack—"

"How much?" I interrupt. "I thought it was a thousand. Why in heaven's name did you spend ten?"

"I wanted you to have a better chance at winning." He grins at me like a Cheshire cat. "Besides, I may have had another ulterior motive. Whenever you're around, Jack acts like a horny teenager. I enjoy riling him up, truth be told. Plus, it's a worthwhile donation."

"Why do you want to rile up Jack Loving using me? And, you already make enormous donations to this charity. You didn't *need* to do this," I explain.

He smiles brightly at me. "It's done, Lizzie. Look, Jack is a good guy. He…well, let me just say, he could really benefit from your company."

Suddenly, my confidence is deflated like a helium balloon. Of course, the sexy man would not want to be friends or have a professional relationship with me. How could I have allowed my body to light up around him? In these moments, I'm given a reality check about what Mark really thinks about me. I'm an escort—nothing more. It's so easy for me to forget sometimes that this is a job. Mark uses me on his endowment, which I love and am extremely grateful for, but when I attend parties with him, he's renting my body. I'm arm candy for him.

"Lizzie, what's wrong? Where did your smile go?"

Suddenly, my eyes begin to burn as I try and hold back the tears. An errant one slips through and I quickly wipe it away. "Nothing is wrong. There's something in my eye, that's all." I move to stand up and he shadows me, always the gentleman. "I need to powder my nose. Will you excuse me?"

He grabs my elbow, holding me back, looking deeply at my face for my sudden depressing mood. Moving his chair backward, he skirts us away, "I'll walk you," and I'm not given a chance to argue.

In the hallway, he pushes me into the now familiar alcove where he once commandeered my body into orgasm without ever having touched my skin. Turning me to him, he has a serious look on his face and he's not messing around. "Tell me what's wrong and do not insult our friendship by saying it was some bullshit ornery eyelash." I open my mouth, quickly closing it, not able to find the words. "*Now,* Lizzie."

I roll my eyes uncontrollably and he narrows his at me, "Sometimes I forget."

"Forget. Forget what?" I hesitate a little too long and his face nears mine. The heat of his breath tingles across my skin only adding to my discomfort. "Lizzie!"

"You make me forget that I'm your escort, Mark! We've become such good friends and when I'm with you I forget it's a business arrangement for you." He pulls back as if I had smacked him. The range of emotions play out on his face, too numerous to count. Of significance, he's pissed! I mean, super pissed off. Underneath it, though, he's hurt. Damn, I should have kept my mouth closed. Reaching his hand to lightly touch his forehead and mouth, he says nothing, his hand trembling. Shaking his head at me, he wills himself to calm down. He paces back and forth, and when I reach out for him, he flinches away.*Oh god, no.* "Mark, please."

A minute passes, but it seems like hours while I wait for his response. Seemingly calmer, he finally takes a step closer to me. "For the record, I no longer look at you as *just* an escort. Besides, you're the first so-called *escort* that I have seen more than once yet *never* fucked. Additionally, I'm pretty certain I clarified how impressed I have been with your business savvy when I gave you my checkbook full of signed checks!" he hisses. Trying to regain his fragile composure, he reaches out and grabs my hands in his. "You may have begun as arm candy, and you are sooo....deliciously arm candy" he smirks. "However, that changed over time. We began a partnership formed out of our love and admiration for children's charities. We've made a lot of people happy and done a lot of good for Richmond. No matter how we were initially brought together, our roles have absolutely changed. Significantly. I'm not gonna lie to you, Birdie. I told you on day one, 'my dad is the gentleman, not me'."

I roll my eyes and we share a chuckle. He moves his face closer into mine. He inhales deeply, scenting me. The warmth I feel from his breath sends chills down my spine. No woman could resist the sex appeal of Mark Chesney in this moment. His magnetism is that strong. God, this man!

His tongue licks the shell of my ear and he speaks softly, yet firmly, conveying he's barely holding on in this moment. "If you'd let me, I'd fuck you so hard you'd lose your voice for a week. No bullshit. You want to know my reality, Mrs. Macintyre? When I plan to spend time with you, I go to the gym. I work out to the point of exhaustion. I do this to take the edge off. Otherwise, my control will surely slip. On the nights, after I leave you, I immediately hit an ice cold shower for at least thirty minutes because I have to stroke a nut at least three times. I replay what it felt like to hold you in my arms, watching the ecstasy on your face as you came apart, flooding your juices over my thigh. I still feel the warmth, Birdie. I still fucking feel it…all the time. I'm driving down the road and suddenly it hits me and I place my hand on the exact spot I drove my thigh into your wet heat. I still feel it, babe, and it drives me fucking wild with desire. You're quite the fuckable goddess, Lizzie Macintyre, but you're un-freaking-available right now. More imperative than that is I have this really crazy gut feeling that we need our friendship more than a quick fuck. As much of an idiot as that makes me not to push for something to happen between us, I don't want to jeopardize who we are to one another. I need your friendship forever and I don't trust anyone else to spend my endowment money. So, that's my fucked up reality. I want you so bad I can taste it. I'm pissed as hell at myself that I didn't caress your skin when I had the chance. Karma is surely mocking me. Especially, when I recognize I have the opportunity to have an amazing, deeply connected relationship with a woman that doesn't include just sex." He takes a step away, breathes deeply to collect his thoughts, and finally turns back to face me. "So do you now understand that I don't look at you in the same light we were first introduced under?

I'm taken aback by the honesty and depth of his words. I pull his shoulders down to mine, hugging him with all my strength. "Oh,

Mark. Your friendship means the world to me as well. The fact you have trusted me with your painful loss of Joshua, we will forever be friends no matter what." My eyes sparkle at him, reflecting in our connection. I release him and decide to discuss the elephant in the room. Timidly, I ask "Mark, can we talk about the money?"

He looks at me with confused narrowed eyes. "What about it?"

Feeling very uncomfortable, I shuffle back and forth on my toes, "Well, ya know. The money from Ms. Martin?" I whisper conspiratorially. He throws his hands to the side in the universal sign of 'so what?' "You've paid me A LOT of money, Mark, and I guess I am beginning to feel bad about it..."

"Look here," he interrupts. "What Ms. Martin pays you is for attendance at social events. You are now required, because you work on the endowment, to attend said events. Consider this a business arrangement which includes a clothing allowance. I guess I could pay you directly from the endowment funds. That is if you choose to be difficult about this, but know that your salary will be quite impressive and if what she pays you makes you uncomfortable, look out!"

"Seriously, Mark! Stop teasing me. I actually think it would be better to pay me via the endowment...BUT we will agree on a rate."

"Yeah, right. Whatever you say, sweetness. I know you'll always give me my money's worth," he laughs and pulls me in for a nice hug and kiss on the neck.

"Funny, that's the second time I've heard that statement about you today." The deep, harsh-sounding growl comes from behind me and I instantly go on alert. I pull away from Mark and barely move away from him before something quickly moves in front of my face, heading toward Mark. It takes a second for my mind to clear before I realize Jeremy has just punched Mark in the face and he was thrown back, totally blindsided.

"Jeremy!" I scream. Crouching before Mark, I ask, "Oh my god, are you okay?"

Mark shakes off the cobwebs and jumps to his feet. "If you're looking for an excuse to get your ass whipped, you just found it, motherfucker. That's the only free shot you'll *ever* get on me."

I move to stand between both men, quickly realizing I'm a pion in comparison. Shoving and loud voices are heard, including Jeremy's assertion, "She's no better than a whore!" before I'm silently begging for someone, anyone, to break these two up. "PLEASE! I need both of you to STOP!" I yell.

Suddenly, Jeremy is ripped away from me and the large imposing frame of Jack Loving stands between the two men. He tries to mediate and settle them down, but Jeremy is like a heated missile guided by an angry warhead. It happens so quickly, I hardly realize it as it is happening. Jeremy reaches to swing at Jack, and out of nowhere, Jack has him in a headlock, ripping off his waist belt and using it to tie his hands to his feet behind him. Holy shit! *How did he know to do that?* He just cow-tied him in a matter of seconds. In a dazed fog, I apparently miss the vile statements spewing from Jeremy's lips because suddenly Mark reaches over and clocks him hard. He's out cold. The next thing I know, everything turns black.

Chapter Thirty-two

Knights In Shining Armor...

Jack

I'm heading to the men's restroom when I hear a commotion. Considering this event is private, I know something is very wrong. Never would I have imagined I would find Lizzie standing in between two towering men, actually holding them off from one another. The woman has spunk for sure.

What really pisses me off is when the guy calls her a whore. No. That's not gonna fly around me. Granted, I don't know her well but she's a sweet girl and doesn't deserve the shit coming from the asshole's mouth.

I notice immediately that he's drunk because he reeks of alcohol. I initially thought he had wandered up from the hotel bar, but I realize that Lizzie knows him. The look of pain on her face is very unpleasant to witness. There's a back story there for sure.

When I see the angry welt quickly growing on Mark's face, I know this guy sucker punched him. Mark's a very agile guy, quick on his toes as I've learned many a day playing racquetball at the Country

Club. What really throws me is when I hear Mark snarl at him, "You don't fucking deserve her, you sack-of-shit drunk!" Yep, there's a story there between these three.

Working quickly to subdue him, I am able to defuse the situation or at least prevent Mark from going to jail or Lizzie being hurt by mistake. Oh, if that would've happened….I would have only seen red and gone the hell off on every damn body responsible. When Mark decks him out cold, it's actually a good thing because I was tired of the scene he was making.

Just as a security guard appears, I hear Lizzie fall. I fall in front of her, holding her hands and wiping the tears from her cheeks. No words of encouragement help to wake her. She's passed out completely. The in-house physician is called—thank god for fancy hotels still employing them—and he suggests moving both of them to separate rooms. Like a well-oiled machine, the staff at The Jefferson comply, placing Lizzie in luxurious quarters and the dumbass is sent next door.

Mark is a nervous wreck. I've never seen him become unglued like this. It's terribly obvious that he cares for Lizzie. On that, I'd stake my life. The style of relationship, however, I don't have a clue. He strokes her hair, whispers in her ear, and even rubs lotion on her hands using the suite's complimentary bottle. He also paces a lot. If he's begged her to wake once, it's a million times.

The doctor wants her to awaken naturally but after thirty minutes he places a dampened swab under her nose and she winces her face away from the smell. "Oh, thank god! You're awake! I was so afraid, Lizzie. How…how are you feeling? Can I get you something…water…tea…anything?" He rapid fires drink suggestions to her and she just looks cross-eyed and out of it.

"Just give her some time and she should be fine." Turning to Lizzie, the doctor says, "If you need anything, please call the number on this card and I will come right up, understand?" Lizzie responds solemnly, shaking her head yes. "Take it easy for the next few days, ma'am." He smiles and turns to leave the suite and I follow him.

As I am opening the door, I have the coincidence of my life when standing across the hall leaving her room, is none other than Victoria. The doctor notices my deer in the headlights response and just walks away, probably surmising we are all nutcases. I haven't laid eyes on her in months and I am immediately struck with how thin she is. Victoria has always been a beautiful woman with very little excess weight, but this is different. She looks bad—very unhealthy bad.

I stare at her in horror, my eyes traveling up and down her body. She becomes self-conscious and moves to cover her torso with her hands, hugging herself to hide what is painfully obvious. I don't know what to say or do. I'm not supposed to speak to her especially since I'm proceeding with the divorce and so much of my money is at stake. Even so, my heart twinges in pain knowing this is the woman I married, the mother of my children, and for all her faults, she had a busy job as a millionaire's wife. Some would hear that and harrumph with laughter, but my family Trust requires much work and I know she did great for many years. For those reasons, I want to embrace her if for no other reason than to encourage her to eat, but I know my lawyers would shit themselves.

Basic human compassion wins out. "Oh, Vickie." I shake my head in frustration, "What are you doing to yourself, honey?" She bursts into tears and nearly falls to her knees before I reach her and support her frame. Not even knowing he was there, Mark comes up beside me and helps me move her into her bedroom suite. I knew she was here and had been ever since Dad arranged it after the big conference room showdown. I didn't know what floor and only fate can explain this happenstance.

Mark looks at her closely, then at me with questioning eyes. He knows the drill and the wall of silence I've self-imposed between us. I can tell he's struggling with what to do in the moment. He doesn't want me left alone with her yet he's needed across the hall. "I'll be over in a second, Mark. Go ahead, I'm fine."

Chapter Thirty-three

When You Hit Rock Bottom, There's Only One Direction To Go...

Victoria

W hen I see my beautiful Jack standing there with someone holding a medical bag, I nearly expire on the spot. I surely managed to confuse reality with my dreams, especially considering I only ever see him with my eyes closed. I've made so many mistakes and looking at him this close up is almost too painful to bear.

Earlier in the evening, I watched him while at the Gala. A shot of pain went through my body as he chatted with his first love—the woman I would never replace in his heart. They smiled at one another, occasionally touching arms. I was very curious to know how he explained my absence. What do people know about our situation? I read the Richmond Times Dispatch every day and there's nothing hinting on scandal. I'm sure mother dearest is in charge on that one. I guess that's something at least.

What really hurt was when he danced two songs, back to back, with Erin. They weren't in formal hold; her arms were around his neck signifying a close relationship. When he whispered something in her ear and she giggled, I ended the torture and came back upstairs. Even though I desperately needed to discuss Daddy's kidnapping, my heart was broken and I needed to regroup.

"You need to take better care of yourself for the children's sakes," he speaks quietly to me as if he is rationalizing himself with an errant child.

I shake my head yes and stared into his eyes, pleading with him for some type of physical touch. I've missed his body so much. I am desperate to be held, loved. "I'll try. For the kids, I'll try."

He looks at me awkwardly and I sense he is very uncomfortable and I know our time is quickly ending. My eyes fly to the letter on the floor. Apparently, I dropped it without realizing it. He follows my eyes and before I realize it, goes to retrieve it. Picking it up, he turns it over and sees it had his name in my handwriting. He looks at me with confused eyes and I look to my lap, clinching my hands out of nervous habit. "What's this?"

I begin to cry and he moves to sit next to me on the couch. Our limbs aren't touching, but I can almost feel his heat and the smell uniquely Jack fills my nostrils. He lightly swipes his fingertips across my shoulder blades from left to right and back, lingering over my spine. He seems to be pressing in, feeling for something. I move into his touch, relishing the heat of his hands and the friction from rubbing his callused tips against the fabric. "It's okay, Victoria. Time will heal each of us; that's what I'm banking on." I lift my face up to his and without even thinking, I lean into him, quickly pressing my lips carefully against his. He pulls back swiftly and jumps off the couch as if he were burned. I burst into loud sobs, holding myself for comfort, but it doesn't help. Nothing will ever help again. Speaking softly, he says, "We have to move on. Our marriage is over, Victoria."

A blaze of anger rips through my body something fierce. Images of him holding Erin torment my mind and surely will torment my dreams. "You've already moved on. It's obvious you're seeing Erin again!" I scream at him. "I bet she inspires you to fuck her seven ways to Sunday just like the good 'ole days, doesn't she, *husband?*"

His eyebrows shoot up and his face reddens. He licks his lips as a nervous habit, which is what he always does when in deep contemplation. "Who I FUCK is no longer your concern, soon to be *ex*-wife! However, in consideration for the obvious emotional pain you're going through, I will share with you that my balls are nearly shriveled up and dead tissue at this point because I haven't fucked anyone except my right hand since I had sex with you the last time. Happy now? Are you thrilled to know I've remained the faithful husband even though you destroyed our lives and your family's +trust? I gotta tell you, though, it's a struggle EVERY DAMN DAY!" he roars through clenched teeth. "I have needs as a man and you've emasculated me. Was it worth it? Did you enjoy laughing behind my back while spending my millions? Well, I guess you'll have the last laugh on a beach somewhere spending my money the investigators can't seem to find! ARE. YOU. F-U-C-K-I-N-G. HAPPY, Victoria?"

Falling to the floor, I dry heave because I'm so emotionally drained from arguing. His imposing figure stands over me, but he says nothing. I watch him turn toward the door then stop, the sound of the envelope smacking in his hand. The curiosity fills his expression along with his desire to drop it and walk away. His fingers squeeze the corners and he turns it over, examining it closely. Taking a deep breath, he rips it open and shock crosses his features while he peers at the photograph of my father bloodied, eyes swollen shut, gagged, bound, and bruised. Turning to the next item, he opens my folded letter. Familiar eyes meet mine and the intensity is so strong, it causes me to look away in shame. I must have written it twenty times.

Knowing it may be my last words to him, I memorized them, vowing them sketched to my soul.

December 14, 2014

Jack,

It's long past time I admit my failures. They're not pretty, in fact they're pretty awful. I am taking a huge risk with what I'm about to tell you but you are a good and decent man. I just wish I had trusted you so long ago with my secrets and things would be very different.

My parents have controlled my life in an unhealthy way for a very long time. I should have listened to you and stayed far, far away, but I am weak and stupid. I have craved my father's love and my mother's approval my entire life. I never kept a penny of that money. My father needed the money for his fledgling business; however, considering what's going on, now I question that, too.

Enclosed, please find a picture kidnappers have sent my mother. They are based in Atlantic City and are collecting on his gambling debts. They've given us a deadline of tonight at midnight, or they will kill him. They want $100,000.

If you have any love for me in your heart and would consider paying the ransom demand, I would be most appreciative. I know I have absolutely no right to ask for this; however, I have nowhere else to turn. If you are able to do this, I need to take it to Mom's house and she will deliver it. The deadline is quickly nearing and all I can hope for is that they will have mercy.

I will instruct my lawyers to accept your proposed financial settlement. It's more than fair under the circumstances.

I will love you forever and will always cherish our years together and the beautiful children our love created. Sometimes you don't know what you have until it's gone. If you can find it in your heart to forgive my actions, it would mean so much to me. I miss your touch desperately, Jack. I will never stop trying to win back your love. Please don't forget me . . . or . . .

My unending love,
Victoria

Just as he finishes the note, my attention is drawn to my ringing cell phone with Mom's familiar preprogrammed ringtone. I return my gaze to him and refuse to acknowledge her during these precious few remaining moments I share with him. I can see so much indecision there in his eyes.

"I'll be in touch," are his only words before he turns to walk away, envelope held tightly in his grasp.

I stand there watching the door close behind his departing figure. I fall to my knees sobbing loudly after him begging him, "Don't leave me, please." Calling out to no one but the deadly silence that surrounds me and my loneliness.

Lying on the floor, I find comfort in the scratchy fibers of the carpeting. Anything that can make me feel is welcomed. My eyes land on the wooden jewelry box that belonged to my father's mother. He gave it to me when I got married, saying it represented family bonds. It was the only item he had left from his mother and he wanted me to have it. I remember the moment well because it was a rare opportunity to share an emotional connection with my father. As fleeting as those minutes were, they represented only a handful of occasions I ever felt affection from him.

I jump up, rush over to the box, and pull out the bottom drawer, desperately hoping it will still be there. As I pull out small mementos from my childhood—friendship bracelets, mood ring, picture of my first boyfriend—I'm desperate to find my most treasured possession from my dad. *Please still be here...oh please, please, please....YES!*

I take a deep breath, closing my eyes, holding it against my chest. I still have it. I don't know why I suddenly doubted not having it, but it's been years since I pulled it out and held it in my hands.

My picture. The one that got his approval when he came home from work one day. *The only one that ever did.* Every day, when I met him at the door, new picture in hand, he would inspect my drawing I had lovingly created. I tried so hard to make it perfect so he would like it enough to hang on the wall of his office. Every picture failed his liking except one. *This one.* He never told me why it passed his scrutiny, just a simple, "Victoria, I love it." I became so excited, jumping up and down, knowing I had pleased my father. The next day, I was disappointed to see it lying on the sideboard. I'd hoped he would have taken it to the office, but he didn't. Every morning for a week, I'd check to see if it was there and it was. I finally cried and my mother asked me why and I explained my disappointment that it was still there. She dismissed me for being silly, telling me to get my chores done. When I later took the trash to the curb, I found my drawing mixed in with the other trash. I was crushed. I lovingly removed it and hid it safely in my room. Years later, I added the picture to my grandmother's jewelry box.

There are very few things that have ever met my father's love or approval—his disabled twin siblings whom he still supports, his grandmother's jewelry box, his business, his gambling, and this picture.

I have spent my whole life seeking my father's approval. No matter how hard I try, it's never enough. It will never *be* enough. My life was never mine to enjoy, rather I was here to serve him and by extension, my mother. I have become a wretched human being—cold, calculating, manipulative, oppressive, rude, arrogant, and bitchy. Oh, so bitchy to everyone around me thinking I was better than everyone else. How I wish, I could turn back the hands of time and correct everyone I have wronged. But how? How can you make up for years of bad behavior when all you've ever known or been taught was to manipulate others?

Jack…how I love that man. Somehow, I will try to make this right. Only time will tell if I can. *My dear, Grace and Bryce, you are everything to me and I vow to be a better person. I cannot put you through any more hell than I already have. I must change starting now.*

I pick up the picture that I have cherished and held sacred. Walking to the fireplace, I examine it very closely for one last time. Ignoring the feeling of tightness in my chest, and my racing blood pressure, I place it across the gas logs. I stand up and walk to the switch on the wall, turning the fire on. I immediately turn around, refusing to watch it burn, knowing that the charred smell is the only evidence I need to know I am free of its control.

From this point on, I vow to be free of the negativity that is my parents. I am now my own person, under no one's control. I am at the bottom, of this I am sure.

Chapter Thirty-four

Spring Cleaning: Sweeping Out The Trash...

Jack

I think I've just slipped into an alternative reality. This night just keeps getting worse by the fucking minute. The odds of opening that door at the exact moment Victoria would be exiting from the hundreds of hotel rooms in this building has to be nearly one in a million. I exit her room, emotionally battered and bruised, listening to her cries as she begged me not to leave her. I'm wracked with confusion and guilt, not knowing what to do.

I'm still reeling from her changed appearance. Never could I imagine she could look this bad. Her hair was unstyled; she probably hasn't seen her hair dresser in months. Her clothes were simple, far from the Fifth Avenue attire she normally wears. Her skin looked dry, brittle, even cracked. Her makeup was minimal and her signature perfume she never leaves home without was noticeably absent. The most shocking aspect was her weight loss. Wow, she is too thin.

Returning to Lizzie's suite, I'm immediately met with Mark's concerned eyes. His shiner has gotten worse and I know it's probably his wounded pride at being sucker punched that he's most angry about. "There you are. I was beginning to think I needed to send out a search party. If your parents knew that I'd left you alone with her, they'd kill me. You do know that, right?"

Shaking my head, I say, "Man, you are not going to believe what I just found out." With narrowed eyes, he begs me to continue. "Is Lizzie resting in the bedroom?" He nods. "Okay. Victoria's dad has been kidnaped. There's a ransom demand. Apparently, she gave all the money to her dad for his business but since he has gambling debts it probably went to that."

The look of recognition crosses his face. "Remember, I did tell you he had local debts but paid them off so that makes sense. However, my search came up he was clean."

"True, but not in Atlantic City."

"Fuuucckkk!"

"Yeah, I know." I show him the envelope and he inspects it carefully. "Does the picture look real to you?"

"It's hard to say. What's the plan?"

"The deadline is midnight for a hundred grand. Since that's not a lot of time, I need to get rolling. I'm heading home to see what I can pull together. I've decided to call Detective Wallace and rope him in on this."

"Let me know if you need any cash. I have it at home if you need it."

"Thanks, man, I appreciate it. I'm going to look in on Lizzie before I leave."

Opening the door as quietly as I can, she's lying there on the bed. Her long brown hair is fanned out across the pillow and her breasts are straining against the top of her dress as she breathes. She looks just like an angel sleeping so peacefully. I cannot resist reaching down and picking up a lock of her hair, twisting it around my fingers. It feels like silk and my cock begins to harden as I watch over her quiet form. *Dammit, not the time.* I turn to walk away and she must have sensed me because she wakes up and calls my name. Turning back around, I can't help but smirk at her sleepy face so delightfully enchanting.

"Thank you for your help tonight. I'm…sorry. It's all very embarrassing."

Shaking my head, I tell her, "There's nothing to be sorry for."

She inhales deeply, "You're just being nice. If you knew everything, you wouldn't say that."

Looking at her questioningly, I know there's a lot more to this girl than meets the eye. For some unknown reason, I'm pulled toward her. She captivates me and my mind always leads to what it would feel like to have her underneath me. Feeling my skin against hers, watching her as she…stop! I can't keep thinking about having sex with her every time she's near. Smiling at her, I reach for her hand and lay a lingering kiss across her knuckles. She looks at me with want in her eyes. She seems to be just as affected as I am by her. "Please, Lizzie, let's just …enjoy this moment—this admittedly, odd moment". I shake my head, trying to make sense of the electricity we always seem to generate around one another. We look at each other, silently sending words of compassion. "Unexpected events have necessitated my presence elsewhere, but, Lizzie?"

"Yes?"

"I'll be in touch soon. You owe me a date and I plan to see that it happens."

"Jack, this may be incredibly out of line but I've heard bits and pieces along the way recently. Is everything okay? With your wife, I mean?" she asks very tentatively. I get the distinct impression she is embarrassed to be clarifying my marital status. I take a ragged breath. Wow, I wasn't expecting that question, from her anyway.

"It's not public knowledge due to extenuating circumstances, but Victoria and I have been separated for several months now. We are negotiating a complicated divorce."

She returns to me with a look of compassion, her eyes having their own deep troubles. "I'm very sorry for your children. This must be quite difficult for them."

Of course, she would understand what's at stake having children similar in age as mine. "Thank you. It is tough right now for everyone. If you would please keep this..."

She immediately interrupts, "Absolutely, you have my word." She smiles kindly.

...to yourself." I give her a big smile and unfortunately I really must leave her suite. I say my goodbyes with promises to connect later. *And you bet your sweet ass, Lizzie Macintyre, that I'll beat your phone number out of Mark's ass if I have to.*

I race home and pull the money from my office safe. I keep it there for emergencies. Granddaddy Bowes said he didn't always trust banks and you should have an emergency fund in case they steal your money. I don't reckon he was thinking I should use it for ransom demands.

I call Detective Wallace and he is meeting me. It's a quick plan, but we've buried a tracker in the cash. After I deliver the money to Victoria's mom, he will discretely follow her. Victoria wasn't thrilled that I was delivering the money, but I needed to do it.

It's been years since I've been to their home. It reeks of fake grandeur. They always want people to believe they are wealthy and living an affluent lifestyle. I know the truth and it's far from stability that this house is built on. Even my parents, who have tremendous wealth, are not ostentatious people. Their home is very elegant, far from the showiness here.

When Victoria's mom answers the door, she is visibly shocked to see me. She peeks around me, looking for someone, and finds me alone. "Ahhh…J-Jack? What can I h-help you with?"

With a small gym bag over my arm, I look toward it, "I think you know the answer to that question." She makes a small nod and steps aside for me to enter.

"It's good to see you, Jack. It's been a long time."

I shake my head. "Yes, it has been a long time, Mrs. Winfield." My eyes narrow at her, waiting to see if she'll act remorseful for her part in my money being stolen. I only see a tired, bitter old woman. Her eyes are red and swollen from despair but what is noticeably absent is guilt. She doesn't feel bad on any level for anything, especially how she has treated her only child. *Bitch.* "I'll make this short and sweet because I know you have a deadline. The money is all here—"

"You're sure? A hundred grand? It's all there?"

"I was trying to say…yes, it's all there." I take a menacing step toward her and bend my head closer to her face. "This will be the LAST money you people extort from me. I'm done! If you try and use Victoria to get to me again, it won't work. Make your husband face his gambling issues and stop trying to make people believe you're better than everyone else. You're not!"

"Ohhh, don't try and come in my home lecturing me from your grand ivory tower. You rich people think you deserve it all and I'm sick of it!"

"Let me tell you something, my mother has more compassion and understanding in her tiny fingernail then you could ever hope to dream about. She is the epitome of selflessness. Her day begins and ends thinking about how to make other people's lives better! You, on the other hand, start and end *your* day thinking about what the world owes you and dreaming of your next scheme to bleed someone dry. You make me sick. You've destroyed your daughter. Have you actually seen her lately?" Her eyes enlarge and I know...she hasn't seen her in probably a long time. "You are killing your child! She is physically sick, wasting away, and probably suffering from chronic depression. Guilt over stealing from me is written like it's tattooed on her forehead. She would have never done that had you people not pressured her into it. If you want to be a better mother, start by losing Victoria's phone number."

I move toward the door and realize I have forgotten something very important. Facing her with the angriest look I can muster, I seethe, "Do not *ever* contact my children. From this point on, they are totally off limits to you. Got it?" She begins to show the crack in her thick shell and whimpers slightly with a head nod. Finally, these people and I are *finished*. With the slamming door, I leave the black cloud that hung over my marriage behind.

Chapter Thirty-five

A New Direction...

Lizzie

The sound of the bedroom door opening causes me to look up and find Mark's smiling face peering in. Even with his bruises he is incredibly handsome. Then I'm immediately horrified that he and Jeremy fought. "I'm so sorry about what happened tonight."

"Don't be silly. I've wanted to knock some sense into that prick for some time now. This just gave me an excuse to do it. My pride is pissed he got one past me before I saw it coming, but I'll live. I just couldn't tolerate him disrespecting you right in front of me, Lizzie. I won't allow ANYONE to mistreat my friends. Period." We sit, staring at one another, just processing each other's words.

"I've actually thought a lot about it and think I understand why he reacted that way. He didn't appreciate the idea of, how should I say this, me paying to have sex with you. He heard a portion of our conversation and didn't know that our relationship is more complex."

He smiles at me sweetly. "I can only assume he doesn't know about Ms. Martin, correct?"

Shaking my head, I reply, "No, he does not know anything about her. He has no clue how I have been supporting myself and the children. It's not that I've been lying to him or anything like that. He's just never asked me a single thing about my job. He's been in an alcoholic haze for so long now." Suddenly feeling ashamed, I stare at my clenched hands.

Mark moves to sit down beside me on the bed. He lays his hand on top of mine and squeezes. "Hey, stop that now. I won't allow you to put yourself down because you made money to feed your children. You're a good mom, Lizzie."

My eyes suddenly burn as I try to fight back the tears. I don't like to cry, especially in front of other people. Nevertheless, the tears start falling and Mark gently pulls me into him, just holding me. After several minutes pass, he jokes and I can't help but chuckle, "I knew I'd get you in bed eventually."

"You're a great friend, Mark Chesney, and I'm so lucky that you came into my life." I reach to his cheek and kiss him sweetly. Then the tears start anew, happy tears because I hope we will always be friends. "That reminds me, you've been holding out on me as I understand it!"

Looking totally confused, he replies, "What are you talking about?"

I narrow my eyes at him, teasing him, "Did you have something to tell me about your conversation with Ms. Martin?"

Returning my teasing look with his own narrowed eyes, he says, "Meaning what, specifically? Ms. Martin and I speak about many things."

"Oh, don't be coy with me. She approached me this evening with an offer to run her business. She says you spoke to her in my favor."

He smiles and laughs boldly, "So, what if I did? You're smart, intelligent, and have a way with people. I think you'd be perfect."

"As a sex escort owner/operator! How ever did you come to that realization, Mark? Seriously! I don't know anything about this trade." He busts out laughing, as do I. I end up with streams of tears rolling down my cheeks thinking about me running the opulent office sitting in the non-descript building on Main Street.

"She would teach you, you know that. Plus, I'd be here to advise you which is what I told her as well. As much as society wants to ignore dirty little secrets like these, they serve a needed purpose. Now, you are the exception…always have been my exception to every damn rule there is, but it's true. Wealthy people or persons with the potential for exposure, can't afford the liability of psycho dating. Some just need an escort, eye candy if you're really lucky…" he winks at me and I mock swat at him and he fakes being hurt, "…to go to business dinners, etc., without the date getting pissed because you didn't call the next day. Others just really need sexual release, for the same reason, no strings attached—NSA for short. Many start out saying they accept that arrangement, but they just aren't cut out for it and everyone suffers in the end. It's a big risk of exposure in the media and social networking if eye candy feigns injury and scrutiny follows the wealthy person around calling him/her scum. It boils down to a guarantee that unless the client wants it, it's totally NSA."

"I hear what you're saying and if I do this I must be sure I'm careful because I'm not going to the big house! I love cock too much…but don't address that topic because I'm too horny! I truly do and trust me, no judgments coming from me because lord knows I'd be homeless if not for you. I'm embarrassed for you to know just how close I was to losing my apartment before you gave me that first bonus check. It's hard for single moms, Mark."

"I know it is and that's why you'll do it. Her other escorts *need* you to do it. No pressure from me, Birdie. I'm being straight with you. I'll help you. Full disclosure…don't be pissed, okay?" Oh shit, I fear I'm not going to like this and he suddenly looks scared shitless. "I investigated you and I knew how much you needed…"

"You what!"

"Don't, just don't fucking say it. It's done, it's over with, I didn't have to tell you but I respect you, so drop it. Your husband is a punk ass and you needed me as much as I needed your friendship. It's been hard on me since losing my wife."

I sit there stewing, majorly pissed but thinking back to those early days of meeting him and knowing our friendship is very different now. "My life is a real mess, Mark. I've put up with Jeremy's drinking for way too long. He always says he's going to get it together, but he never does. Addiction is a terrible disease. If I didn't let him stay with me, he'd be homeless. That's a fact. I allow it because of Hope and Ethan. Although recently I've realized I'm not doing them any favors by letting him stay because they witness his drunkenness. It's a tough call to make.

"Jeremy and I don't have a marriage in the traditional sense and definitely not the physical one, either. I probably shouldn't say this to you, considering our temptations in the past, but I'm lonely and I'm ready to start feeling like a woman again." I shake my head, dropping my forehead in my hands. "I want to start dating again and I can't exactly do that with a drunken husband sleeping just next door."

He laughs softly in agreement. "I think you should. You've been more loyal to him than most women probably would have been. Don't feel bad because you want a future, Birdie. You're a beautiful, smart, talented, and sexy woman. You deserve to be happy. Besides, you're already moving in the right direction…you have a date planned with a super nice guy."

Shock moves over me as realization hits that he's right, I do have a date planned. A date with Jack Loving! "Oh my…shit! Did you plan this when you bought ten thousand dollars' worth of raffle tickets? Did you hope I'd spend time with Jack?"

A smug, knowing grin moves over his face. "I wouldn't know anything about such an allegation, dear Lizzie!"

My mouth drops and I gasp loudly, "Liar! You know exactly why you did it. You have to tell me, was Jack in on this, too? I won't go unless you confess everything. I mean it, Mark."

He shakes his head and motions with his hands for me to 'calm down'. "Jack didn't even know about the raffle until an hour beforehand. His mother planned it to raise money and tease her loving son. I just let fate and karma work their magic. He gets so tongue tied around you. I've never seen him so off kilter." I smirk at him, knowing he's probably right. "I want to tell you something about Jack and I need you to keep it between us."

"Of course."

"There are some complicated matters going on right now with Jack's wife, Victoria. He is under a tremendous amount of stress. Jack is an heir to his family Trust. He and his mother are the epitome of what being a Good Samaritan is all about. The work they do in the Richmond community is extraordinary. They are extremely wealthy people, but it doesn't go to their heads. I have known the family for a long time and I am quite friendly with Jack. He's a good man, Lizzie. Because of his family Trust—his choices in life—his freedom to live life on his own terms is not available to him."

"I don't understand what you mean?"

"Well, I can't go into specifics without sacrificing our friendship, but I'll share one pretty large example with you. Jack is a criminal defense attorney. Now, consider for a moment that you are the heir to a massive account whose purpose is to provide for the less fortunate. Now, also consider that in order for those things to happen, you have to live life safely so you can be around long enough to do those good works. Therefore, if you have a safe occupation, the likelihood of you not dying too soon is high. Conversely, if you have an unsafe occupation like police officer, fireman, member of the armed forces, you could die prematurely. Understand?"

I sit quietly, comprehending everything he just said. "That's so unfair, Mark. Everyone deserves the opportunity to pick a career that suits their desires. You're saying because in the bigger picture it's more important to help thousands of people, Jack's personal wishes are sacrificed, being stuck in a job he hates. That's so wrong and I feel terrible for him."

I sit quietly, comprehending everything he just said. "That's so unfair, Mark. Everyone deserves the opportunity to pick a career that suits their desires. You're saying, because in the bigger picture it's more important to help thousands of people, Jack's personal wishes are sacrificed, being stuck in a job he hates. That's so wrong and I feel terrible for him."

Mark shrugs his shoulders, "I agree, but the terms of his Trust are clear. Look, he is not a martyr. He is a lawyer and has had years to perfect his craft and he's one of the best, most respected in the city. There's a lot more to Jack Loving that has earned my respect. Besides, you would have crossed paths with him, anyway, working on the endowment. I just crossed my fingers and pushed a little. The unblemished truth is that I think you need to put your guilt card away over Jeremy. You've done more than enough. It's time to move on. You're a gorgeous woman, Birdie, and if I can't have you, then I want to put you in alignment with the stars, so to speak, with another good guy who desperately needs a good woman like you."

"Boy, you have this all planned out, don't you?"

"Actually, yes. I've been considering this for some time now. I see something that makes sense to me and I push for it."

"Well, just so you know, payback is a bitch because if you are messing with my personal life, you're giving me permission to mess around with yours!"

"Oh, no, no, no! I never agreed to that!"

"Oh, you sure did the moment you dropped ten grand on raffle tickets. You started this, baby!" He grabs me and hugs me. Our tender embrace is interrupted when my cell phone rings. Looking at the display, I don't recognize the number. "Hello?"

"Yes, is this Elizabeth Macintyre," a very deep sounding, serious person asks.

"Yes, this is she."

"Mrs. Macintyre, my name is Detective Mills with the Richmond City Police Department." Suddenly, a warm feeling rushes through my body and I just know that this call is not good news. "Ma'am, are you alone? I have some difficult news to share with you."

I can't breathe. My mind quickly flashes with all of my loved ones, knowing that in just a second, one will be lost to me. I stare at Mark and can see his lips moving, but I don't hear him. His face is filled with fear and concern. I know the Detective is speaking, but I'm only able to hear a few words, "husband…car accident…collision…intoxicated."

I'm oddly aware that I can hear the sounds of someone wailing in the distance as if they are in pain. They are screaming, but I cannot help them because I cannot help myself. My reality is totally blurred. I'm faintly aware of Mark taking my phone and speaking, running his hands through his hair so tightly his knuckles are white.

Uncontrollable gagging tells me I'm going to be sick, so I move toward the bathroom but fall to the floor when my legs feel strangely numb like noodles and won't support me. I try to pull myself up, but I'm too weak, I cannot do it. I wish the damn screaming would stop, it's so loud. Strong arms grip around my back and under my legs, and almost in slow motion, I'm being carried to the toilet. My hair is pulled away from my face just before a cool rag is placed on my neck.

It's the oddest feeling of dizziness mixed with blurriness as I'm only partially in control of my own body. Strange, oh so very strange. Muffled sounds I can't truly make out are spoken in my ear along with the feeling of hands on my shoulders massaging gently. Of everything around me, the feeling I find most disconcerting is the painful shard on my knees surely caused by the sewn-in beading of my exquisite couture gown, as it presses into the marble floor. In a wicked way, I almost welcome the pain. Somehow it's easier to focus on the absurdity of the decimation of this beautiful garment rather than…well, the other pain.

The blasted screaming just continues and continues and I fear I may lose my mind if I can't get away from it. I place my hands over my ears to block the sound and it just amplifies it more! I survey Mark, desperate for help, and he is regarding me, totally horrified. I manage to read his lips, "Baby, I'm here, Lizzie." Just then, his words bring me back through the foggy haze long enough to comprehend the meaning behind the shrieking, that it was me who was screaming. Oh God, please, no! *"Jeremy is dead!"*

The End

Stay Tuned for Book 2 in the Good Samaritan series by Jolie Mae Miller.

Due for release spring, 2015

Acknowledgements

*O*kay, this will be a tear jerker for me! I clearly remember the day when I firmly made the decision to *publish* a book. Many of us write as I did but never *really* make the mental commitment to push forward, full-steam ahead. Besides, who the hell automatically knows how to self-publish? For me, that day happened to come just one year ago on November 9, 2013, when I went to a friend's home (thank you Kim B.) when she hosted authors, Erin Nicholas, and Mari Carr. *It was also my birthday.* My best friend Jenny invited me and outed my book-writing to the fabulous Mari. Thank you, Jenny, because this was truly my beginning. Wow, I still remember that conversation like it was yesterday. Not only did she encourage me, but she gave me extremely helpful information to set me on this journey. That night, I left with the encouragement to *really* figure out the process toward being an independent author. Thank you from the bottom of my heart, Mari, for your continued support over this past year. You're amazing!

Decision made to publish—now what do I do? I continued to write and dipped my toe in the social media world announcing little ol' me. I was immediately embraced with best wishes and encouraging messages. One in particular changed my path, yet again. Leighton Riley—you rock, girl! A random message from this fellow debut author helped me create important contacts to REALLY get this ball rolling. We were in the same boat and, Leighton, I really appreciate your help with everything.

Suddenly, I have an editor in the form of a fiery redhead, Tiffany Tillman, of www.RedheadBookServices.com. If you've heard of the Mashup Tour, it's Tiffany behind the scenes. She is a grammar nazi and helped me so much with many, many aspects. Our lengthy conversations to bring me up-to-speed on all things "Indy" have been so valuable. I can never express adequate appreciation for you helping my book finally get published! Our middle of the night phone calls mean so much to me not just because you are a professional, but because I feel I can call you, *my friend*. You can take my words and touch them with your magical wand, (AKA editing/track changes in Word) and suddenly we have fairy-dusted grammar. There's no underestimating the necessity for an editor, no matter your skill level. The inner-dialogue suggestions were fantastic. You have my unending appreciation for everything you have done to help me along this new journey. If there is anything you ever need, I hope you'll call. Word-of-mouth is a powerful thing…if you need an editor, call Tiffany. She's fantastic!

The story is obviously the soul of a book, but without good window dressing, many people won't bother to even pick it up. Laura Hidalgo, of www.BookfabulousDesigns.com, designed my cover and it still amazes me that without reading the story and after a short conversation, she knew exactly the concept I was looking to achieve. Tiffany told me early on to have faith in Laura because she was really good. Quite simply, she is *amazing*. A good cover is crucial and it cannot be understated how important this aspect of the process truly is. My goal was to make this cover about Richmond, Virginia. The Jefferson Hotel, a supremely iconic Richmond landmark is mentioned frequently in this story. Even though we weren't allowed to photograph the actual famous steps (trust me, I *really* tried), Laura used an image that conveys the message. Thank you from the bottom of my heart, Laura, for having enormous patience with this debut author. I know it was a challenge to fit everything onto the back cover, but you did a great job. The skyline, which was incredibly important to me, is so beautiful. The envelope: sheesh! I learned so much about placing and manipulating objects. That was an experience and I love the final product! Additional kudos to Tiffany as well for her design input on the cover. Her guidance on branding was so helpful. Thanks again for everything, Laura; book two is around the corner!

So a book, isn't a "book" unless it has been formatted. Well, the other redhead in my life, is a crazy girl who I think is a *really* cool chick. Deena Schoenfeldt, of www.ebookbuilders.com, makes me laugh every single time I speak with her. She's helped me with my website and offered me incredibly sage advice about the logistics of bringing words from my computer screen to you. She's very knowledgeable and I think she's great. Deena, I'm very appreciative that you were on this journey with me and can't wait to send you book two.

Before a book can be released, it's best to have beta readers provide their honest input. I asked three ladies to beta for me, all of which are avid romance readers. Many people find it interesting that the first person to read the manuscript was my mom. Growing up, she always had a romance book nearby, so I thought it seemed only logical. I'll never forget when she called to tell me she finished. I was so happy that *she* was so excited. Admittedly, I was worried she wouldn't be objective, but she gave me very helpful information. Thanks, Mom!

Next, Kathi Bowers, a friend for over twenty years who has an impressive book library and an amazing eye for detail. This was her first time reading as a beta, and she was worried she wouldn't do a good job. This girl is an incredible beta! She picked up on many things that were overlooked which is easy to do when you've looked at a document many times. Originally, Victoria was actually named Laura. To cut down on character confusion, Kathi was absolutely correct that she needed a name change. You did a fabulous job, Kathi!

Additionally, my dear friend Tammie Taylor. My-oh-my, this girl is special. She was incredibly helpful to me, discussing some areas I needed to expand on and tying-up of loose ends. Sometimes you can live with a story for so long, you can somehow miss the tiniest obvious things. She has an amazing eye for detail and did an incredible job offering keen advice. Tammie and her husband have always been incredibly supportive of my book writing and it means more than you know!

Thanks again to my incredible beta readers. Personal free-time is a rarity in everyone's busy life. I recognize how lucky I am that you took the time to not only read my book, but also the many conversations we've had discussing plot points, etc. From the bottom of my heart, THANK YOU!

When you write a book, you don't really think about the tedious business and tax aspects. Thank God for one of my oldest and dearest best friends, Jill McLain. She's never once complained when I asked a question and always on the other end of the phone to brighten my day. Thank you for many years of friendship. Love ya!

Thank you, to many of my friends from Powhatan, who have written me messages of encouragement along the way. One in particular I especially enjoyed from an old friend growing up (Sheffie W.), who requested that this book be: "Spicy with extra hot sauce, please"…I hope it was made to order!

To my friends in Prince George, who have also been very supportive and offered their support, THANK YOU! You'll never know how much your kind words or questions about my progress, would lift me up and strengthen me to finish this book.

Greg: Sorry cuz… no pop-ups:0)

To my family: my husband, daughter, sons, parents…thank you so much. Many times you will hear authors express appreciation to their families for their unending support and it's especially true. When deadlines approach or you need time in the "writing cave", more pressure is placed on other family members. I have a fabulous support system who encourage me daily to follow my dreams. When you're an erotic romance author, you especially need their support and understanding so I'm pretty lucky! *I love all of you so very much…….THANK YOU!*

To the readers, thank you so much for buying this book! Words cannot express how touched I am that you spent your very, hard-earned dollars on *The Good Samaritan*. There are many fabulous books out there, and to know you're reading *mine* is an emotional thing for me. Whether it's book one or twenty-one, I'll never be immune to this powerfully grateful feeling. Thank you! Thank you! Thank you!!!

Independent (AKA Indie) Authors, really need your reviews! PLEASE! Take five minutes and return to the site you purchased from, a leave a book review. It is incredibly important for us to know what you think.

All my unending love and appreciation from my home in Virginia to you, I am,

Very truly yours,

Jolie Mae

P.S. Stay tuned for Book Two coming spring, 2015!

About the Author:

Jolie Mae Miller is an independent author, living in Prince George, Virginia, with her loving husband and amazing children. Her busy home also includes a Yorkie, a Poodle, and a St. Bernard. Her favorite job is being a Mom and Meme (because she's too young to be a "GRANDMA!").

She grew up in Powhatan, Virginia, working in her family's auto parts business for many years. After her sister received a life-saving transplant, she pursued and was hired by Richmond-based, non-profit, United Network for Organ Sharing (UNOS). She enjoyed thirteen years working in the Accounting department managing various functions. Today, she has the best job, Mom.

In her free time, she enjoys reading and watching baseball. Whether it's her husband who umpires, her son or the Orioles. Additionally, she's an ancestry junkie, knowing quite well it's a never ending project. Jolie Mae is incredibly blessed to have a supportive family behind her while she pursues her love and passion of complex-themed writing. She credits her amazing parents for continuing to be positive, guiding forces in her life. Her love of reading definitely came from her Mom and is constantly inspired by her Dad's outgoing personality and knack for great storytelling.

Contact Jolie Mae

*J*olie Mae absolutely loves to hear from fans! To learn more about Jolie Mae, please feel free to contact her as follows:

Official website: www.joliemaemiller.com

Email her directly: jolie@joliemaemiller.com

Marketing, Autographed Books or other inquiries: info@joliemaemiller.com

Newsletter requests: newsletter@joliemaemiller.com

Facebook: Jolie Mae Miller-
Author www.facebook.com/JolieMaeMillerAuthor

Twitter: @joliemaemiller

Goodreads: www.goodreads.com/author/show/9848695.Jolie_Mae_Miller

---

www.ingramcontent.com/pod-product-compliance
Lightning Source LLC
Chambersburg PA
CBHW070653180626
46817CB00006B/2355